Bellegarde

Bellegarde

JAMIE LILAC

An Imprint of HarperCollinsPublishers

Library of Congress Cataloging-in-Publication Data
Names: Lilac, Jamie, author.
Title: Bellegarde / Jamie Lilac.
Description: First edition. | New York : HarperTeen, [2023] |
Audience: Ages 13 up. | Audience: Grades 10–12. | Summary: Told
   in alternating voices, in eighteenth-century France, popular ultra-
   wealthy teen, Beau Bellegarde, bets he can transform working-class
   Evie into school royalty.
Identifiers: LCCN 2022044823 | ISBN 978-0-06-323839-8
   (paperback)
Subjects: CYAC: Interpersonal relations—Fiction. | Social
   classes—Fiction. | Schools—Fiction. | Paris (France)—History—
   18th century—Fiction. | France—History—18th century—
   Fiction. | LCGFT: Historical fiction. | Romance fiction. | Novels.
Classification: LCC PZ7.1.L546 Be 2023 | DDC [Fic]—dc23
LC record available at https://lccn.loc.gov/2022044823

Typography by Julia Feingold
23 24 25 26 27 LBC 5 4 3 2 1
First Edition

To Mama,
it's always for you.

And to my little girl,
my stories will always lead back to you.

CHAPTER ONE

EVIE

Some say there's nothing more beautiful than Paris in the morning, but those people must be watching the sun rise from underneath their silk sheets, and not from a dirty bakery window through half-shut eyes, with flour-coated hands that ache from meticulously placing hundreds of sugared pearls on top of a cake meant for the queen of France.

It's never sweet enough for her. The strawberry jam is layered perfectly between fresh crème cake and toasted marshmallow, but we'll still hear about how one of her bites was bland. She'll place another order, though. And then another. And I'll continue to be thankful for it. Because without her, without any of the people in the golden palace under the silk sheets, I don't know what we'd do.

The reason I see the sun rise most mornings, see it peek up over the clockmaker's workshop, is because if I didn't, it would mean Mother and Father would have to. And they've already got their hands full with afternoon orders and with Violette, whose greatest talent is knowing where we store the extra dough and exactly how much she can scarf down in secret before she gets a stomachache.

I've saved a blueberry scone for her this morning, left in the oven for a few minutes just the way my mother taught me—burnt enough that father wouldn't want to serve it, but not so burnt that it can't be eaten anyway.

Quincy's here. His horses always make so much noise, clacking on the cobblestones and rattling the carriage. I'm betting Violette didn't sleep through it.

"Mademoiselle Evie," he says, tipping his hat as he approaches our storefront, "got something good for me today?" The horses' heads are topped with feathered plumes that shed all over the streets, and they only keep adding more. Quincy himself doesn't have feathers, but if they put one more piece of pizzazz on his outfit, I think he'd be more decorated than the king.

"Always, Quincy," I say, carefully handing over the heavy boxed cake. The satin bow I tied looks perfect on this one. Mother says I have a knack for it, but so far, tying bows hasn't proved a useful skill for anything but packaging cakes and putting the finishing touches on my handmade dresses.

Quincy places the cake in the carriage, wedging it between pillows of plush velvet. It'll be inside the palace gates of Versailles and sitting pretty on top of a crystal stand before the queen wakes.

"Another ball tonight?" I ask Quincy. The queen is always throwing masked parties, inviting every high-status Parisian to be found. Which of course means we're never invited. But sometimes I like to imagine one of my father's cakes, or mine, making it to the queen's soiree, getting to be the centerpiece.

I imagine everyone circling around it, admiring the marzi-
pan roses and filigree icing complete with real gold leaf. For
a moment, they don't know that it was made by low-status
hands, and they look at it the same way they look at each other.

"No, ma'am," says Quincy. "This is just breakfast." He
gives me a wink before hoisting himself up onto the coach,
and with another tip of his bedazzled hat, he's gone.

Breakfast. Would that we could all eat cake for breakfast.
But, oh, Violette's scone! It'll have gone cold by now. I rush
inside, stash it in my apron pocket, and tiptoe up the steps to
our home.

She's already awake, as suspected. It wasn't the horses
that got her, though. It was her stupid nightmares.

"You've got to stop listening to Remy," I tell her. "He's
messing with you. None of that stuff is true."

"But he said it really happened!" Violette squeaks. She
rubs her little fists against sleepy eyes. This is where my
mother might tell her that Remy, the silversmith's boy, only
tells her those ghost stories because he likes her. But that's
foolish. And I don't want Violette's life to begin and end with
the silversmith's boy.

"Well, I heard that ghosts don't like anything that smells
sweet," I say, "and we live above a bakery, so they're never
going to come here."

"Really?" Her hazel eyes grow wide, and it's so cute that
I almost want to laugh.

"Would your big sister lie to you?"

She hesitates to answer, looking me over, always the

smartest member of the Clément family.

"Well, I've got some of the best ghost repellent in all of France right here," I say, reaching into my apron pocket. She perks up as soon as she smells it, grabbing for it with her stubby fingers. I pull it back, joking with her. "You better not get any crumbs in the bed or else Father might find out."

"I promise, Evie," she says. "I promise!"

She's already inhaled half the scone by the time the clocks chime.

"Gotta go," I say, mussing her corkscrew curls. We both got our father's coffee-brown hair and olive skin, but only she was lucky enough to get Mother's curls. "Be good today."

Violette gulps down the milk on her bedside table. "Are you wearing that?" She mumbles before wiping her mouth.

"This thing?" I ruffle the apron. "Of course not, silly."

"Well, I just meant— I thought—" Violette begins, her cheeks flushing a kitten-nose pink, "maybe you could wear one of your new dresses today."

My mother's told her. I asked her not to, but she's gone and done it. And now Violette's hopes will be up, thinking that in just four short weeks I could actually be chosen as the Bellegarde Bloom at the Court of Flowers Ball. Am I expected to tell her that people like us never win, that we don't even have a chance? It'll crush her. So, I say the only thing I can think to say.

"I'll have to finish them first. You know that baby-pink one with the big bow, your favorite? I stained the bottom of it. I forgot to sweep the floors and I dirtied it right up."

"What about the blue?" she asks, clearly disappointed.

"Oh, that one, it's, uh—" I stutter. "The hem on that one fell right out. Yes, I'll have to restitch it this week. How does that sound?"

I'm successful in my lies because a smile spreads across her heart-shaped face. "Okay," she says with a nod.

The pink dress *is* kind of dirty at the bottom, so it isn't a complete lie, but it isn't anything a little elbow grease wouldn't get out. The other, though, the powder blue, has never had a stitch out of place. Even Madame Bissett was impressed with that one.

"I'll see you after school," I tell her with a wink.

I know what Violette is thinking. She thinks if I wear some of the clothes I've made, the ones with scrap fabrics Madame Bissett gave me or the ones Quincy brought for me, the ones I covet, that maybe the Court will nominate me to be in the running for the Bloom, a title that would surely make me the most desired bachelorette in all of Paris. And maybe the dresses would help elevate me to a status above invisible, but they'd never match up to the couture gowns the other girls will be pulling out this month. Even the best of what we've got can't compete with their worst. And there isn't a high-status boy in the city who'd pick homemade over couture.

I decide I'll tell Violette the truth one day. Maybe when she's a little older, before she gets to university and gets humiliated the way I did. I'll teach her we don't need those people for anything except to buy our cakes.

·໑ঠ৶ঽ·

Josephine is practically racing to school, and I'm almost at a jog trying to keep up. She's wearing the skirt I made her, the best one she owns, and her round ebony cheeks are streaked with blush. Her tight curls, which are usually tousled together with a few pins and pomade, have now been braided up the back and finished into two puffs like tufts of cotton candy that she's sprinkled with a shimmering powder. I finally have to ask her what I've been wanting to ask for weeks. "What's up with you lately?"

"Up with me?" she says, never breaking stride. "What do you mean?"

"The clothes and the makeup. I mean, you look great. You looked great before, too. But I didn't think you were into that stuff."

"I'm not," Josephine says, "but Mia Bellegarde is." She looks back at me and smiles one of her signature mischievous smiles that she's been giving me ever since we were toddlers.

"I knew it! I knew it, I knew it! I knew she was your type the second she arrived in the city. Why haven't you told me?"

"I wasn't sure if it was worth telling yet, and I didn't want you getting your hopes up for me."

"So," I say. I'm walking as fast as her now, drinking in her giddy face. "What's changed? Did something happen?"

"Well, kind of," Josephine says. "Yesterday in Monsieur Dorey's class, she asked if I had a spare piece of parchment, and when I gave it to her, she kind of, well, she did like this." Josephine reaches over and brushes her hand against mine, her fingers lingering. "She didn't have to! She could've just grabbed the parchment from the other side."

Now I'm thinking maybe it's Josephine who has her hopes up instead. She must see the uncertainty on my face, because she starts explaining.

"Look," she says, "it was different. I know it sounds like I'm reading too much into it or something, but it was different."

"I believe you!" And I do. Or, at least, I believe that's what she thinks. But it doesn't matter, because Jo hasn't been this enraptured by anything in a really long time, and whatever it is, I'll take it, even if it means my best friend ends up with a Bellegarde. "So, is that why we're about to be at school before everyone else, or what? The soles of my shoes are wearing out over here."

Josephine stops so abruptly that I trip over her feet and almost go tumbling to the cobblestones, but she anticipates it and catches me. *Two halves of the same brain*, her mother always says.

"Okay," Josephine says. She lowers her voice to a whisper as a group of snickering ninth-year girls passes by. "I wanted to keep it a surprise, but . . ."

"Spit it out, Jo!"

"Okay, okay." She takes a deep breath. "Rumor is Rachelle is breaking up with Beau this morning."

"What?" I gasp. I can't help myself. Rachelle LeBlanc and Beau Bellegarde are king and queen of the school. Their parents probably already have their wedding planned. There's no way they're breaking up.

"It's true. Apparently, Rachelle met a baron when she was in the Loire Valley, and word is she's over Beau now."

I sigh. "Of course she did."

"It's supposed to happen in the courtyard this morning," she says. "I think everyone in school knows by now. Well, everyone except for Beau."

Beau Bellegarde. Rachelle is terrible, but it might be satisfying to see the look on his face when she does it. He's the most notorious ladies' man at the university, probably even worse than his half brother, Julien. Before Rachelle, it felt like Beau had a different girl on his arm every week. And the stories I've heard, well . . .

"Beau's going to be shocked," I say.

"He might be shocked, but I don't think he's going to be too upset. Grace says he's been standing Rachelle up left and right lately."

I shake my head. "No. No way. He wouldn't do anything to risk his relationship with her."

"Why not?"

"Because she's—she's her! She's the prettiest girl in school, and she's got more money than almost anyone at the university. Did you see the emerald ring she wore last week? That could pay our rent for years. Maybe a lifetime."

Josephine's brows scrunch together. "Yeah, but she's also the most wicked girl in school. All of those things—money, beauty, power—they don't make her a better person. They don't make anyone a better person. It's just stuff."

"Well, they seem to make life a lot easier for people," I tell her.

She shrugs. "Maybe. For a while. But not forever."

"Wait," I stop. "Why'd you want to keep it a surprise from me, anyway?"

Josephine grins. "Well, it's just, you know—*Beau*."

"Okay? What about him?"

"Oh, come on, Evie, you know I've always wanted the two of you to get together! And imagine, you with Beau and me with Mia. We could be family!"

"You have really lost your mind, Jo."

Josephine is laughing hysterically. "I know, I know. But you used to have a huge crush on him!"

"I was seven! And you act like you don't remember what they did to me—what *he* did to me."

Josephine exhales. All these years later, she still feels bad about not being there when it happened. "I understand," she says, "but you know that I don't—"

"You don't think Beau had anything to do with it," I finish her sentence, mocking the way she says it any time the incident has been brought up in the past. "I know. But I still think he's just as bad as the rest of them."

She rolls her eyes and locks her arm in mine.

We're at school now, and I've never seen so many people here before class. Word has definitely gotten around because everyone's eyes are trained on the line of carriages arriving in the courtyard.

Even without the carriages, it isn't tough to tell who comes from which side of town. It follows us. The kids from mine and Jo's side are the ones with the slumped shoulders and faint dark smudges under their eyes, borne from long nights or early mornings working to make enough money to get by. The kids that arrive in the gilded carriages always look fresh, well rested, and bright eyed. We may go to the same school, but we're still worlds apart.

Rachelle arrives first, her platinum hair barely powdered, padded high, and finished with a ribbon that's been woven like a crown surrounding her soft curls. She's flanked on either side by Lola and the Chastain twins.

Rachelle LeBlanc is everything I'm not. Where she's long-legged and tall, I'm a can't-reach-the-top-row-of-a-bookshelf kind of height. Where she's filled out, her curves exactly placed where the boys want them, I'm flat-chested and awkward. And where she comes from a long line of wealth and status, I, well . . . don't.

Josephine leans over to me. "You think she'll even want to be the Bloom anymore or you think she'll just wait for the baron to propose?"

"How do we know she's actually dating a baron?"

"Grace claims to have seen them at the opera house together," Josephine says. Grace talks a lot, but she's usually right.

"Well, baron or not, there's no way Rachelle would ever let someone else win the title of Bellegarde Bloom. She's lived her whole life for that moment."

Josephine grabs my wrist. Beau's carriage has just arrived.

Beau's half brother, Julien, is the first out. He's good-looking enough, broad-chested and icy blond, but his pale white nose is always pointed to the sky like he's just smelled something foul. Next is Beau's cousin Mia. She's shy, with raven-black hair down to her ribs. I glance back at Josephine. Her eyes don't leave Mia.

Last out of the carriage is Beau Bellegarde. His resemblance to Mia is uncanny—bushy-browed and tanned. He's dark-haired and sharp-jawed, handsome in a way you never quite get used to. But every time I see him, I see the face of the boy who was staring into mine the day everyone laughed at me. Handsome or not, his face only makes me angry now.

Everyone has stopped pretending they're not staring, and now they've given in to full-on eavesdropping as Beau swings his arm around a particularly cold-looking Rachelle. It's about to happen, and he has no idea.

Beau, with his smug smile, like nothing in the world could possibly touch him, probably thinking we're all looking at him because we're so obsessed with him. And then there's Rachelle, dating a baron but still wanting to get chosen as the Bloom at the Court Ball in hopes of maybe catching a bigger fish like a viscount or even a duke if she's lucky enough. They have everything they could ever want, and it still isn't enough.

It might feel good to see one of them lose something.

Chapter Two

BEAU

She's still mad about last night. It was an honest mistake. Nights spent at the château—an abandoned mansion where university students throw elaborate parties—almost never go to plan. Last night after we left the château, I crashed out at Dre's and forgot all about meeting up with Rachelle at the Gardens. She'll get over it. She always gets over it. And when she sees what I have for her, last night will be a blip. It'll be nothing. But she pulls away when I try to give her a hug.

"You okay?" I ask, but before she can answer, Julien busts through the group, sizing the Chastain twins up.

"My, my, my, Darcy," Julien says. He runs a hand through his slicked-back hair and bites his lip as he looks her up and down. "You do something different to your hair this morning?"

She glares back at him. I'm laughing because he's the biggest idiot I know, and he's been trying to get in with the Chastain twins for years. This must be his new tactic.

"Well, I don't know what's different about you," Julien continues, "but if you keep looking like that, none of these girls are going to have a chance at winning Bellegarde Bloom."

She steps forward, eyes locked with his, and grins. "I'm Diane," she says. She points to her sister. "*That's* Darcy."

"Well." Julien coughs. "I guess that's what's different about you, then." Even Julien has to laugh at himself. He never gives up, even when he's clearly defeated. Though not so defeated this morning, because Diane, or is it Darcy— truth be told I can't ever seem to get it right, either—lets him plant a kiss on her hand anyway.

He leans back to me and Dre, grinning. "Can you smell it, boys?" He lifts his chin and inhales. "The Court Ball is in the air."

He's right. Almost every girl in the courtyard is at least a little more dolled up than usual. They're wearing their best, looking their best, and admittedly, I don't mind it. Even Rachelle's got on a diamond pendant I've never seen. Probably something her grandfather gave her. Don't know why she's trying to impress, though. She'd still win Bellegarde Bloom if she wore a burlap sack. She doesn't need diamonds. Which reminds me.

"I've got something for you," I whisper to her, but she's inching away from me. She has that look on her face, the same annoyed one she gave me when I asked her if she'd go with me to the shops to see the new printing press at St. Clair's. The necklace I bought her isn't diamonds, but it's from De la Croix, so it will cheer her up fine.

Rachelle frowns. "Actually, Beau, I need to talk to you about something first."

Here we go. I'm going to get an earful about last night. I laugh a little because she sounds so serious and there's nothing about Rachelle that's serious. "What's wrong?"

She twirls a finger through her curls. More new jewels there, too. "This isn't working anymore."

"Excuse me?"

"The two of us. It isn't working anymore. Don't you agree?"

I might be imagining it, but it's like everyone's gone quiet. Dre and Lola have stopped locking lips long enough to breathe. Even Julien has stopped heckling his latest victims. Instead, they're all looking at me. I stuff the De la Croix box back into my jacket pocket. She can't be serious. "Sorry, what?"

She folds her arms, unaffected. "It was fun. But it's time to go our separate ways. You understand, don't you?"

I'm stunned into silence, my mouth hanging open. I look to Dre, but he just throws his hands up. Lola's chin is resting on his shoulder. Did they know about this?

Rachelle isn't at a loss for words. "Oh, Beau," she keeps going. "It's not like we were going to get married."

Get married? Of course we weren't going to get married! I'm not sure I could imagine anything worse. But I've put too much time into this. I need this. "You're really doing this in front of everyone?"

Rachelle sighs. "You don't want to drag this out, do you, Beau?"

And I'm panicking, so I guess I do.

.ᴼᵉˢ.

We're finally alone, sitting by the fountain we meet at when we're skipping class, and she's somehow less affected than when we were in front of a hundred classmates. It isn't that I want to be with Rachelle. She's arrogant and pretentious and kind of dreadful. But she's a LeBlanc. Her family is on top of the Parisian social world. Forget Paris! The LeBlanc name is known all throughout France. It's why I've laughed at her father's terrible jokes and pretended that her mother is charming. Being with Rachelle means not having to explain that I'm the son of my father's mistress, that I was kept a secret for years, until her death. It means the rumors stop, at least when I'm in earshot. With Rachelle on my arm, no one cares that I don't entirely fit in with the posh crowd. No one cares that I'm barely a Bellegarde.

In less than four weeks, I would have escorted her through the doors at the Court of Flowers Ball, a masked affair that means everything to teenagers in this city. We might have shared a dance or two for appearances, but later that night, she would be named Bellegarde Bloom, and when she won and all the suitors came flocking to her, she would inevitably have broken up with me. She would have pinned her bouton-niere on some unsuspecting chum, and *that* is when I would have gotten out of it scot-free. I'd be free of Rachelle, but it wouldn't be my fault. Everyone would be expecting it, and I'd still have my classmates' admiration.

I take Rachelle's hand in mine, putting on my best face. "You don't really want to break up, do you?"

Her hand slips away. "Beau, we both know this wasn't going anywhere."

That's true, but I lie and say, "That's not true," because what else am I going to say?

She rolls her eyes at me. Has she known my plan this whole time? She traces a finger across her chest, fidgeting with her new necklace. The new necklace. The new ring. I was a fool not to notice these things before. "Is there someone else?"

She grins. "Well, of course there's someone else."

"And?"

She repeats after me. "And?"

"And who is he?"

She perks up like she thinks she's the queen readying herself to accept an award. "If you must know, he's a baron."

"Ha! Just a baron? A baron of what?"

"Don't be jealous, Beau!"

"Jealous? Of a baron? Don't make me laugh."

"He's important!" she sneers.

"Important?" I chuckle. "Rachelle, I'm a Bellegarde. If you haven't noticed, the title you're vying for is the Bellegarde Bloom. Named for my grandmother who was the very first Bloom, the woman who started the Court of Flowers that's so precious to you! I could have a baron shine my shoes if I wanted to."

For a moment, she almost looks like she's buying it. They all think I can have whatever I want because I'm Tom

Bellegarde's son, because I'm part of the Bellegarde legacy, and I'm going to keep it that way for as long as I can.

"I must admit," she says with a careless flutter of her wispy eyelashes, "having a Bellegarde escort me into the ball would have been nice, but the Baron has a title, Beau. You must know that, for an escort, that outshines the Bellegarde name, even for the Court of Flowers. And besides, you can't have actually believed I was going to end up with someone who didn't have a title."

End up with. She says it so nonchalantly, as if I was dreaming about "ending up" with her. "Outshines the Bellegarde name?" I say with disbelief, attempting to gather my rattled thoughts. "How'd you even meet this guy?"

The corners of her mouth turn upward, and she gazes off like she's remembering something delightful. "Oh, just kind of ran into each other when I was visiting Aunt Geneviève."

Rachelle's Aunt Geneviève has been trying to get rid of me for months now, always writing her and asking if she's found a proper suitor. Rachelle reads me the letters. She thinks it's hysterical. But I've always known that woman was up to something. Geneviève has made a career out of marrying rich old noblemen right before they croak. "Just ran into him? What, he just happened to trample through her giant hedges, waltz his way across the front lawn, past the guard, and into your aunt's estate? Or by 'ran into each other' do you mean that she invited him over for afternoon tea?"

Rachelle crosses her arms. "Well, it doesn't matter now.

The Baron and I are getting to know one another. I've asked him to be my escort to the Court Ball, and that's that. Even Father loves him."

Father loves him. Of course he's met Monsieur LeBlanc.

It's over for me. Not for Rachelle, though. This guy is probably just the first step on the ladder. Even if a baron is her best choice at the Ball, he won't be who she marries. Next, Aunt Geneviève will be inviting a viscount for tea and the baron will be yesterday's news. But for me, it's over.

I turn to Rachelle, who is admiring her new jewelry. I don't mean it, but I say it anyway because I feel like my mother would've wanted me to: "I hope you and the baron are happy."

CHAPTER THREE

EVIE

When Madame Bissett tells you that you're doing something, you don't really have a choice, and that's how I've ended up letting Josephine lace me into half-boned stays, laughing as she ties the finishing bow, knowing this is the last thing I want to do.

"What's that you always say to me?" Josephine snickers. "You're going to look like a princess!"

I glare at her, but it only makes her laugh harder.

I'm really doing this for Jo, because her mess of a dress, the one that was supposed to be in Madame Bissett's fashion show today, is currently balled up in a heap and stashed deep in a closet. She tried throwing it away, but I wouldn't let her. The construction is so bad that it isn't salvageable as a full garment, but it's made from the most beautiful lavender snow brocade, and I wouldn't dare let that go to waste. I can at least use the scraps for something. Maybe.

Morgan was supposed wear my dress, but she's sick, which, under any other circumstances, would probably mean I was off the hook. But now we've had to lie to Madame Bissett and tell her that the dress I made was actually made by me *and* Josephine—she can't afford another failing grade in this class. And since Jo is too tall for my dress, here I am, laced up and out of breath and about to have to do one of the most embarrassing things I've ever done.

"I'll be right back!" Jo says. "I need to find your shoes."

Across the dressing room, Madame Bissett slaps a measuring stick at her palm as she inspects everyone's garment, and soon, her icy stare locks on me. She makes her way over to me with one sharp brow pinched, and every muscle in my body tenses.

"I see that you managed to finish the beading, Evie," she notes, studying the fabric, pulling at my waist before zeroing in on the quilted petticoat, and more important, an inch of wonky stitching I tried hiding. "Although, it's still not your best work."

I open my mouth full of excuses, but her lips purse and I know she'll hear none of them. "Yes, Madame Bissett," I sigh in agreement. "I'll try harder next time."

As much as I want to be angry about her judgment, her scrutiny over minute details, Madame Bissett is one of the only people whose approval truly means something to me. Without her belief in me, I don't know if I'd have these dreams outside of the bakery. Without her sneaking me boxes of scrap fabric over the last four years, I'd barely have had enough to sew a hanky. So when she hands out her harsh but fair judgments, I accept them. And when I tell her that I'll do better next time, I mean it.

"Got them!" Josephine exclaims, rushing over, waving a pair of heels in the air.

"Are you sure these are the only ones you could find?" I ask her as she slips my foot into a tightly pointed, heeled shoe and gives me a crooked, hope-for-the-best smile because they're at least two sizes too big.

Josephine nods. "All the others had already been taken. But look! You'll never be able to tell they're too big."

I wobble as I try to stand and have to grab for her shoulder to find my footing. I cut my eyes at her. "Yeah, can't tell at all."

"Anyone have a comb?" Josephine calls out. Petticoats are being fluffed and clouds of powder are hanging in the air. My head gets yanked back as she runs her fingers through my hair and catches on the tangles.

I turn around and glare at her. "Absolutely not, Jo."

"What?" Josephine can't hold her laughter in, and it tells me just how ridiculous I must look. "I wanted to try something. I bet I could make it look like the queen's."

"She has Léonard Autié to do her hair!" I try to laugh, again, but I'm laced far too tight in my stays. How does anyone wear these?

Josephine pleads with me. "At least let me powder your hair or paint your lips." She bats her eyelashes at me. "Pretty please." She's mocking the things I say to her when the roles are reversed and I'm dressing her up.

Just then, Rachelle and Lola pass by, two beautifully

devastating reminders that no matter how much powder or paint I could apply, I'd still never look like them. Rachelle adjusts her corset. Her curls barely move as she does it, never a strand out of place. Like me, everyone else is watching her, too, and I decide some people are just dealt a better hand.

"No," I tell Josephine assuredly, "I don't want any of that stuff. Let's just get this over with."

Madame Bissett herds us into a line. She's put me near the back, and now I have even longer to agonize over every possible scenario of how this could all go wrong. I'm not the very last one, though. That place has been reserved for Rachelle. The Chastain twins are side-eyeing her for it when she isn't looking.

My back is turned when Rachelle starts complaining. "Why did they put me in this thing? Ruffles at my hips? And buttercream yellow? It's gross. Why couldn't they put me in something like *that*?"

I don't have to turn around to know she's pointing at me, at the dress I made. It's pistachio green and not at all my color—it was Morgan's color—but it has tulle that gathers sheer like frost at my collarbone and lace that blooms in tiers at my wrists. The beading alone took me most of the last few months. The things Rachelle and Lola and the twins wear on a daily basis are beautiful, and their couture especially is brilliant. It's new and fresh and exciting, a departure from the standard French dress—no doubt inspired by the queen— but it isn't mine. My style is different. It may not be able to compete with their couture now, but if I could ever leave the bakery, ever get some real training, find a real mentor . . .

"Ready?" Jo asks, knocking me from my thoughts.

My mouth twists. No, of course not.

I catch Rachelle still staring at my dress. She cocks her head to the side a little, surveying. "Hmm," she mutters under her breath. Rachelle LeBlanc is admiring my work, and I have to smile a little because it's the only thing they can't take from me.

Madame Bissett claps her hands together. "Places," she says, "we're almost ready, and we've got quite the audience. Monsieur Travers and Madame Wright have also brought their classes."

My stomach drops. It was supposed to be one class and one class only, an impromptu show for maybe twenty people. Now the whole university theater might as well be filled.

Lola squeals. "Dre is in Monsieur Travers's class. I'm going to give him a show."

Rachelle lets out a sigh. "Great. Beau is in that class, too."

"Well," says Darcy Chastain, "you can just show him what he's missing, then."

Rachelle jerks her head in Darcy's direction. "*I* broke up with him, Darcy. I don't have to show him what he's missing. He already knows."

I thought it would feel better than it did, seeing Beau Bellegarde with that foolish look on his face as she told him it was over. But it didn't. It was just sad. I almost felt sorry for him. Almost.

Someone starts playing a violin and the line starts moving

and I can feel my heart in my throat.

Josephine runs up and grabs my arm. "I had a peek out there. It's not bad. I'm going to be on the other side of the stage. Just keep your eyes on me, walk right across, and it'll all be over before you know it."

"Easy for you to say," I tell her.

The first girl goes, and the second, and the third. I'm quickly shoved farther up the line, and I get a good look at the audience for the first time from behind the curtain. One thing's for certain: Jo lied about it not being bad. The seats are filled as far as I can see, and suddenly, I'm regretting all my choices that led to this moment. Why did I have to take Madame Bissett's dressmaking class? Why couldn't I have been satisfied with taking over the bakery for my father? Why did Madame Landry have to teach me how to sew all those years ago?

Madame Bissett's hand is on my back, her bony fingers pushing me forward, but I can't move.

"Evie," Madame Bissett hisses. "Evie, go!"

I stumble out onto the theater stage, and they're all staring up at me, every face, even the violinist glances over at me as she plays. I search for Jo on the other side, but it's too dark and I can't see anything through the curtains.

Walk, Evie. It's about the dress. Just walk.

I will my feet to move, holding my hands out at my side trying to steady myself on the heels. I must look like a newborn baby calf trying with knock-knees to walk for the first time. Finally, I find my balance, gripping the shoes with my toes as best I can. Madame Wright is smiling. Maybe this is it. Maybe this is the moment that everyone finally realizes what I can do. Maybe all the girls will ask me to make their dresses for the Court Ball. I could even teach myself to make matching masks, I could sell them as a set. I tilt my chin up, square my shoulders back, and just as the tightness in my chest gives, I hear a sound from the audience, like a muffled laugh.

I turn my head, and my eyes lock on Julien's. He's whispering something to Beau and Dre, and I can't tell if they're looking at me or not, but I think they are. They have to be. It's only me up here. They're laughing at me. Suddenly, I can't breathe. Things start to go hazy and my heart picks up even more speed, and I forget all about gripping the shoes because my heel gets hooked into a divot in the stage. The moment I feel my foot teetering, I know it's over, I don't have a chance. I manage to avoid a complete faceplant, catching myself on my hands as I go down, skinning my palms on the stage's surface. It happens so fast that I don't remember standing back up or hobbling offstage, only that the boy holding the curtain ropes is doubled over cackling and one of my feet is bare on the floor, a single cherry-blossom-pink heel left behind.

Jo's fumbling around, one hand gripping mine and the other sliding a crate across the floor. "Sit down," she says. "You're bleeding."

"I'm what?" I ask her. I sit because I may faint otherwise. I reach back and start grabbing at the corset laces, but Jo is already on it, unstringing them enough to give me relief. I take a deep breath, and that's when I feel the stinging in my knee. It's nothing, just a scrape, but Jo is already wrapping spare fabric around it and propping it up like I've been mortally wounded. "How bad was it?"

"It was nothing," she tries to say, but my face is already buried in my tender hands. She ties a tight knot at the scrape and taps me on the shoulder. "Look, they've all forgotten about it already."

I pull my fingers apart enough to look onto the stage, and there's Lola. She's twirling, jumping around, and dancing even though she can't really dance. She's laughing at herself, and everyone's cheering her on. One of her more aggressive twirls sends her puffy skirt rising a little, and right when it looks like Madame Bissett might rush her off the stage, Lola dizzily runs off, right toward me and Josephine. She's howling laughing and out of breath, but she gives me a quick wink before heading into the dressing room, so subtle Josephine doesn't notice it. What was that? Did she do that for me? Did she want to make them forget about my fall? No. Couldn't be.

The crowd gets even louder, and I know exactly who it is they're all yelling for. Rachelle is wearing Amelie's dress, and it doesn't matter that she doesn't like the ruffles at her hips because she still looks perfect. She looks like all the other women in the Court of Flowers, the ones who walk through town with glittering parasols, the ones everyone watches from their windows and wishes they could be. And I don't know why I do it, but I stand up and walk to the curtains just to see.

I'm not looking at her, though. I'm probably the only one not looking at her. I'm looking out in the crowd, looking for Beau, but his seat is empty. Dre and Julien are still there. Julien is on his feet with his hands cupped around his mouth yelling for Rachelle while Monsieur Travers tries to get him to sit down.

So, I look back at Rachelle. Her skin is shimmering champagne, her smile effortless like she knows how much everyone loves her. Up until this morning, she was dating the most popular boy in school, and now she doesn't even look like she cares that it's over. And why would she, when every person in this theater wants her or wants to be her?

I wonder what that would feel like.

We're in the dressing room, and I'm finally back in my own clothes, my comfortable, wonderful, boneless clothes. Everyone's huddled around Madame Bissett like a pack of wolves as she hands out the invites to the Court of Flowers Ball. It's perfect timing, too, because they're all so excited about it that none of them seem to be thinking about the fall I just took.

"Grabbed you one," Josephine says, handing over a rolled piece of parchment dyed a barely there blush pink. It twinkles as I unfurl it, the edges embossed with flowers and interlaced with gilded vines.

court OF flowers Ball

"It is the belief in roses that makes them flourish."

·⊹∽⊱·

*The Court requests the pleasure of
your company in attendance to the Ball,
On Friday, 30th of May, current, at 7 o'clock P.M.
Bellegarde Bloom announced at first starlight*

I hold the parchment to my nose. "Is that perfume?"

"Probably," Josephine says. "Who are you going to vote for?"

I shrug. "No one." I never nominate anyone for court, the five girls who get to be in the running for Bellegarde Bloom. It's pointless. Each year, it's always the five girls you assume will be chosen—the ones with dazzling mansions and last names that mean something in Paris. It's madness, really. Girls spend all season trying to secure an escort, someone whose arm we'll hang on as we enter the Ball, but after that, it's a frenzy. The Ball is the biggest event of the year for French teenagers to find a match, so once we're in the doors, the room erupts into a chaos of flirtation.

Although we're the only school in the neighborhood, and although only Parisian girls are considered for the title of Bloom, others our age pour in from all over France hoping to find someone worthy of marriage.

The Ball began as such, as a way for students to meet others in hopes of creating strong matches. The first year, an elected board made up of various French university officials chose a girl who they thought represented the elite of the elite—the most eligible bachelorette at the event. She was named the Bloom and was given a boutonniere to pin on her choice of suitor, a king and queen of the Ball so to speak. The first girl ever chosen for it was Anne Grand, Beau Bellegarde's great-great-grandmother. She pinned her boutonniere on François Bellegarde, who she then went on to marry. The title became known as the Bellegarde Bloom after their successful pairing, and François, after amassing his enormous wealth, bought a flower shop as a gift to Anne, one of his many investments. He named the shop Bellegarde Blooms, and now I have to see their rose-and-wisteria-filled carriages bouncing down Rue Saint-Honoré each week, the Bellegarde name inescapable.

Out of that, with Anne at the helm, the Court of Flowers was born—an exclusive women's club made up of only those who are named the Bellegarde Bloom. They took over for the board and have been running the Ball ever since. The Court of Flowers is what most high-society Parisian girls aspire to. They marry powerful men and spend their days dripping in jewels, being adored, and planning parties.

This year it *really* doesn't matter who is nominated. Put the queen herself in the running, and the Court will still probably give it to Rachelle. Still, I smirk over at Josephine. "Or maybe I'll just put your name down five times."

"Well, I'm putting *you* down," she says. "And Mia, of course. Did you see her out there?"

"Didn't see much out there, Jo. Too busy looking at the floor."

Josephine frowns. "You think she'd go to the Ball with me?"

"You mean as an escort?" I ask. "She's a Bellegarde. She'll have boys crawling all over her trying to escort *her* in."

"I don't know," she says with an unsure shake of her head. "I thought maybe we could escort each other in. Maybe it's a silly thought."

I don't know much about Mia. She's a Bellegarde, which makes me apprehensive, but I know that Josephine wants to know her, and that's enough for me. "No, it's not silly," I tell her. "She'd be crazy not to want to attend with you."

"Thanks, Evie," she says with a grin. "You ready?"

"I need to grab my shoes," I say. "I'll be right out."

I slip my boots on at the dress rack, my ankle still aching. For a moment, before I leave, I admire my dress. I may not have done it justice, but it's still the prettiest one on the rack.

"Hey," a nearby voice says. I look up to see Lola dancing her fingers across my dress's tulle. "Did you make this?" She's apple-cheeked with amber eyes that match her braids. Sparkling lavender powder still lingers at her temples and dusts her brown chest.

I nod. "I did, yeah."

Lola runs her hand down one of the sleeves. "This

beading must have taken you forever."

I let out a small laugh. "Something like that."

"My grandmother used to sew," she says. "She made most of my clothes growing up. She tried to teach me, but I was hopeless."

"It's tough," I say, thinking about Jo, about how no matter how many times I show her a technique, it almost never goes right.

"Well, you're definitely a natural. This looks like something that could be in the palace. I wish I had one like it."

"I could always make you one," I blurt out. I say it before I have time to think, but Lola St. Martin wearing one of my gowns would be pretty grand. She'd even pay me to make it. A nice sum, I bet. If I could dress someone like her, it could be the start to my future.

"I'd love that!" Lola says.

Rachelle snatches a skirt off of the rack and starts changing into her school outfit. "What would you love?"

"Oh, she was saying she could make me a gown like this," Lola tells her before looking back at me. "It's Evie, isn't it?"

We've only been going to school together most of our lives. "Uh, yes—yeah, it's Evie."

Rachelle chuckles. "Yeah, right, like you don't already have a closet full of couture." She turns to me. "No offense, of course."

Of course.

"Well, I think—" Lola starts, but Rachelle cuts her off.

"Zip me up?"

"Sure," Lola says. And once she does, they both leave. Lola never looks back at me. I was foolish to think she might be different.

The boy, Cliff, who'd been holding the curtain ropes just offstage, approaches me as the girls take their leave.

"Ouch." He cringes. "That was brutal. My advice? You might want to stick to pastries."

I blink. "What?"

"I said"—Cliff raises his voice, but only high enough for me to hear—"you're the girl always covered in flour, and to them, you're never going to be more than that. It's best you go ahead and stop trying. They're never going to accept the flour girl."

He doesn't even give me a chance to respond before he's out the same door Lola and Rachelle just left through.

Never going to accept me? I'm the *flour girl*? Is that what they call me? And how very rich coming from Cliff, the biggest, most unsuccessful social climber in all of the university.

I step out into the courtyard and look for Josephine. I won't tell her about Cliff because she'll go after him, and I can't risk having her thrown out of university this close to graduation. I try to shake him and his red-haired, freckle-faced scowl from my mind, but I can't get rid of his words. *Flour girl.* Is that all I am? After seventeen years, twelve years of being in school with them, is that all they think of me?

CHAPTER FOUR

BEAU

Everyone in Paris thinks I've got it all, but here in this drab law office, I just finished signing a piece of paper that says I've got nothing. Well, almost nothing.

"Cheer up, brother," Julien says to me on our way out of his uncle's office, "I'm sure we can have you a nameplate made for your desk."

It's the same joke he tells every time. Except, really, I don't think he's joking. He thinks he's so funny. What he doesn't know, or maybe he does, is how badly I'd like to land my fist between his eyes.

Anyone that thinks I've got no problems should ask my father about my inheritance, about how the day Julien and I graduate, Julien will inherit most of the family wealth—the money, the land, the properties—and I'll get my mother's cottage on the outskirts of London. Julien's uncle claims it's because Julien is the firstborn son, born two months and four days before me. But I know the truth. I know it's really because I'm the child of a mistress. This is how Julien's mother wants it, and this is what my father agreed to, because he just can't stand up to her.

We have to sign the papers once a year, and I have to be reminded that no matter how much my father denies it, Julien and I will always be treated differently. I will always be the mistress's boy, the one who only gets to live in the main house in Paris because his mother fell ill and died when he was six.

Dre is waiting for us on the other side of the street, shielding his eyes from the sun, and pointing to the clock. "What took you so long? The girls left me here!"

"Had to take care of a few things," Julien says. He throws his arm around me. "Family business, right?"

I nod. "Sure."

Julien shakes me. "Loosen up, brother. Dre, where'd the girls go?"

"Not sure," Dre answers. He brushes a hand over his close-cropped Afro and grits his teeth before motioning farther up the street. "Wasn't paying much attention, but I think they went into one of those shops down there. Lola wanted to try on dresses for the ball."

"Well," Julien says, "are we going to find them, or what?"

"And sit in a dress shop for hours?" I ask. "No way." No one tells you how strange it is when your friend group involves your girlfriend and then that girlfriend breaks up with you and you're expected to still hang out with her.

"Speak for yourself," says Julien, starting off down the street. "I'm a few good lines away from bedding Darcy. Or Diane. Both if I play it right."

I shake my head. He doesn't have a chance.

Dre laughs into his hands. "Yeah, yeah, you keep telling yourself that."

Julien turns his head to watch a passing girl. "Whatever, I'm going to find them."

Anyone who's anyone is on the Rue du Faubourg Saint-Honoré on a late weekday afternoon, after the clocks ring, after university lets out. The shops are bustling, the bread is warm, the café always has a quartet playing outside, and if you know to ask for Luis, Dre's cousin, like we did, you can get a little liquor slipped in your tea.

"Why don't we go to the café?" I propose. "They always end up there anyway."

"I think someone doesn't want to see Rachelle," Dre teases. He and Lola have been obsessed with each other since we were ten. They've always known they would be together. Sometimes I wish I was that certain about anything.

I lie. "No, that's not it."

"Oh, come on," Julien says, "get over it." He leads the way, though, and I follow because what am I going to do? Go sit at the café alone?

Julien knows I don't have to get over it, not Rachelle at least. He knows why I was with her. He's still mad about it, about her not choosing him. I can see it in his eyes, the way he looks like he couldn't be happier that she's dumped me. He tried with her once. It's why his nose is crooked.

"There they are," Dre says. The Chastain twins are standing with Lola on the sidewalk, each one weighed down by an armful of shopping bags.

"Girls, girls, girls." Julien grins as he walks up to the twins. "What color am I wearing to escort you to the ball? Emerald? Plum? I've been told I look good in blue, but with this face, I can make anything work."

"You should ask Leo and Blaise," Lola teases with a raised eyebrow. "They've already got their dress coats."

Julien scoffs. "Leo and Blaise? Why would I ask them?"

I clear my throat. He's always the last to the party. "I think she's saying that the twins are being escorted by Leo and Blaise."

Julien straightens. "Those rapscallions? You're joking."

"They aren't rapscallions," Diane snaps back at him.

"Yes, they're our cousins," adds Darcy.

Julien instantly cools down, clutching his chest to feign relief. "Oh, well, that changes everything. Don't go breaking my heart now, girls."

Dre shoots me a look, and the two of us can't help ourselves, so we burst out laughing.

Julien turns to me. "Who is it you're escorting at the ball again, Beau?"

"I don't know, Julien. Maybe we should just walk in together since it seems neither of us have someone to escort," I challenge.

"Hmm," he says, looking me up and down. "Shouldn't be too hard for you to find a new date should it, little brother? You must have every girl in Paris knocking down your door. Oh, except, we live at the same house, and I haven't heard one knock." Our eyes keep on each other for a second too long before he turns around to the girls to see their reaction, hoping they think he's as hilarious as he thinks he is.

They've already stopped paying attention to him, though. Their focus is directed elsewhere. We *really* should've gone to the café, because the boutique door opens and out comes Rachelle arm in arm with a lanky, goofy-grinned brute who needs a haircut. I can only assume he is the famous baron.

I don't have to assume for long because as soon as they get close, Rachelle takes a moment away from leaning her head on his shoulder and says, "Boys, this is Nicolas, Baron of Brittany. He's come into town to surprise me. Isn't that sweet?"

"So, *so* sweet," Julien exaggerates before looking back at me, eating this up. "Don't you think so, Beau?"

I sigh. "Oh, yes, I can't believe he had a second to step away from all of his baron duties. What are those again?"

Rachelle's lip curls up. "If you must know, Beau, Nicolas here is very busy. Tell him how busy you are, darling."

The baron shakes his hair out of his face. "Uh, busy? Sure." His eyebrows crinkle like he's confused, but then he lets out a dopey chuckle, like he was only trying to remember what he did mere hours ago. "Fed the cows, took some letters to my sister. Oh! I got to take a boat out with a real fisherman today. He even let me steer."

"Well, would you look at that," I say to Rachelle. My dimples press in as I try to maintain a straight face. "He even got to steer."

"Shut up, Beau," she jeers back at me. "Nicolas just bought my dress for the Court Ball. Even picked up a gilded mask to match. He's escorting me." There's nothing Rachelle hates more than not having the upper hand.

"Congratulations," I say. Nothing surprising about that. What will be a surprise is if the baron actually makes it to the ball before Rachelle trades him in for a newer, better model.

Julien can't help himself. "We were actually just discussing who Beau is going to be escorting at the ball."

Rachelle folds her arms and glares at me sourly. "Well? Who's the lucky lady, Beau?"

"There isn't one," I tell her. "Some of us have the ability to be alone for more than a week."

Rachelle wrinkles her mouth and nudges the baron. "I think it's time to go, darling. Didn't you say you've got something special planned for us?"

"I— Well," Nicolas starts, but Rachelle quickly cuts him off.

"Can't wait to see what it is," she says. "Ugh, I just can't get enough of you." She shoves her hand through his hair and presses her lips to his. We all stand there awkwardly looking at each other while their tongues get acquainted. Once they finally break apart, Rachelle stares straight at me. She flashes a wink over her shoulder as she saunters away.

"Well, well, well," Julian says to me, walking in proud strides. "Looks like it didn't take Rachelle long to move on. How are you feeling now that you won't be escorting the girl that's going to take home the title of the Bellegarde Bloom?"

We cross over the street and walk along the sidewalk. Ivy blooms scatter the pavement and creep up the storefronts. Up ahead, two girls from the university in tight embroidered bodices and shorter-than-usual petticoats walk in step with each other. I think I have a class with them, or at least one of them. They're quite pretty, but I've never noticed them until today.

"It's my last name on the title!" I blurt out before correcting myself, hoping my nonchalant attitude is convincing. "*Our* last name. So why would I care? Besides, Rachelle isn't necessarily going to be Bloom. It could go to any girl. She hasn't won yet."

Even Dre laughs at the thought. "I don't know. Isn't she destined to win or something? Isn't it practically in the Le-Blanc blood?"

It might not be in their blood, but the women in Rachelle's family have won Bellegarde Bloom for generations. Her mother, her mother's mother, and her mother's mother's mother. They've all won Bloom, and then they've all found the most prestigious suitor at the Ball, pinned their boutonniere on his lapel, and later went on to marry him. Only her aunt Geneviève didn't marry the suitor she pinned, and that's because she found an old marquis foolish enough to fall for her tricks. I don't think there's a drop of love in that family. Just money and status.

"Now I know you're losing it," Julien says. "Any girl could

become Bloom? Any girl could beat Rachelle? Tell me, Beau, how in this fantasy land of yours, would that ever be possible?"

I shrug. "Firstly, no one knows the baron. Part of Rachelle's appeal was that she was dating a Bellegarde."

Julien smiles. "Oh, right, yes, so you're the only reason she would've won?"

"I'm not the only reason," I say, "but I don't need Rachelle. Rachelle was relying on my name just as much as her own to stand out. Without me she's just another rich socialite made up of hair and rouge and couture."

"Don't forget the jewels," Julien says with a sly grin, "particularly the necklace the baron gave her."

I shake my head. "Doesn't matter. I'm telling you, I could make any girl at the university into the Bloom."

This seems to pique Julien's interest because he stops in his tracks and turns to me. "You sure about that?"

"Of course I am," I say. I'm not, but he's been acting so high and mighty today that I double down. "Any one of them."

Julien looks at me like he's sizing me up. "Want to bet?"

"Bet?" I ask.

"Yes," he says, "if you're so sure that you, Beau Bellegarde, King of the School, can make any girl at the university into the Bloom, then let's bet on it."

"I don't know, I don't think—" Dre starts, but I step in.

"Sure," I say, "when I find out what's in it for me."

Julien scratches his chin. "In it for you?"

"If I win," I say, "which I will—what do I get? I'm not doing this for nothing."

"Hmm," says Julien, thinking on it. He hesitates but then gets a look in his eye, and his mouth spreads into a smirk. "How about if you win, you get my inheritance."

I don't know what to say. I can't tell if he's playing me for a fool or not, so I let him keep talking.

"Right. I'll pick the girl," he continues. "Any girl I want. And you have less than four weeks to turn her into the Bellegarde Bloom. If your girl wins, you can have it all, instead of just your mother's little shack in London."

Her shack. His words make my blood boil, but I can tell he's serious. He's just foolish enough to be serious.

"And if you lose," Julien says, "I'll tell father about your big career aspirations, about how you've no intention to go into finance, about how you've been searching for any way out of it. You lose and I tell him everything. And when I do, he'll be so furious that he'll take the little shack in London away from you and add it to my pile."

Julien knows. How does he always know everything? Somehow, he knows about me wanting to write, about how hard I'm trying to conjure up a plan to get out of working at Father's office. And he's right. I hate that he's right. If I don't fall in line with Father's plans for me, I'll lose the cottage, the only thing that's mine.

It's cruel, but I know Julien all too well. All he wants is to have everything I've ever called my own. He's taken every

single thing from me over the years, and now he wants to take
my father from me, and what little I have left of my mother.

But he's going to lose. Dre tries to intervene, but I stick
my hand out and clasp Julien's before he can get a word in.
"Deal." We shake on it.

Dre slaps a hand to his forehead. "Did that really just
happen? You two are actually doing this?"

Julien looks triumphant already, like he can't believe I've
agreed to it. My chest is puffed, but my stomach begins to
sink because I don't know what I've done. Did I really say I
could make *any* girl into the Bloom?

I can't let Julien see me sweat, so I hold my shoulders back
and ask, "So, who's it going to be?"

Julien rubs his hands together excitedly and starts walking. "Let's check out the menu, gentlemen."

He takes us into the apothecary first, and I'm hit with a
barrage of scents all at once: citrus, mint, coriander. My head
starts to spin.

Julien points over to a particularly odd-looking girl
standing by a shelf full of tiny glass jars. "What about her?"
he says.

I know she goes to our school, but I've no clue what her
name is. Her dark hair is wiry and frizzed, and she's wearing
two different socks. She opens one of the jars and gives it a
sniff. I think that's all she's going to do, but then she dabs a
little onto her palm and gives it a taste.

All three of us lurch back in disgust.

"Now, Julien, you can't do that to him," says Dre.

I've got my fingers crossed he won't, but when she turns around, looking over her shoulder to see if anyone spotted her, she's actually kind of cute. Odd-looking, sure, but with a comb and a different outfit, I might be okay.

Julien seems to notice the same thing I do, too, because he quickly says, "She's not the one," and drags us back onto the street.

The next girl he eyes is a girl whose name I know, Madeleine. She's only been at the university a few years.

"She could work," Julien says.

Madeleine is outside the café standing around a small gathering of musicians. Her hair is much shorter than most of the girls at school, pinned into rolls that stop at the base of her chin, and barely adorned. She's always dressed in something plain, and she never wears a stitch of rouge. Today is no different.

"She's got potential," I say, lying, hoping Julien might take the bait. She might have potential, but it would be a complete overhaul, and plus, Madeleine is a bit wicked. She has a tongue sharp as thorns and already scares most everyone, so improving her likability in a month's time would be near impossible.

We watch her for a moment, and Julien decides, "No, not her."

"Oh, there's one," Dre says, motioning on down the street.

I elbow him when I see her. "Really? You're getting involved now?"

Julien turns around and spots her. "Caroline Dupree," he says gleefully. "Now *that* would be a fair bet."

Caroline is walking her enormous poodle down the sidewalk. The dog is snow white and comes up to her ribs. She's dressed the thing exactly to match her, both with glittering pink choker necklaces and a bouffant over-powdered hairdo, the weight of which could send her toppling over any moment. I'm already imagining having to spend time with her the next few weeks, having to listen to her high-pitched shrill of a voice, and having to act interested in her poodle's pedigree. I hang my head in my hands.

"Looks like we might have found her, eh, Beau," Julien mocks.

The shop door next to us flies open, the bells clanging and chiming against each other as it does. We all turn to see the person who's bursting from the bakery, hacking and coughing, covered from head to toe in flour. She shakes and shakes, a white dust cloud forming around her. Caroline Dupree yelps, jumping out of the way, before turning to head in a different direction with a disgusted look on her face.

"Violette!" the flour-coated girl yells back into the bakery. "What did I tell you about mixing by yourself?"

"Oooh," Dre says, laughing, "that's brutal."

"Oh, would you look at that," Julien says, staring at her. He glances back to us. "Looks like a Bellegarde Bloom to me!"

"Evie Clément?" I gulp. "No. No way. Not her. Find someone else. What about Caroline? I thought we were going with Caroline."

I look back to her. She's yelling something I can't make out to a young girl who's just inside the shop, looking particularly mischievous. Evie whips her hair to the side and gives it one last rattle before heading back in, her flour footprints following behind.

Julien cocks his head smiling. "Oh, what's that, brother? Something wrong with Evie?"

"Are you kidding?" I thrust my hand out. "Look at her! Beyond the fact that she's always got icing in her hair or flour on her dress, or the fact that she fell flat on her face in front of most of the school today, she's completely unapproachable and she despises me! She's never going to speak to me, let alone say yes to going to the ball with me. No. Pick again."

And I instantly know I should've never opened my mouth about Evie because Julien has smelled the blood in the water. "Evie Clément it is, then," he says. "Can't wait to see how father takes it when you lose."

"Julien, please," I say. "I'm serious. She *hates* me."

He couldn't be happier. "I guess that means you better get going, brother. You've got less than a month to turn that weed into a rose."

CHAPTER FIVE

EVIE

I can't be too mad at Violette. She's got one of those faces that turns everyone into mush, and that's why she's sitting pretty and I'm the one covered in flour and left sweeping all the rest of it off the floor after she had a mixing disaster.

"You know you could give me a hand, right?" I tell her as she swings her legs from the countertop. "And get down from there. Father'll have us both if you scuff up the cabinets."

She uses the stool to climb down and pokes her bottom lip out. "I can't help. We've only got one broom."

"How convenient. Then go over there and flip the door sign to Closed. We've got to get this place cleaned up before any customers try to come in. Or worse, Father."

About that time, the bell above the door chimes.

"Violette, I said to close it." I stand to see what she's up to, knocking the flour from my knees, but it isn't her that's opened the door. It's Beau Bellegarde.

"Ah, sorry," I say. Of course Beau would come in now, when I look like this, like the bakery exploded. "We're closed."

He points to the door. Violette is standing behind him with blushed cheeks and eyes wider than a fawn. "Oh," he says, "well, that's not what your sign says."

I drop the broom and glare at Violette. "That's because someone hasn't switched it yet."

Violette runs up behind Beau like she's trying to get a closer look at him. He twists around and locks eyes on her. "I'd suppose that someone she's talking about is you, huh?"

Violette nods shyly.

Beau smiles down at her. "You wouldn't have been the one to make this mess, would you?"

She's biting down on her thumb and swaying from side to side. She's entranced by the Beau Bellegarde charm. If she only knew how fake that charm is. "Uh-uh," she says, shaking her head no.

"Well, that's a lie if I've ever heard one," I say to Violette.

"Chérubin," Beau says, reading the sign that hangs above my head. "I like the name."

"Thanks," I say hesitantly, cautious of his kindness. I've always been fond of it as well—Chérubin, the bakery named by my grand-père who always said my grand-mère had the sweet face of an angel. "Anyway, like I said, we're closed. Unless you'd like one of these cakes, and in that case, they're double the price."

"Oh, double the price?" he asks. "Is that right?" I was counting on that getting him out of here, but he approaches the display case and crouches down, surveying the cakes father made this morning. Fine. If he wants, I'll take his money.

"Sure is," I say. "You know, afternoon surge and all."

"Afternoon surge," he says. He looks around the bakery, empty except for the three of us and a heap of wet flour I'll be scrubbing from the tile for the next couple of hours. "Right." He turns back to Violette and asks, "Which one is your favorite?"

She's laying it on thick, casually twirling in her dress. "Mmm," she says. She points to the cardamom-pistachio brioche with rosewater glaze. "That one."

Violette's true favorite are the blueberry scones, but the brioche is one of our most expensive pastries. Clever girl.

"And what about you?" Beau looks up at me. His eyes are the same blue as when we were kids, like sea salt and starlight. The only difference is that now I see the deception behind them.

"Don't have a favorite," I tell him. "We don't eat much cake around here."

He nods, straightening up and shoving his hands in his pockets. He's studying me. Why is he studying me? "Well, what do you do around here, then?"

"What do I do around the bakery?" I ask.

He laughs. "No. What do you do for fun? I never see you out. Never seen you at the Gardens or the château, or anywhere other than university, really."

I take a breath. What's he getting at? "I'm sorry, is there something I can help you with?"

"What? A gentleman can't ask you a question?"

I catch a hazy reflection of myself in one of the bread tins, at my flour coating, and I couldn't look more absurd if I tried. I'll have to tell Jo that she finally got her wish of my hair being powdered.

"Okay," I start. "Well, fun isn't really a priority of mine. My best friend and I sneak in the theater sometimes, so I suppose that's fun, though I'm not sure by your standards. But usually, I'm here. Working." I pause, looking up at his smug face. "And the Gardens? The château? You don't see me at those places because I don't want to be at those places."

At least, I don't think I want to be at those places. I've heard what goes on at the château—the elaborate parties and the champagne swiped from parents' secret stores. But I've never been invited.

He's grinning and nodding his head. I've just insulted his very existence, and he finds it humorous. "Well, maybe we should change that."

"Maybe not," I say.

Violette is hanging on our every word.

"Sneaking into the theater sounds fun," he says, ignoring my slight. "You could teach me how to do that."

What's he playing at? This is the first time Beau Bellegarde has spoken to me in years. Unless, of course, you count that time a couple of years ago when he bumped into me in the hall and managed to mumble something that sounded like an apology.

"Look," I say. "I don't know what you're getting at or who

told you to come in here—" I stop because I can see them. They're standing outside the window, Julien and Dre, both craning their ruffle-collared necks to see in, to see Beau. To see me. Of course. They've sent him in here as a joke, and I'm the punch line. My fists tighten, but I take a deep breath. I want to say everything I've never said to him. But I can't. Not right now. Not in front of Violette. So, I tell him something different. "Hey, actually, I've got something you can do for me instead."

He perks up. "Really?"

"Yeah," I say, leading him to the door. "Could you help me take this sign down? My father keeps forgetting, and I can't reach it. We ran out of lavender petit fours weeks ago, and people keep coming asking for them because I can't get to that sign." Violette starts to follow us, but I motion to her to stay back and give her a quick wink.

Beau holds the door as if he's got a gentlemanly bone in his body, but I don't thank him.

I point up to the crooked, far-out-of-my-reach sign, advertising my father's famous lavender petit fours. "It's that one there."

I can see Julien and Dre out of the corner of my eye. They're watching us intently, but I act like I don't see them. They're not worth my attention.

Beau stretches, grabbing for the sign, but even he isn't tall enough to match Father's giant reach. Exactly as I thought.

"Maybe you could flip that crate over and stand on it," I

suggest, pointing to the wooden box Madame Landry leaves out, filled with hay . . . and underneath that hay, her sleeping, ornery cat Timmons.

"This one?" he asks, bending down. I nod, covering my grin. Beau's fingers don't even touch the hay before Timmons shrieks from underneath the pile, his paws flailing. Beau goes flying backward but not before Timmons's claws nick his culottes.

"Ouch!" Beau squeals. Timmons arches his orange back and hisses before running in Madame Landry's open door. Beau turns his attention to me. "Did you know that cat was in there?" In his distraction, he's crossed the threshold of the door, now standing on the street and looking in at me with a pained expression.

"Sorry, must've forgotten," I manage to say through the laughter. "But anyway, I can't help you. Like I said, we're closed." I shut and lock the bakery door, flipping our sign to read Closed. I lock eyes with Beau for a tiny moment before he turns to Dre and Julien and starts ranting something. I can't hear the words, but it's safe to guess whatever he's saying isn't in my favor.

"Evie!" I turn to see Violette standing behind me, hand on hip like she's scolding me for something. "You know Timmons likes that spot!"

"I know, I know. That wasn't very good of me."

"No," she says, wagging her little finger. "That boy was nice, Evie. And he has a really pretty face, too."

"That boy is a monster, Violette."

"Didn't look like a monster to me," she says back.

"Well, sometimes people surprise you," I say, but she doesn't look convinced. "Now, why don't you surprise me and help me clean this mess before Father gets back."

The sun's going down, and I can tell Jo is mad that I'm late.

"Nice of you to show up," she calls out as I round the corner. Jo's street is worse off than ours. The apartments are lopsided and squeezed together like tilted books on a shelf. Living above the bakery isn't the high life, but we don't have it as bad. They keep the streets relatively clean, and the shop-keepers' families all look out for each other.

"Emergency at the bakery," I tell her. "Violette thought she could bake without me again."

Josephine cracks a smile but quickly covers it. She remembers the last time Violette tried and what a disaster it was. We were scraping dough from the ceiling for weeks. Jo covers her smile, though, because she wants me to know she's mad.

"I'm really sorry, Jo," I say. "Promise I'll do better. Forgive me?"

She rubs her chin, her eyes narrowing on me. "Ugh." She jumps up from the steps. "I guess. But now we're going to have to hurry if we want to get back before dark, so you better have brought your running shoes."

"Back before dark?" I say. "Where are we going?"

"Well," she says, pulling an envelope from the satchel

slung over her shoulder, "I may have bribed father to give me something." Her father works for the Petite Post. He's gone most of the time, at least ten runs a day. Sometimes more. Josephine's always scouring the letters he gets to deliver, seeing if there's any she wants to deliver herself. She got to go to the palace with him once, but they didn't let them past the gates. She made the trek with him just to hand a letter to a guardsman. I'll never let her live that one down.

"Who's it for?"

Her smile grows. She hands me the letter. "See for yourself."

I flip the envelope over. "Mia Bellegarde?"

Josephine's shoulders raise, tense with excitement. "Yep."

"Okay," I say, confused. "And is there a plan attached to this?"

"Plan?"

"Well, sure, is this how you're hoping to ask if you can escort her to the Court Ball?"

She looks at me as if I'm crazy. "What? No! No way. When I ask to escort her, it's going to be better than showing up to her house with a letter."

"Mm-hmm." I nod. "So, have you thought up anything to say to her, then?"

"Well, no. Not exactly. I'll just—I'll knock on the door and then—then I don't know, I'll think of something."

"All right, so, no plan. Off to Mia's house we go."

Josephine leads the way. I don't have to guess what area

we're going to. The rich kids at school all live in the same few blocks of each other.

It isn't much of a walk, but it's enough time to tell her about Beau. She's just as bewildered as I am as to why he was in the shop asking me questions, but she doesn't come to the same conclusion I have. She still holds out hope that Beau Bellegarde is decent, and I'll never understand why. But she doesn't say much about the whole ordeal—her mind seems preoccupied, and I think I know why.

"What do you like so much about Mia, anyway?" I ask her, changing the subject. "Other than how pretty she is. What do you see in her?"

She exhales a long sigh. "I don't know," she says. "I think I like the possibility of her."

"The possibility? Whatever does that mean?"

It takes her a moment before she answers. "Right now, I don't know her. But I want to. She's so—*so* beautiful, you know? And at first, I thought she was beautiful like those ornate old gilded mirrors in Monsieur Dubois's shopwindow. You remember those?"

I nod. I do remember them. Josephine and I used to walk slowly past his shop so that we could catch our reflection in those mirrors—they were hand-carved with roses and eucalyptus branches. One day, someone in the social elite, perhaps even a royal, would be looking at themselves in those mirrors, but on those days, it was us. That was before Monsieur Dubois started chasing us off, not wanting us loitering at his storefront.

"I thought Mia was like that. This beautiful thing I would never know up close, something I'd watch be carted away by someone who wasn't me, someone I could never compete with. But she's more than that. When she came into Madame Grangier's class that first time . . ." She smiles.

"I saw her," Jo continues, "and there was something about her, like I knew her from somewhere."

"Hasn't she lived in the country before now?"

"Yes." She shakes her head. "I don't mean I'd met her before. I mean it felt like I *knew* her. Like, have you ever seen someone and even though you know for sure that they're a stranger, they look familiar? It was like that, like I knew her from a past life or a dream or something. And slowly, I began to realize that she was less like one of those fancy mirrors in Monsieur Dubois's window and more like a sunset over the Seine or a warm memory. . . . The kind of beauty I could actually have in my life. I don't know, but I can't let it go."

I've never felt that way about anyone, and I'm not sure I ever will. But I'm glad whatever it is, that Jo's got it.

"Do you think she feels the same way?" I ask. "About you? Do you think she feels a connection?"

Josephine shrugs. "I don't know."

"Aren't you worried about it?"

"Sure." She grins, but it's a heavy grin. It tells me she means it. "But I have to try. What's the worst that could happen? She doesn't want to get to know me. She doesn't feel the same. That wouldn't feel grand, but it wouldn't be the end of me, either. The way I see it—if I have the chance to fall in love and the worst thing that could happen is that I get rejected, then I'd be a fool not to try."

Sometimes I wish I was brave like her, the way she jumps without knowing what's on the other side. Maybe if I was more like that, then I could do more than work at the bakery. Maybe I could travel. I could actually learn about fashion. I could be someone's apprentice. But my mother and father need me too much. Goodness knows Violette does, too. She won't have to spend her life at the bakery, though. I'll make sure of it.

Josephine comes to a stop in front of a three-story stone home with columns and long, skinny windows across the facade. Thick hedges and hydrangea bushes flank the front steps. I know this home.

"Wait," I say. "This isn't it. This is Beau Bellegarde's house."

"Yes," Josephine says, blinking. "And Mia's."

"No, but they're only cousins."

"They are. But because Mia's parents still live in the countryside, she stays here, at Beau's."

"Jo, no," I plead. "I told you what happened today. I can't show up at his house now."

"We're not going to see Beau," she says. "We'll knock on the door. A footman will probably answer, and then we'll ask for Mia. I'm sure Beau isn't even here."

I know that chances are, she's right. He's most likely off with Julien and Dre at the Gardens or wherever it is people like them hang out. And I go along with her to the door because, after everything she just said about Mia, how could I not?

Josephine and I look at each other. She takes a deep breath like she's readying herself before turning and tapping the bronze door knocker. We stand and wait, but no one shows.

"Should I try again?" she asks. "Maybe we should just leave it?"

But I can tell she doesn't want to do that. We didn't come all this way for her to leave the letter on the steps, so I reach up and pound the door knocker, the metal clanging so loud it surprises both of us.

"Oops," I say.

A voice yells on the other side of the door. "Coming!" I can't quite make it out, but it almost sounds like—

The door flings open, and Josephine and I both stand there dumbfounded. It's the first time I've seen Beau out of his school clothes. He's in his undershirt, an ivory top that hugs his muscles. His hair is wet like he's just bathed, and judging by his face, he's as shocked to see us as we are to see him.

I can't seem to formulate any words, so Josephine does the talking.

"Uh, hi," she says. "We're from the Petite Post. We have a letter for Mia. Mia Bellegarde."

Beau looks at me. "The Petite Post, huh? Strange, because I thought you worked at the bakery. Could've sworn I saw you there earlier today."

"Oh, well, um—" I start, but I mostly end up mumbling something incoherent. Jo nudges my arm to try and get me together, but thankfully I don't have to worry about it because, just then, Mia walks up behind Beau.

"What's this?" Mia asks warmly. She's casual, dressed effortlessly in blue silk, and her dark hair has been woven into a thick braid that rests over one of her shoulders.

"Oh, Mia," Josephine says. She begins to fumble her words. "I have a letter for you. The Petite Post. Sorry, I mean, I'm from the Petite Post. Well, kind of. My father works for the Petite Post, but sometimes he gets me to deliver the letters for him. And this one's for you. It *is* Mia, right?"

Smooth, Jo. Real smooth.

"That's me," Mia says, taking the letter Jo hands to her. "And you're Josephine. We have Monsieur Dorey's class together."

"That's right!" Jo says with a little too much gusto before toning it down. "I thought I knew you from somewhere."

I knew she should've had a plan.

Mia's kind demeanor never gives, though. "It's from Mother and Father," she gasps as she looks down at the envelope. She reaches out and grabs Jo's hands. "Oh, thank you so much for bringing this. I haven't heard from them in months!"

Josephine clams up. She can barely get a word out. "You're, um—you're welcome."

Jo is so painfully obvious, but maybe that's because I know her. I look back to see if Beau is noticing the same thing I am, but he isn't looking at them. He's stuck staring at me. I shift my eyes to the ground, pretending not to notice.

"Hey," Mia says to Josephine, "what did you think about

Monsieur Dorey's assignment? The one on René Descartes. Have you started it yet?"

The two of them get so carried away in conversation that Mia steps outside and they go off into their own little world. I'm left in silence with Beau, and I'm cursing Josephine under my breath, but the truth is that I wouldn't do it for anyone but her. Still, she owes me big.

I can't possibly stare at my feet for one second longer, so I lift my eyes back up, hoping Beau has finally averted his attention, but he hasn't. He's still studying me. And he looks so good all dressed down as he is. Why does he have to look so good?

"All right," I finally say, breaking the awkward tension. "What is it that you wanted to say to me?"

He crosses his arms and leans against the doorway. "What do I want to say to you? Nothing. Don't know what you're talking about."

I sigh. "Right, well, I tried."

"You tried?" He scoffs. "That's rich. Coming from a girl who wouldn't even let me ask her a simple question a few hours ago. Now I've got a cat scratch and a bruised ego. Thanks for that."

"I think your ego can handle a little bruising," I quip. "And ask me a simple question? Yes, I'm sure that's all you were there to do, with your friends standing outside watching our every move."

"Oh, wow," he says, exaggerating the offense. "Do you find it that hard to believe that someone is just interested in you, Evie Clément?" He winks, and I hesitate to answer him because I don't know what to do with his obvious flirting and because my name sounds different leaving his mouth.

His friends aren't here. There's no one around for him to impress or joke with. So, what does he mean? Why did he say that?

I watch him, waiting for him to crack a smile, waiting for a sign that he's mocking me, because if there's anyone in this city I don't trust, it's Beau Bellegarde. At this particular moment, though, he's unreadable. "Interested in me?" I finally ask.

He parts his lips to speak, but Mia interrupts as she heads back in the door. "Thanks so much for helping," she says to Josephine before holding up the envelope from her parents. "And for this, too. See you at school tomorrow?"

Josephine couldn't look happier. She shakes her head. "Yes, tomorrow! See you there." She turns to me. "Want to go?"

"Yes," I tell her. I don't look back at Beau. "I do."

CHAPTER SIX

BEAU

Mia rips open the letter as soon as the door shuts, and her eyes begin darting back and forth across the parchment. She doesn't even look before she plops down, sinking into the parlor sofa cushions. I stand next to the fire and listen.

"They say the dandelions in the field behind our home are in full bloom. They say Verena and Marco have been caring for the livestock. Three lambs have been born in the last few months! Oh, did I tell you Verena and Marco have married? Mother and Father said the ceremony was beautiful."

She's talking to me, but she never lifts her nose from the page. I know what she's looking for, and I hold my breath hoping it's good news.

"They say . . ." Mia begins, but her voice softens. "Oh."

"What? They say what?"

Mia sighs. "They won't be able to make it. Not to graduation. Not to send me off to the Court Ball. None of it. They're needed too much at home."

Mia's father is a physician. He's my father's brother and the only decent uncle I've got. The other two are Julien's mother's siblings, and they look at me the same way she does, like I'm unwelcome.

"Sorry, Mia," I tell her, placing a hand on her back. "I know they'd come if they could."

"Yes," she says. "Ugh. Well, until the next letter, I suppose. I don't want to think about it."

She folds the parchment slowly, her shoulders slumped. She looks at me and cracks a smile, but I know it's hard for her. With every letter, she thinks it might be the one, might be the one where they say they're finally coming to the city to visit her. But she knows it's for the best. The townspeople need them there. And she's going to get the best education here. She could even win Bellegarde Bloom, maybe, if Rachelle would take herself out of the running. I wish Julien and Dre had chosen Mia for the bet, but that would've been too easy. I'd have told her the plan and she'd have gone all out for me to try and win—she secretly despises Julien the same way I do. Instead, I'm left trying to figure out how I'm going to tell my father all my secrets when I lose because Evie Clément is an impossible case. She could never be the Bloom.

"What did you think of that girl?" I ask her.

"Josephine?" Mia says. She isn't looking at me, though. She's staring at her fidgeting hands. She fidgets when she gets nervous. "I think she's really nice. She's smart. Cute, too. Why?"

"No, not Josephine, I didn't mean her. I meant the other one."

"Oh, yes, I don't think I know her. Pretty, though."

"You think?" I ask.

"Sure, why not?"

"I don't know, I suppose you're right. I wasn't thinking of her in that manner." It isn't that I've never looked at Evie and thought she wasn't pretty. It's more that I've avoided looking at Evie altogether because, even after all these years, I still feel bad about what happened.

"Why not?" Mia asks, eyeing me. "Because she doesn't dress like us? Because she likely doesn't live on this side of town? Because she doesn't prance around like queen of the school? Is that all you boys care about?"

"No, it's not that—I don't know. It's—*complicated*."

One of Mia's brows raises in judgement. "Hmm," she says. "Speaking of queen of the school, how are you doing since Rachelle dumped you?"

I shrug. "Fine," I say. "Also, she didn't really dump me. It was more a parting of ways."

"Looked to me like she dumped you," Mia teases. I think she knows that I didn't have my heart in it with Rachelle.

"You're one to talk. Who are you going to be escorted by?"

Mia kicks her feet up and lays back on the sofa. "Myself, maybe."

"No way," I tell her. "You're a Bellegarde. Boys will all be jumping at the chance to have you on their arm. I'm sure many will ask."

She turns her head to me. "And if they're not worthy, I'll say no."

"Well, well, well. Look at you being the judgmental one."

She laughs. "Yes, but unlike you, I will be judging them on the breadth of their character rather than their last name."

I shake my head, grinning. "I'm not like that."

"Sure, you're not," she says, rolling her eyes. "Who are you escorting anyway? Now that Rachelle is going with the Baron of Brittany. Anyone you're thinking about?"

I toss another log onto the fire and watch the flames hurry to hug it. "No," I say. "Maybe. I don't know."

"*No. Maybe.* Sounds like you're really into her."

"No, it's not that," I say through laughter. "I'm quite sure she hates me."

It's best I find someone else to ask. Perhaps Camille if she doesn't have a date yet, or maybe that girl from philosophy class. She's all right.

"Does she have a reason to?"

The embers start to pop. I think back to that day when we were kids, the day Julien and Rachelle decided to play a trick on Evie. "Yes," I say. "She does."

"Well," Mia says. She sits up, straightening her braid. "What are you going to do about it?"

"Do about it?" I shrug. "Nothing. Don't think there's anything I can do."

"Sure, there is. There's always something you can do. There's always a way you can start being good to someone you maybe haven't been so good to in the past. As long as you're living, you've got the opportunity to turn it around."

Evie's not going to forgive me, even if I tell her what really happened that day. She'll never change her mind. But Mia's right about one thing—I need to try to turn my life around. If I had that money, the money Julien is set to inherit, I could do anything. I could move somewhere new. I could move to London, live in the home I grew up in, the cottage my mother raised me in. It would be enough that I could be free, and Julien and his wicked mother could never look at me like I was a nobody again. But it all depends on Evie now. "And how would you suppose I do that?"

Mia stands and smooths out her dress. "Well, what does she like?"

"I—" What does she like? Working at the bakery? "I don't know."

"Then I'd suggest you start there," Mia says, patting my chest before she walks past. "I'm going to go write Mother and Father back."

I know it's here somewhere.

The journal I've kept all these years, the one Madame Martinez made us keep, has to be here. I know Evie was in that class. I ransack my closet, digging my way past coats with missing buttons and shoes that have lost their companion. My small printing press is in the back corner, the ink dried out, put away in hopes that my father wouldn't see it. I keep looking. Finally, shoved deep into a dust-covered box, I find it.

The bindings are tattered, sewn by Madame Martinez

herself, but the pages are still intact. I grin when I see the first page, seeing my name written out in my ten-year-old handwriting. Truth be told, it hasn't changed much. I flip until I find the page I'm looking for.

Madame Martinez gave us an assignment to write one nice thing about each person in the class. I think we were supposed to turn them in, but I took mine home.

I can't help but grin when I see what I've written about Dre. *Has a funny laugh and cool hats.* Still has a funny laugh. Still has cool hats. I flip the page and folded in the crease of the journal is a lopsided paper heart, cut with barely a smooth edge, but still recognizable, likely something from St. Valentine's. I tuck it away and run my finger down the page looking for her name. I have to pause when I get to it. I didn't stick to the one-nice-thing rule for many of the names, but Evie's is by far the longest.

I like the daisies on her dress. She told me it was her mother's. She says daisies are her favorite. I like that she wears her mother's dresses. I like her smile. I like her hair. She stands by the window a lot when it's sunny out. I like that. She says she likes the rain, and I like the rain, too.

I read it over and over again. I read some of the others, too. For most, like Evie, I wouldn't be able to tell you anything about them today. And not because they're no longer in my classes—almost all of these names are still there—but because, well, really, because I don't know why. I suppose somewhere along the way I stopped noticing things about other people.

She likes the rain. My mother loved storms. She used to take me out in them if they weren't too bad. She'd race me from the house to the garden and back. When we got inside, she'd make cider and we'd sit by the fire and dry our clothes and she'd let me stay up past my bedtime. I like the rain, too.

I can't give Evie the rain, though.

She likes daisies. I could go to the flower shop father owns. They could fix something up for her.

But I don't know. She'd probably just throw them back in my face.

I shut the journal when I hear my bedroom door open. Probably him now.

"Beau?" My father's voice is distinct—deep and intimidating to anyone who doesn't know him, and to some that do.

I fumble out of the closet. "Oh, hello, Father, I didn't know you'd be home tonight."

"Yes, well," he says, straightening out his coat, "thankfully I finished my work early and get to sleep in my own bed for a change."

I nod. "What's that?" I ask, motioning to the small velvet box he's holding.

"This," he says extending it to me, "is for you, actually. A gift."

"Oh." A gift? I don't think he's ever given me anything outside of my birthday and holidays. I take the box and lift it open. Inside is a pair of silver cuff links with gold wirework in the shape of the Bellegarde family crest. "Goodness, these are—"

"Just like mine," he says, flashing an identical pair at his wrists. "I was going to give them to you at graduation, but they arrived today and I couldn't wait."

"They're—they're really grand, Father," I say. "Thank you."

I thank him because I'll never be able to tell him how I really feel. His work is his most important priority— sometimes, because he's gone so much, it seems more important than I am—so, were I to reject his wishes for me to join the family business, I'm not sure what he'd do. I fear he'd cast me out.

He looks proud. "You're welcome, son. We'll go down to Marquise and have you a suit tailored soon. You're going to fit right in at the office."

He grabs a hold of my shoulder with a tight grip, his way of showing affection, before leaving the room.

I look down at the cuff links again. *Fit right in at the office.* I don't want to fit in at the office. I don't want to be glad to have one night's rest in my own bed. I don't want any part of that life.

I shut my door and head back into the closet, but this time, I know where it is I'm looking.

I drag out the small printing press, one of the only objects I have left of my time with my mother, and I begin to arrange the letters. I may not know much about Evie Clément, but I know how to spell her name.

Once I've laid out all the names the way I want them, I

decide my handiwork needs an official title. Looking around my room, the inspiration is minimal until I catch the jagged corner of that St. Valentine's heart peeking out from my old school journal.

I begin ordering the letters, and when I'm done, I take a step back to look at it all together.

PAPER HEARTS

It's perfect. And it just might work.

CHAPTER SEVEN

EVIE

After music class, I find Josephine waiting for me in the halls. She's clutching a piece of parchment to her chest.

"We need to talk," she says, grabbing my wrist and pulling me aside.

If I had to guess what this is about, I'd say that Mia Bellegarde has probably looked at her or said hello and Jo is now analyzing every millisecond of it. "Okay, but can I get some fresh air first?" I squeeze past a group of younger students all huddled together. They giggle when we walk past, but those girls are always giggling. "Monsieur Simon's class smells like the stables."

"Well, but—but Evie," Josephine says, stumbling over her words. "I think you need to see this first."

I open the door to the courtyard and inhale. Ahh. There isn't a breeze to be found, but the sun is beaming, and the clouds are full, and if nothing else, it isn't Monsieur Simon's stuffy classroom.

"See what?" I ask her, my face still pointed toward the blue sky.

Before Josephine can speak, Grace, the school gossip, walks past us. "Heard the news, Evie," she says. "You'll have to tell me later how you pulled it off."

I whip around to Josephine. "What was that about?"

Someone else, a voice that I can't place, shouts, "Go, Evie! I'm voting for you."

Suddenly I look around and notice that almost everyone in the courtyard is staring at me, and if they aren't, it's because their faces are buried in a piece of parchment. "What's going on?" I ask Jo.

She flips the parchment at her chest over. At the top, in crooked, wonky letters, it reads *Paper Hearts: A Parisian Periodical*. "It's what I needed to talk to you about," she says.

"What is that? Let me see," I say, snatching the parchment.

It's some kind of newspaper. There's a student spotlight right at the top. Of course, it's about Rachelle—something to do with her bright future with the Baron of Brittany, how the pair look strikingly perfect together, how the author already predicts a wedding is in their future. There are a few sentences detailing the new astronomy teacher and a small space for upcoming events. I keep scanning, but I don't have to look for long because Jo's finger plops down onto the page.

"There," she says. "Read."

It's right at the top, in the corner at the left side of the page, and I've missed it.

PAPER HEARTS
A PARISIAN PERIODICAL

Author's Picks
Most Likely to be Named the Bellegarde Bloom:
Rachelle LeBlanc
Lola St. Martin
Diane Chastain
Mia Bellegarde
Evie Clément

My mouth falls open as I look up to Josephine. "Who wrote this?"

The four names above mine have always been obvious choices, that's no secret to anyone at this school. But I am not and never have been the fifth choice. The fifth choice is someone like Camille Petit or Margaux Page or, better yet, Darcy Chastain—she's probably somewhere fuming right now. Either way, the fifth choice is not me. This must be some kind of joke.

Jo shrugs. "No idea. But whoever they are, I think they may have just made you the most popular you've ever been."

She walks over to a bench in the shade.

I follow her, heart suddenly racing. "Do you think it's because of the fashion show?" I sit down next to her, glad to have a tree blocking the glances coming our way. "Do you think whoever wrote this saw me fall and this is their idea of a hysterical joke?"

"I don't know," she says. "Who would really care that much?"

There's no time to think, though, because someone has made his way over to us—Florent, a guy we've gone to school with our whole lives. I scrunch up against Jo as he intrudes, sitting down on the arm of the stone bench.

"Evie," he says. He slicks the sides of his hair down behind his ears. "How do you do?"

I haven't spoken to Florent in I don't know how long— years, maybe. He spends most of his time fencing and, as I've heard from Grace, sneaking into the brothels on the street my mother and father never let me walk down.

"Florent," I say. My brows scrunch together. Is he going to tell me that he wrote this, that he's the one behind this ridiculous periodical?

"I was strolling the courtyard," he said, his lips pucker briefly, "and I couldn't help but notice you sitting over here. I had an irresistible urge to stop and tell you how ravishingly beautiful you look today."

I look down at my outfit—same dress on rotation, same shoes as always. I've looked this way for years now. I grimace at Florent. "You what?"

Josephine snorts. "He said he wanted to tell you how ravishingly beautiful you are." She puts emphasis on the word *ravishingly*, mocking Florent's insincere tone. He isn't amused.

I hold up the periodical. "Did you have something to do with this?" I ask him.

He moves closer, squinting at the page as though the text is foreign to him. "I'm not sure I know what you mean," he says. "I've never seen this before."

My eyes narrow in on him, but before I can call his bluff, Beau appears behind him and seizes something from the back pocket of Florent's trousers. "Oh, you mean you've never seen *this* before?" Beau asks him. He holds up the item from Florent's pocket, revealing a crumpled copy of the mysterious *Paper Hearts* periodical.

"Uh, uh—how did that get in there?" Florent begins to stumble over his words.

Beau doesn't let him get out whatever lie of an explanation he's trying to cook up, though. "He went to see Mia first," says Beau. "Asked if he could escort her to the ball."

Josephine shifts in her seat next to me.

Beau points to the wrinkles in Florent's copy of the periodical. "If I had to guess what this ruse is, I'd say he's likely hoping whoever he escorts will win and then pin their boutonniere on him. Or perhaps, he's not even hoping for a boutonniere, but rather to escort someone on the court and then use that to flirt with the lady of his liking. Is that about right, Florent, or is there something I'm missing?"

Beau's grinning at him cheekily. Florent's lip curls, but he doesn't say anything as he walks away, clearly defeated.

Beau turns back to us, triumphant.

"Ugh!" I shout, snatching the periodical from Beau's clutches and pummeling it into a crumpled ball. "I'm going to hurt whoever did this!"

"Well, I—I don't think you want to *hurt* them." Beau

fumbles over his words. "That seems a bit harsh. I mean, it's just a little harmless fun."

"Harmless fun?" I snap back. "Easy for you to say given that your name isn't in it. I bet whoever's behind this is sad and lonely and has nothing better to do than make up rumors."

"Oh, well, I wouldn't call them sad and lonely," he argues.

"I would!" Jo agrees with me. "They had the time to write up all this gossip. I'd say they're probably miserable."

"They are *not* miserable!" Beau yelps.

His staunch defensiveness catches me off guard, and I watch his face for a moment—the way his brows knit with defiance as though he's been personally offended, and it hits me. "Wait," I say to him. "You did this. You're the mysterious author behind *Paper Hearts*, aren't you?"

"No, no, of course not," he stutters, but his mouth twitches when he says it and he can't look me in the eyes.

I stand, getting closer to him. "You *are* the one who has been writing this nonsense, Beau Bellegarde. I can tell you're lying." At least, I think I can. I hold my accusatory stare, though, not wanting him to know I'm unsure. "*Paper Hearts* is you," I say sternly. And I must admit, I'm pretty convincing.

After a moment's hesitation, like he's contemplating telling me the truth or not, he leans in. "Okay, okay, keep your voice down," he says in a rushed whisper.

Josephine gasps.

"You did this!" I screech, throwing the wadded-up copy at his chest.

Beau panics. "I said, voices down!" He lowers his voice. "But yes," he says, moving over to take my place on the bench and grasping the ends of his floppy hair. "Yes, I did it. I wrote *Paper Hearts*."

"To get back at me for a little cat scratch," I hiss, finally able to string my thoughts together. "You know, I always knew you were immature, but I didn't realize it was this bad."

Beau rubs his jaw, nodding and now looking particularly disheveled. "Wow. Okay," he says. "That had nothing to do with it, but I'm glad to know what you think of me, I guess."

"I'm sorry," Jo says, coming to my defense. "Were you expecting to be thanked?"

"To be thanked?" Beau says. "No, was never expecting a thanks, but now that you mention it—"

I scoff, cutting him off. "Oh, yeah, right. Like this isn't revenge of some sort, or a cruel joke! I wouldn't put that past you, either."

"So, let me get this straight," Beau says. "You think I'm trying to get back at you for intentionally wounding me by putting your name down as one of the most likely girls to capture the title of Bellegarde Bloom, thereby making you one of the most desirable girls in this school? I have to say, I've had a lot of foolhearted plans in my life, but that sure would be one of the most foolish."

My jaw clenches as I stare at him. He has a point. But what's causing this sudden interest in me? He's never cared before, but now we're weeks away from graduation and we're in the courtyard, and instead of being with his friends over at the fountain, he's here underneath the oak tree with me and Josephine.

"So, what's it about, then?" I ask. "Why put my name down?"

"Because I think you can be Bloom," he says, straight-faced. "That's why."

A laugh escapes my lips. "That's nonsense."

"Well, it is if you keep thinking like that," he says.

I look him over and he looks sincere, but there's still not an ounce of me that softens to him or trusts him.

"Come to the theater with me," he says. "Tonight. You and Josephine, both."

"Oh, no," I say, shaking my head, "absolutely not."

"You have something better to do? Like go out with one of those two?" Beau ticks his head to the side, motioning in the direction of two determined-looking boys heading my way—Art and Hugo. "Better decide now. Because they'll be here in three . . . two . . ."

"Evie," Hugo begins. "Josephine," he says, nodding in her direction, but she'd rather stare off into the abyss than look at Hugo. He's got thin lips and a wide face, and I'll never forget the time he made Jo cry. I sneer at him.

Art intrudes. "Might I say, both of you girls look lovely today."

Beau looks down at me with a delighted smirk. He's eating up my discomfort.

"Let me stop you there," I say to Art and Hugo both. "I assume you've come over here because someone"—I cut my eyes at Beau—"has fed you the lie that I'm a Bloom hopeful. Well, I'm here to tell you that I am not, so you can save whatever it is you were going to say."

But they don't budge. In their brains, if it's written on some sheet of paper, it must be true. And it seems that's how most are feeling, because every look I've gotten since I've stepped foot into this courtyard has either been a dirty or congratulatory look from a girl or an intrigued look of possibility from a boy.

The Court of Flowers is the most prestigious and exclusive women's club in all of Paris. Winning the title of Bellegarde Bloom is the only way you get in. If I thought of the ball at all, it was always about the girls—those vying to become Bloom. But it wasn't until this moment that I realized how stiff the competition for her boutonniere would be. After all, that's why Hugo and Art are here.

"Nonsense," Hugo says, "that has nothing to do with it."

"Doesn't it, though?" Josephine interjects.

Hugo doesn't answer her. Instead, he stays trained on me and says, "Let me take you out. I'd like to show you just how much of a Bloom you are. I can arrange a tasting with the finest chocolatier in all of France."

"Well, I have *already* arranged for a jaunt through the heart of the city." Hugo pushes in front of Art, but Art quickly shoves him.

They're both awaiting my reply, and I think I might vomit.

Josephine leans across me to Beau. "This theater thing," she says, "it might look scandalous if you bring both of us— best to invite your cousin Mia as well so that it will appear a mere family-and-friend outing."

"Deal," Beau says instantly. "Mia loves the theater."

Josephine sits back but not before shooting me a look that tells me I'd better go along with Beau's theater idea. I don't know what she's going to do to pay me back for all of this, but it better be big.

Art and Hugo are still squabbling when I finally give them my answer.

"Gentlemen!" I say. "Your proposals are flattering, really, but as it turns out, I already have plans this evening."

"Plans," Hugo huffed. "Plans with whom?"

I look to Beau, who appears quite pleased with himself, before turning back to the two boys. "Um," I begin.

"With me," Beau says. He doesn't gloat. Well, maybe he does a little. But the way he says it is just so—so confident, like he knows the two of them won't be able to compete with him.

And it works, because all Hugo says is "Hmm," before he and Art leave, still both arguing as they walk away.

Just then, a voice nearby shrieks, "A wedding in our future? Who would say that? I've never said I was going to marry the baron!" Rachelle is walking past with the Chastain twins trailing her, both of them trying to scurry fast enough to keep up with her while she's on what seems to be a rampage of some sort.

Beau can't help himself. "Rachelle," he says. "I hear a congratulations are in order. I suppose you'll be dropping out of the running for Bellegarde Bloom, now that it seems you've already found your prince."

"Ugh," she fumes, turning toward Beau, and it looks like smoke might come out of her nostrils at any moment. She holds up a copy of his periodical. "*This* is garbage. Whoever wrote it is severely misinformed." She directs her attention to me. "Clearly, judging by their predictions for Bloom, they have no idea what they're talking about." Rachelle whips back around to the twins. "Come on, girls. We're going to get to the bottom of this."

Once they're out of earshot, I look up at Beau. "You know she's going to lose it when she finds out you wrote that."

"Eh"—he shrugs—"so be it. Let her show everyone who she really is."

I don't know why, but I wonder if he still cares for her. It doesn't look like it. So why did he stay with her for so long if he knew what kind of a person she was?

The class bells sound, startling me from my thoughts.

"Pick you up at seven?" Beau says.

"We'll be waiting," Josephine answers for the two of us.

I turn to her when he leaves and throw my hands in the air. "What were you thinking?"

"Oh, like you'd have rather gone with Hugo and Art?" she asks.

"I didn't have to go with either of them! And now you've got me going on a date—or, no, not a date—a . . . whatever this is, with Beau Bellegarde. What if my father needs me at the bakery? What if Violette needs me for something?"

"Calm down," Jo says. "The Bellegardes have one of the best boxes in the theater. Worst case, we have a great view and get a free show out of it."

"Yeah, and I'm sure Mia being there has nothing to do with it."

A grin spreads across her lips. "That was smart, huh?"

I answer her with a smug pout.

"Look," she says, "if I hadn't said yes, you'd have turned down Hugo and Art, too, and you'd be spending tonight stuck at that bakery like you always do. You've got to stop worrying about everyone else and live a little, Evie."

Live a little? I *am* living. I can't help that my version of living might look differently from others. Jo knows that better than anyone. I'm living. I am. Aren't I?

"Better get home," I tell Jo. "Violette's going to be thrilled that she gets to help me choose an outfit for the theater."

Josephine smiles. She knows I've given in.

CHAPTER EIGHT

BEAU

"Here," Mia says, reaching across the carriage to help tie the fabric at my collar. "Let me."

I lift my chin so that she can work. "Is it too much?" I ask.

"Too much? For whom? I've seen you dress far more lavish than this to go to the theater before."

I gulp. "Yeah. You're right. I want to make sure she doesn't feel out of place, though."

"Who, Evie?"

"Yes, Evie," I say. I shake my head, annoyed with myself. "I should've gotten her a gown. I should've gone to the boutique, or I should've brought her one of your things."

"She'll be fine," Mia tells me. "Have you seen the clothes she makes? Josephine says she's talented enough to dress the queen. I'm sure she can whip something up to go to the theater."

She sews. I should've known that from the fashion show, but I was a bit too busy focusing on Evie's nosedive into the stage and the fact that I'd just been dumped in front of every student at the university.

"Sweet that you're concerned for her, though," Mia says. "I thought you'd only be worried what everyone would think."

I am. I'm absolutely worried about it, about people staring, about them talking. But I guess I didn't realize until I said it out loud to Mia that I'm also worried about how it will make Evie feel.

"Why *are* you concerned, anyway?" Mia asks. "I've never heard you talk about her until yesterday. Trying to use her now that everyone thinks she might be chosen as the Bloom?"

"No, it's not like that."

"Hmm." Mia studies me, her arms folded. "Better not be. She seems like a nice girl. Nothing like Rachelle."

We arrive at the bakery, and Evie and Josephine are already outside waiting for us. Francis opens the carriage door to let them in.

"You girls look marvelous," Mia gasps. She takes Josephine's skirt in her fingers, examining it. "Evie, did you make these?"

Evie nods. "Mm-hmm," she says quietly.

Mia turns and flashes me a wink, and I know what she's saying—that I should be impressed, and also, that she was right about Evie's abilities. Where Mia's dress is cinched tight, these gowns are delicate and loosely draped. Josephine wears a pale peach, and Evie a periwinkle shade that shows off her dark hair and highlights the freckles like constellations on her chest. Her hair is pinned back and soft, not in the soaring, overstuffed pompadour most of the girls at university wear. She doesn't wear any jewels, and her cheeks are barely blushed—not like they've been pinched, but like they've recently seen the sun. Neither of them look quite like the women who usually frequent the theater, but they're still so elegant, and there's something intriguing about the fact that Evie did it herself. She needed a dress, so she found a way to make one. I know many people who could buy many dresses, but I don't know anyone who could make their own. Not anyone but her. Mia is right. Evie is nothing like Rachelle.

I can barely get a word in edgewise with Mia and Josephine, so Evie and I don't speak until we arrive at the theater. I offer her my hand as she goes to step from the carriage, but she pretends not to see it and jumps out herself. Her boots peek out from underneath her dress, the same ones I've seen her wear to school. I make a mental note to buy her a new pair.

"You look nice," I tell her. I mean it, too.

She turns to me and takes a breath. "Thanks," she says. "I suppose you clean up well also."

"Glad to see that you're speaking to me."

"Don't get used to it," she laughs. "I'll give you your one date, and then I won't have to deal with you anymore."

I open my mouth to give her my rebuttal, but we're being led inside the theater and I can't think of anything to say. I can always think of something to say. But with her, everything sharp-tongued and quick-witted leaves my mind.

We make our way through the grand foyer, past the hand-painted wall murals and underneath the twinkling crystal chandelier. For a moment, I lose the group, their bodies melting with the others rushing in. In my haste to catch up, I get stuck between two women covered head to toe in jewels that don't reflect the light the way they should.

"And to arrive like that to the theater, nonetheless," one of them says, fanning herself and dabbing at the sweat on her lip.

"You don't suppose they know something that we don't?" the other responds. Her nose is flat, and one of her eyes is twitching. I look to see what they're both so interested in and find that their gaze leads to Evie and Josephine, who are both stood with their faces inches away from one of the wall murals, admiring the work. "They're young. Suppose there's a trend we've missed?"

"A trend," the first woman scoffs. "I'm afraid it's more likely that those two are being paid to be here, if you know what I mean."

I urge my feet to keep moving, to not give them any attention, but I stop anyway. I can't help myself.

"Can you believe the queen let them wear those?" I whisper to the women.

"The queen?" says the sweaty one. "Whatever are you on about?"

"Oh, well, I thought everyone knew," I say. They both lean in, ears perked for the gossip.

"Knew what?" the other asks before backtracking. "I mean, yes, we do know, but what is it that you think we know? Just so we know that *you* know."

"That those are two of the queen's personal dressers, of course," I tell them. "She's commissioned them to make something for her newest portrait, determined to outdo the last. She's had them wear the garments here to test them out. Rumor is the boutique on the Rue du Faubourg Saint-Honoré is already swarming with orders."

Both of their mouths hang open like trout.

"Anyway," I say, "can't wait to see the portrait myself."

I have to snicker as I walk away. I wish I could see the look on their faces when they make it to the boutique and the owner has no clue what they're speaking of.

I hurry up through the gallery, and when I finally make it into my family's personal box, the others are already there.

"Right on time," Mia remarks. "It's about to start."

The Salle Favart is shaped like a horseshoe, stacked with tiers of opulent marble, gold filigree, and crimson velvet until your eyes reach the cherry on top—a circular ceiling painted to depict a heavenly scene of angels dancing among the clouds. Evie and Josephine both step to the balcony and look down at the gathering crowd. Josephine pinches Evie's shoulder, and they both exchange a look of wonderment. I can't recall the last time I looked that way about anything.

Mia takes Josephine to the side, and Evie is left standing at the railing alone. She fiddles nervously with the sleeves of her dress, smoothing them out and making sure the fabric lies just so. I'm glad she didn't hear the women talking about her, because her gowns, no matter if they're different, are the most beautiful ones here. I like that she doesn't try to look like anyone else except for her.

What would she think if she knew why I've asked her

here tonight? What would she think to know that she's the centerpiece in my bet with Julien? And how would Mia feel about it, to find out she was right, that I'm using Evie in hopes that I can make her into the Bloom? The idea of it bubbles up in my stomach, the guilt crawling in and making a home, but I push it down, lock it up, and throw away the key.

I walk over and stand next to Evie. "Who told you this was a date?"

She turns to me, offended. "I beg your pardon."

I keep my eyes on the flow of people slowly taking their seats. "Earlier, you called this a date. I don't remember ever referring to it as such."

Evie sighs. "Oh, don't flatter yourself, Beau Bellegarde. It's just a word. Sort of like the word *buffoon*. Do you know that one?"

I bury my laughter in the ridiculously oversized collar I've made the mistake of wearing. "In fact, I do. Been called it a time or two."

"Don't doubt it," she quips back.

"And what if this was?" I ask her.

"What if this was what?"

"A date," I say. "How would you feel about that?"

She's looking me over the same way she did when she and Josephine came to the house, when I asked her if she really couldn't believe that someone would be interested in her. She looks like she doesn't believe a word I say, and I can't blame her.

Before she can answer, we're directed to our seats. Evie

takes the one farthest away from me, choosing to put Mia and Josephine in the middle and she and I on the ends. I don't make a fuss. Getting Evie here was enough trouble as it is. I don't want to push my luck. She despises me, that much she's made clear, but if I can convince her to hold on for a little while longer, enough time for me to keep putting out periodicals detailing her rise into high society, I might actually have a shot at beating Julien at his own game.

Midway through the play, Mia leans over and whispers to me, "Can you hear what they're saying?"

"Barely," I say quietly back to her. I forgot how stuffy this box is, how the performers look more like dolls or playthings from up here and how their words don't carry. She turns to Josephine and cups her hand over her ear, whispering something.

Mia nudges me. "Let's go," she says. "Josephine and Evie know of a better place we can watch from."

"A better place to watch?" I ask, puzzled. "Better than one of the best boxes in the theater?"

"Just come on," she says, yanking me from my seat.

I don't have much of a choice, so I follow them down the steps and out onto the dark streets of Paris. "You know they're not going to let us back up there," I say. "Once the play has started, they won't let anyone in."

"Good thing we know of another way in." Evie grins.

She and Josephine lead the way, taking us all the way around the building and to a door at the rear of the theater.

"This is your plan?" I say to Evie. "Sneak in?"

She leans her head to the side. "What? Are you scared?"

"Not a bit," I tell her, my curiosity piqued.

Josephine reaches up and knocks on the door. She does it in a pattern—four quick knocks, two long, and a quick four more.

The door swings open, and a boy with candy-colored dreadlocks stands in the frame.

"Jo! Evie!" he yelps, his arms extending wide, taking them both in an embrace. "I didn't know when I'd see you two again. You ain't been coming round."

"After that last time, we thought we might lie low for a while," Evie tells him, laughing.

"Oh, nonsense. That batty Peter is harmless," the boy says. "It's the theater manager Monsieur Thomas you've got to look out for. Almost caught me letting the group in a few weeks back. Made up a good story, though, and he bought it, the old crank."

"We'll be quick," Evie says. "Promise."

"Ooh, fancy," he says, looking past her to me and Mia. "You sure you want to dirty up those fine threads?"

I brush the front of my coat. "Dirty up?"

The boy throws his head back, laughing. "You're in for a treat," he says. "Follow me."

We file in the door and snake our way through the back of the theater, making sure to stay in the shadows. Finally, the boy crouches down and crawls through a small opening. Evie and Josephine both take the bottoms of their dresses and crumple them up into their fists, following after him.

Evie looks back at me once she's just through the opening. "You coming?"

"Ah—yeah," I say. "Right behind you." I take one last
look to make sure no one's around and go in after Mia.

The area we're crawling through would be pitch black if it
weren't for the slivers of torchlight coming in from above. At
one point, I stop and look through a particularly wide crack
and can just make out a figure above. I recognize him as the
actor playing the father—we're under the stage.

Finally, we come out the other end, and it puts us just
in front of the action, tucked away in a small nook near the
musicians. We're hidden enough so that we can't be seen, but
I can't help to keep my head down. My father would explode
if he knew I'd snuck in the Salle Favart.

The boy directs me to sit on the floor, so I slide over by
Evie, who is so entranced by what's happening onstage that
she doesn't seem to notice I've finally gotten my seat next
to her.

"This is incredible," I say to her.

"Isn't it?" she agrees. She waits a moment and then leans
over to me. "You have to see things up close. You stay far
away from everything, and there's a lot you'll miss." Her eyes
are trained upward, watching every movement the performers make, but I'm watching her, seeing her up close, and she
actually looks happy.

For the first time in my life, I find myself lost in a play.
I've seen quite a number of them, but I've always either fallen

asleep, fallen bored, or left partway through. Perhaps it's because, down here, I can actually make out the words. Down here, I can see the emotions of the performers—the anguish, the heartbreak, the joy.

The story is of a father and his well-to-do daughter who are both living in Paris when a soldier arrives. The soldier falls in love with the man's daughter, but the father won't allow them to wed because of the soldier's low status. The father himself knows what it's like to be a commoner, yet even with his familiarity, he still won't allow them to be married. It isn't until the soldier reveals he comes from nobility that the father finally agrees to their union. Almost the entire theater claps when this happens, but it only makes me angry. It makes me think of the women earlier in the foyer, how their entire demeanors changed when I told them the made-up story about the queen and her portrait. In this play, the soldier never changed. The only thing that changed was others' perception of him and their idea of how worthy he was.

The play is almost over when two heads pop out from underneath the stage. "Dom," the girl whispers. A crescent moon-shaped beauty patch sits underneath one of her eyes and the dress she wears makes it look like she's covered in clouds. "You better come quick. He's found us. Monsieur Thomas. He's headed here now."

The boy, who I now know to be Dom, jumps up. "Well, ladies and gents," he says. "Looks like it's time to go."

"Oh, he's there now." Josephine points over by the

musicians. A bald man with unkempt eyebrows is clumsily weaving his way through the orchestra, headed straight for us with a wagging finger pointed our direction.

I'm last out in our scramble back underneath the stage, but we make it all the way through and onto our feet.

"This way," Dom says, and begins to run to the right, back the way we came.

"No, not that way," one of the others who warned us tells him. "Monsieur Thomas knows that way."

We hesitate for a moment too long, and one of the stage doors flies open. Behind it is the same bald-headed man, except now he's panting and wheezing and his eyes look like they could spew fire.

"Go, go, go!" Dom yells, and we all make a break for it, gliding past Monsieur Thomas, who has now managed to burst into a full run, though it looks more like a furious waddle.

Dom holds the door for us, and the night air fills my lungs. His friends lead the way. We duck behind buildings and jog down the streets. The girls' dresses float on the wind, and we don't stop running until we reach the Seine. I don't know why we keep running, because chances are Monsieur Thomas didn't make it but a few yards out of the theater doors. I don't care, though, because my heart is racing and my blood is pumping. It feels good to be alive, here, with them. With her.

CHAPTER NINE

EVIE

I reach up, stretching into the night sky, fingers facing the stars. Beau is hunched over next to me, his hands on his knees, sucking in air and letting it out in a fit of laughter.

When he manages to catch his breath, he takes one of my hands and places it on his warm chest, just at his heart. "Feel," he says.

I catch the racing beats and pull my hand away, joining him in laughter. "Am I to believe that Beau Bellegarde has never run from authority?"

"I—I actually don't think I have," he admits.

I find that very hard to believe given how many times he's probably been to the château, but then again, people like Beau rarely ever find themselves on the receiving end of consequences.

"You two coming?" Josephine shouts from the dock.

I start toward her, and Beau follows behind.

"What is that thing?" he asks, squinting through the dark, looking out toward the water where everyone is gathered.

I peer back at him over my shoulder. "Ever been on a houseboat?"

"A what?"

The others are already climbing the makeshift winding staircase leading to the top landing. The boat is small and ramshackle, with one small room in the middle where the three of them sleep. Trellising up one side are makeshift planks that you can climb at your own risk to get to the top. It's not the best craftsmanship, but it's not the worst, either, considering all they had to work with was whatever they could steal or barter for.

Something creaks behind me as I make my way up to join them, a sound like something is about to snap. "Whoa," Beau says, his hand slaps the wood's siding. I look back to see him teetering trying to catch his balance. I don't know why, but I instinctively reach out to help steady him.

"Yeah, sorry," I say, hiding my smile. "Got to be careful on that one. Always skip the third step."

The top of Dom's boat is one of my favorite places in Paris, probably my second-favorite view of the city. Scattered around are cushions of all shapes and sizes, and candles inside iron and glass boxes light up the deck. They're no doubt stolen from the streets, from Bash's time as a lamplighter.

"Your friend having the same as you, Evie?" Dom calls out. He's pouring wine into mismatched glasses, and Celeste is using one of the candles to light her cigarette. Bash is drumming a pair of sticks against a scrap piece of metal.

"Wine okay?" I ask Beau.

One side of his mouth lifts into a surprised grin. "Sure. It's great."

Dom pours each of us a cup. He hands me mine but stops before he gives Beau his.

"How'd you know Evie?" Dom asks him. His ever-present smile lurks, but it isn't as wide. Dom's usually a cutup, but he's serious about his friends.

"Uh," says Beau. He fidgets with his hair, combing it back with his fingers. "Been going to school with her since we were kids."

Dom looks at me for approval on what Beau has said. I don't want to get into it, don't want to make the night heavy, so I nod to Dom and let Beau off the hook.

"Well then, great to meet you, mate," Dom says, handing Beau a cup. "I'm Dom. This right here is Celeste." He motions to a girl who is cozied up next to him, head resting on his shoulder as she puffs on a cigarette. Smoke rings rush from her lips before fading into the Paris skyline. She extends her hand to Beau. "And that maniac back there is Bash." Dom jerks his head over to where Bash sits cross-legged, still drumming away. Bash is paying attention, though, because when Dom says it, he holds one of his sticks up in the air to acknowledge Beau.

"Beau," he says, taking Celeste's hands in his. "Thanks for having me."

"Anytime, mate," Dom says.

And just like that, it's as though he's been inducted into our little club of misfits. He'll probably never be back, but I won't tell the others that.

"What are you doing?" Beau asks, watching me take off

my boots and step onto the wooden floor. He finishes a sip of wine. "You're going to get a splinter."

"Nonsense," I say.

We take a seat on a couple of cushions next to Josephine and Mia, who are deep in conversation and who, over the course of the night, seem to keep drifting closer to each other. I swing my legs over the side of the boat and let the air rising from the river tickle my toes. The wind has died down to a gentle breeze, and the dark waters of the Seine are calm. The boat shifts every so often, but it's not bad. It's the kind of motion that could rock you to sleep.

"You're different around your friends," Beau says.

"How so?"

He shrugs. "I don't know. Lighter, somehow."

I inhale a deep breath and let it out. "Well, for what it's worth, you are, too. Different. But without your friends."

"Is that right?"

"Yeah, you're not as Bellegarde-y as usual."

"Ha!" He smiles. "So, still pretty bad, just not *as* bad?"

"Yep, that's it," I say.

"Well, I suppose I'll take that," he says.

We sit there in silence for a while, listening to the sounds of the city, listening to Josephine and Mia share laughs, before he asks, "Do you think they're interested in each other?"

"Interested in each other?" I chuckle. "Do you know how many times I've begged Jo just to wear a proper skirt? But then Mia shows up, and all of a sudden, her cheeks are rouged and her hair is curled and she's asking me to dress her. I'd be shocked if she hasn't asked to escort Mia to the ball while we've been sitting here."

"Really? Josephine wants to escort Mia?"

"Oh no," I say, slapping my hand over my mouth. "Please don't tell her I said that. I don't want to ruin anything. *Please*."

Beau mimics a zipper over his lips. "Not to worry," he says. "I had a feeling when the two of you came to the house. I'm glad for it, though. Mia needs someone like her. Deserves someone like her, rather. She seems really lovely."

"Jo?" I look over to her. I haven't seen her this happy in a long time, not genuinely. Never seen her so nervous, either. She's always been the cool, confident one, always having to calm me down. When we were getting ready, she was a wreck. You wouldn't know it now, though. "She's the best. We've been friends since before we could walk."

"How do you know the others? Dom and Celeste and . . ." He trails off.

"Bash," I say. "Shopkeepers' kids. We all lived on the same block. Dom's parents were watchmakers, Celeste's had a teahouse, and Bash's mother ran a bookshop. They all got run out by the new couture and luxury shops some years back. They almost got the bakery, too, but we managed to stay afloat."

The whole sorry story rattles off my tongue before I can catch myself. And I'm watching Beau, waiting to see how he'll judge me for it. He unties his collar and pulls it from his neck.

The Bellegardes have retail properties, too, strips of shops they manage because they have the money to. Their name is plastered all over Paris. I bet none of their properties have ever been threatened.

"I didn't know you were going through that," he says, but he doesn't look at me.

"Well, why would you have?"

"I don't know. We knew each other back then."

I scoff. "Hardly."

He looks at me like he wants to challenge what I've said, and I think I want him to. I want him to say we were friends. I want to tell him the things I've wanted to say to him for years, to tell him how that day made me feel, the day he and all his actual friends made me look like a fool. He doesn't challenge it, though.

The pale silver moonlight scatters across his face, and his gaze drifts like there's something he wants to say about it, but instead, he says, "You've got really pretty eyes. Anyone ever tell you that?"

I sigh and sit my drink down. "I have pretty eyes? That's what you've got to say?"

"Should I have something else to say?"

"What is it that you're playing at, Beau Bellegarde?"

He meets my eyes for a second before looking away. "Playing at?"

I quickly begin to lace my boots up, because this conversation is reminding me that I shouldn't be here, not with him.

I don't trust him, and I'm ready to go. "Yes," I say. "What is this? What you're doing here. You ask me to the theater so that, what? So that I didn't have to go on a date with Hugo or Art? As if I'd have gone with them anyways. You didn't save me from anything, and I don't need your help. I don't need your empty compliments, either. So, I don't know what it is you want from me, but whatever it is, you're not going to find it here."

"I don't want anything from you. And I didn't ask you to the theater because of Art and Hugo."

"So, why, then?" I stand up, but I speak quietly enough to not make a scene. If Dom knew the truth of it all, he'd probably throw Beau into the Seine. "Why am I here? Why are you here? Why did you put my name in that paper?"

"I—um, well— You see, I—" he fumbles.

"Right. That's what I thought." I lean down and tap on Josephine's shoulder. "Forgot I've got to get back early tonight," I tell her. "I need to start a few things at the bakery for the morning."

"Oh," she says. "Yeah, all right. Didn't realize it'd gotten so late anyways. My mother and father will probably be worried about me."

"Beau and I can fetch a carriage," Mia says.

"No, thanks," I say. "It's fine. We're close. We'll walk."

Jo eyes me like I've lost my mind. I know what she'd say if we were in private—why walk when we could take a carriage? More important, why walk when we could take a carriage with Mia Bellegarde? But I give her a look and she knows instantly that something's up. I'm thankful for the secret language of friends in moments like this.

"Yes," Jo tells Mia. "You two live pretty far. We're just up the road."

I say my goodbyes to Dom and the others, all the while feeling Beau's presence on the other end of the boat. His eyes haven't left me, and I don't know why. But that isn't my problem.

Before stepping down, I take one last look out over the lights of Paris. Maybe it's the free feeling that comes from being on the water, but the city looks different from up here, especially at night. It looks like you could reach out and take it. But I know that in some hours' time, the sun will rise, and it won't be mine to take any longer.

CHAPTER TEN

RACHELLE

"You don't think he's read it, do you?" Lola asks.

"Who, the baron?" I answer, collapsing farther into the soft cushions of the settee. "No, of course not. He's not interested in some silly university periodical. Especially one that's filled with such obvious lies."

Lola twists around in the vanity chair examining her skin in the mirror. "Who do you think is behind it?" she asks.

I lean back, closing my eyes while Magdalena begins to coat my hands in a sugar scrub. "Probably that poor girl, the one who fell onstage." Beau sat next to her in the courtyard. "What's her name again?"

"You mean Evie? The baker's daughter."

I chuckle. "The daughter of a baker? Be chosen as the Bellegarde Bloom? How . . . quaint. Sad, though, really. Do you think someone is playing a cruel joke on her?"

"I don't know," Lola says. "She seems nice. Did you see the dress she made? It was beautiful."

Waving Magdalena away, I lean forward with a sharp, focused gaze. "She seems *nice*? She made a beautiful dress? Exactly whose side are you on, Lola?"

She thinks I don't see her roll her eyes in the mirror, but I do. "Yours, of course," she says.

"Hmm," I say. "Good." Magdalena resumes slathering a mask of milk and honey on my face.

I think I know why Lola has been acting so different lately. Because now that it has come down to it, she knows she will win second place at the ball. And with the Court of Flowers, there is no second place. The St. Martins' are fine stock, but Lola is only seventh in line to her family's ink fortune. Her mother lost Bloom to my mother, and now she will lose to me.

"I heard a rumor," Magdalena says.

"Oh, do tell," I pry. She always has the best gossip.

Magdalena smirks. "I heard the Duke of Berry is coming into town soon."

My eyes burst open. "The duke? Are you sure of it? Where on Earth did you hear such a thing?"

"My cousin. He's a footman in the palace," Magdalena answers. "Says there's whispers of his arrival as early as next week."

Lola spins around quickly, her mouth upturned and giddy. "Next week? Do you think he'll be at the ball?"

"Well, what's it to you?" I quip. The duke is mine. "You're a taken woman."

"As are you," she snaps back at me.

"The baron and I are not engaged."

"According to *Paper Hearts* you are."

She is trying my patience. "Well, lucky for me, the duke does not read trash like this ridiculous *Paper Hearts*."

Just then, the door crashes open.

"Oh, we're so sorry, Rachelle," Darcy says with clasped hands.

Diane follows right behind her. "Yes, we came as soon as we heard."

The mask Magdalena put on has started to harden, stretching and pulling my face until I can barely move my lips to speak. "Heard what?" I mumble.

The twins exchange glances.

"Well?" I say. "Out with it!"

Diane is the one to show me. She pulls a piece of parchment from behind her back. "There's—there's a new issue of *Paper Hearts*," she says. "Ours came in the post, I suppose because school isn't in today. We thought for sure you'd seen it by now."

Lola gets up and hovers over the parchment.

"Give it to me!" I shout.

I can't move fast enough, though. Lola snatches the parchment from Diane's hand and begins to read.

"'Out and About,'" Lola reads. "'Art Laurent was seen at the Gardens with Camille Petit. We hear Art will officially be escorting Camille to the Court of Flowers Ball.'"

I wave my hand at her. "Boring. Go on."

"Um." Lola pauses. "'Beau Bellegarde was spotted at the Salle Favart with none other than our newest Bloom hopeful,

Evie Clément. The two are said to have left the theater early, hand in hand.'"

My brows raise so high that the mask cracks around them. "Beau with that—that *girl*? Taking her to the Salle Favart? What, to his father's theater box? No. There's simply no way. He would never."

Magdalena steps back. Lola and the twins are staring at me. Not a one of them looks like they're breathing.

"Well!" I spit. "Someone say something!"

"Uh—maybe," Darcy begins, "maybe they're mistaken. Maybe it wasn't her. Maybe it was someone else."

"Then why would they say it was her, Darcy?" I snap.

Lola offers an explanation. "You said it yourself that the periodical was full of lies."

"Of course it is," Darcy says. "Nothing but lies."

Darcy only agrees because she can't believe that the periodical left her name off the list of Bloom hopefuls.

"Don't worry about Evie Clément," Diane says. "She's a nobody."

I cock my head to one side. "Me? Worried about her? Don't make me laugh."

"Oh, I just thought—" Diane starts.

"You thought wrong," I tell her. "That girl is of no matter to me. If this author is telling the truth and she and Beau truly are an item, I pity Beau, not finding someone of his own station. Imagine if he escorted her to the ball."

"I doubt that will happen," says Darcy.

"Well, if it does," I say, "I will be there to upstage them at every turn. There will be no competition when I'm with the baron . . . or the duke."

A knock comes at the door.

"Mademoiselle LeBlanc?" a deep voice calls out from the other side.

"Yes, Claude?"

"A visitor, mademoiselle," Claude answers. "For you."

"A visitor?" Lola repeats. "Who could it be?"

I shrug and walk past them to find out.

"Who is it, Claude?" I ask, wrenching the door open.

The baron is standing in the hallway, and Claude has a mortified look on his face

"Nicolas!" I yelp, tightening the folds of my robe. "Whatever are you doing here?"

"I had to come see you," he says, stepping forward to kiss my hand. His eyes veer off past me, and I turn to see what has grabbed his attention. I've left the door open, and each of the girls are intently eavesdropping on our conversation. I reach behind me and pull the door shut.

"You were saying?"

"Ah, right, yes," Nicolas stumbles. His hair is matted from the rain. I'd like to run my shears through it. I'd also like to run my shears through his entire wardrobe. The old-fashioned garb his mother dresses him in is atrocious. "I've received something from the palace." He begins digging in his coat.

My ears perk. "From the palace, you say?"

"Yes," he says, searching, patting down his pockets. "It's

here somewhere—ah, yes, there it is!" He pulls out a wadded, half-rain-soaked piece of parchment. He walks to the windowsill and flattens it out as best he can. The ink is running and smeared, but it doesn't matter because the last line is still legible.

"The queen sent you something?" I screech.

"Indeed," he says. "An invitation to one of her soirees. The Queen's Ball. I may bring a date, and well, Mother is away, so I've chosen you. If you'll accompany me, that is."

My mouth falls open. Me, at the palace, invited by the queen herself. And the duke! Oh, he's certain to be there. It's likely why he's coming to town. *This is it. It's finally happening.*

"Oh, yes!" I wrap my arms around his neck in an embrace. "Yes, of course I'll go."

Nicolas leans toward me, his lips puckered, but I turn my cheek to him, and with my face slathered in mask, he decides against it.

"Oh, whatever will I wear?" I feign distress, pulling back. "It will have to be something new, something grand. Something special. I don't have any gowns like that in my wardrobe." I flicker my eyes up to him, waiting for him to catch the hint.

"Don't worry about that," Nicolas assures me. "I'll take care of it."

I sigh. "You're extraordinary," I tell him.

And it *will* be grand. It *will* be special. It has to be, because it's the gown I'll wear to make the duke fall in love with me.

Chapter Eleven

BEAU

A few days later, I summon the courage to go back to the bakery.

I walk instead of taking a carriage, and I'm cursing myself for it, because it gives me too much time to think—too much time to go over Evie's words from the other night for the hundredth time.

The sting of them hasn't subsided, the ease with which she told me that she didn't need my compliments or my help. I thought we were having a nice night. She'd introduced me to her friends, and we were laughing, and—and anyway, it doesn't matter. I remind myself that it doesn't matter that she still hates me. It doesn't matter what she thinks of me at all, because the only thing that's important is that she wins Bellegarde Bloom.

When I get to the bakery, Evie's father is outside shooing off a pair of chickens that have gathered in front of the shop.

"Good day, sir," I say, approaching him. "How do you do?"

He waves his arms at the chickens, but they only rush forward at him. "Not well, not well," he says. He's got a thick mustache and hands that look like they could punch through a wall. "Know anyone who wants some chickens?"

I laugh. "Don't think I do. You could throw some bread down the street. I'm sure they'd follow it."

He turns his head slowly, like he can't believe what I've said. "Waste bread on chickens?"

The bakery door opens, ringing the bell. A curly-haired woman pops her head out. "Pierre, darling, where did you put the sugared flowers?" He's preoccupied, though, so she looks over at me. She has Evie's button nose. "Oh, hello there. May I help you?"

"He says to give the chickens bread," her father calls out. "He definitely needs help."

I smile. "I'm here to see Evie, actually. Is she around?"

Her father, Pierre, faces me, ignoring the chickens, which are now bobbing at scraps in front of a nearby shop. "You're here for Evie?" he says.

"Yes, sir."

"You're Beau, aren't you?" Evie's mother asks, her eyes narrowing on me.

"Yes, ma'am," I say. "That's me." Has Evie said something about me? Has she told her parents? Whatever it is she's said, I'm sure it wasn't good.

A small girl presses her face up against the shopwindow— it's Evie's little sister.

"Oh, Violette," her mother says, tapping on the glass. "You're going to get fingerprints all over the window!"

Violette runs off back into the bakery.

"Well, come on in," Evie's mother says to me. "I'd say I'll call for Evie, but I take it Violette's already on that."

Evie's father follows us in. He uses his apron to wipe the sweat from his brow. It's funny to think a behemoth of a man such as him has been outside chasing those chickens off for long enough to break a sweat.

"How do you know Evie?" He asks.

I push my hands into my pockets. Talking to parents has never been my strong suit. And talking to a man who is about three times my size doesn't make things any less intimidating. "School," I say. "We go to university together."

"Hmm," he says. He rakes his fingers over his mustache. "You look familiar."

I nod, hoping he doesn't remember me from years ago. "I moved here when I was a kid. From London. I've been in school with Evie since I was six."

"Would you like something to eat while you wait?" Evie's mother asks. Evie looks so much like her father—the olive skin, the dark hair—but her expressions—the way she walks, the way she does that little thing where she smiles so big that her cheeks scrunch her eyes into crescents—those are all her mother. Her father shoots her mother a look, but she ignores it. I know they don't have anything to spare for anyone who isn't a paying customer.

"Oh, no thank you," I say. "I'm fine." And then, for good measure, I throw in, "But I've had your brioche and *wow*.

It's the best I've ever tasted."

A grin as wide as my hand spreads across Pierre's face. "Pleased to hear it."

The stairs rumble and creak, and down comes Violette, her eyes as wide and full of mischief as the other day when I met her. She turns and looks up the steps, watching Evie descend.

Evie's in a loose blue skirt and a puff-sleeved blouse. A simple barrette holds her hair away from her face, except for a few strands that have broken free.

"Beau?" she says, still standing at the stairs, confused. She looks to her parents and then back to me. "What are you doing here?"

They're all staring at me now. I didn't anticipate having to speak to her in front of her entire family, but here we are. "Um, well. I came to see if you wanted to go to the Gardens with me."

"The Gardens?" she says. "No, I—I've got a busy day."

"Huh," Pierre laughs.

"We've got things covered over here, darling," her mother says. "You go have fun with your friend." She doesn't think I see, but I catch her flashing a wink up to Evie.

"No," says Evie. "No, I couldn't possibly. Thanks for stopping by, though."

She says it with such sarcasm that I can't help but to grin. She starts back up the stairs, but Violette interjects before she reaches the top.

"Will you play dolls with me?" Violette asks. She's looking at me, biting her little cherry-stained tongue and swaying shyly from side to side.

"Me?" I point to my chest.

"Mm-hmm," she nods.

Evie stops and turns, giving Violette deadly eyes. "No, Violette. He doesn't have time." Evie looks back to me. "Right, Beau?"

Her stare urges me to agree, but I want her to go to the Gardens with me, so I don't.

"Oh, no," I say. "On the contrary. I've got all the time in the world to play dolls with you, Violette. Perhaps by the time we finish, your sister will be done with all the busy things she has to do, and she will then accompany me to the Gardens."

"Yay!" Violette bursts, jumping up and down.

Evie sighs loudly. "Okay, fine! I'll go to the Gardens with you. But only for a little while."

A smile widens across my face.

"Good girl," her mother says. "You go have some proper fun."

Violette looks a little sad, but she instantly perks up. "Oh, Evie, can I pick out your outfit? Please, please, please!"

"I'm wearing this," she says. "He can take it or leave it."

Evie looks to me almost as if she thinks I'm going to change my mind based on her wardrobe.

I throw my hands up. "I take it. I take it."

Pierre laughs gruffly. "Good answer, boy."

"And, Violette," I say. I bend my knees, crouching down to her level. "I promise I'll play dolls with you one of these days. It'll be a date. You better not forget about it, okay?"

Her face lights up, the sun reflected in her hazel eyes. "I won't," she assures me. We shake on it.

Evie finally makes her way down the steps and over to me.

"Well." I hold out my arm to her. "Shall we?"

She rolls her eyes and walks past, out the door, leaving me there with an outstretched arm. Her parents share a laugh, unsurprised. They know exactly who they've raised.

I wonder if my father knows half as much about me as Evie's parents do about her.

"You better go while you've still got a chance," her father teases.

"Oh, Pierre, come off it," Evie's mother says, knocking him on the arm.

"I'll have her back soon," I assure them. I tip my hat to them while my brain spins, thinking of a way to tell Evie that all my friends, the ones she hates, are going to be meeting us at the Gardens. She's going to protest, of that I'm sure. But if I'm going to make this believable, if she's going to have a chance at winning Bloom, the periodical isn't going to be enough. People are going to have to see us with their own eyes.

CHAPTER TWELVE

EVIE

The day is ripe, and the sun is showing off its glory, so that means the Gardens are packed to the brim with university students.

"You really want to go in there?" I ask. "With all of those people? We already see them every day at school."

"It's fun," he says. He reaches out and pokes me in the arm. "You're going to have fun. I promise."

"You really love to make promises you're never going to keep, don't you?"

"What's that supposed to mean?"

"You told Violette you were going to come back and play dolls with her."

"Yes." He nods. "And I will. What of it? You don't think I meant it?"

I raise an eyebrow at him. "I don't even know why you've shown up today, so why would I expect you to show up in the future to plays dolls with my little sister? Why did you ask me here, Beau?"

"I—" He rubs his shoulder and looks around the carriage we've yet to exit. "I wanted to introduce you to some people."

"Some people?"

"To my friends," he says. He looks back up at me carefully because he already knows how I feel.

"Your friends?" I hold my hands up to my temples. "You wanted to introduce me to people I've been going to school with most of my life?"

"Well, yes. But you don't really know each other."

"I know them well enough, Beau. I know them well enough to know I don't want to spend my Saturday cavorting with them at the Gardens. No. Not with them."

"But if you'd just give them a chance—"

"Why? Because for some reason I can't even begin to understand, you've decided you have some schoolboy crush on me? Or—or this is all some half-plotted out idea to make Rachelle feel jealous and win her back? And whatever it is, I've got to act like we're friends, like I like you, and like I like your friends as well?"

Once I've finished, I can't believe I've said it to him—that I've even proposed the idea that he might have a crush on me. But he's been so persistent, and other than getting back at Rachelle, there's no other reason I can think of to explain why he keeps coming around.

He doesn't answer my question but he does reply. "You don't have to pretend to like them. Or me, for that matter."

The carriage driver ends the conversation when he pops the door open for us.

The Gardens are sweltering and not much like I remembered them. Beautiful, still—rows of orange trees, plots of daisies, ferns that cover the ground in such lush heaps that it looks like you could swim in them, and, at the center of it all, a lake glistening with the day's sunlight. The patronage is different, though. When I was younger, it was just families here. Now it's nothing but kids my age, all sweating and kissing and mucking up the place.

"Beau!" someone shouts. "Over here!"

Lola is the voice. She's lying, sprawled out on a blanket, waving her arm in the air. It's begun.

"We didn't think you were going to make it," Dre says as we approach.

"Well, I'm here, aren't I?" Beau says.

"Or we thought you were already in one of your usual spots," Julien says. He turns his attention to me. "He takes all his dates to the Gardens. Many girls have experienced the dark corners of the Gardens with him. Haven't they, Beau?"

Beau doesn't say anything. He just eyes Julien.

Dre steps in. "Sorry about him, Evie," he says. "Julien's just cranky because he hasn't been underneath the wisteria himself in months."

Julien huffs. "Like you'd know."

Dre rolls his eyes before turning to Beau. He holds up a cricket bat in one hand and the ball in his other. "Ready to go hit?"

"You bet I am." Beau swipes the ball from his hand. He looks like he's going to follow after them, but then remembers I'm there. "Want to come play?" he asks me.

Me? Play cricket? I can't even walk across a stage in heels

without falling on my face, and he thinks that playing a sport with a bunch of competitive boys is going to go better for me? "No way," I say. "I'll watch."

"Have it your way," he says before running off to join them.

"Evie," Lola calls out to me. "Come, sit with us."

She's sitting with the Chastain twins, who are busy fighting over their one parasol. They all look like your typical garden girl—they've got the braids, the ribbons, the shimmering eyelids, and the bodices that only cinch at the breasts so they can still sit down. I take a deep breath and let it out slowly. Maybe an hour, tops, and I'll get Beau to take me home. I'll make something up. It'll all be over soon.

Lola pats the empty space next to her, and I do my best to cover my boots with my skirt as I sit down.

"First time coming to the Gardens?" Lola asks.

"Oh, no," I tell her. "I used to come here a lot with my family."

Lola laughs. "Back when this place wasn't just a place to see and be seen."

"Yes." I smile. "Back then."

Diane glances over at me, and I can feel her eyes scanning my outfit. I carefully feel for my boots, making sure I did in fact get them entirely covered. "I like your hair," she says. But I don't think she means it. It sounds like one of those things you say when you just need something to say.

"Thanks," I reply.

"It would look so cute braided like ours, too," Lola says.

"Ooh!" Darcy yelps. "You could do it for her, Lola. Give her the garden look."

Lola turns to me. "What do you say, Evie? You up for it?"

"Ah—thank you," I say. I've not been left with much of a choice, but at least this way, we have something to do.

Lola sits cross-legged behind me and begins combing through my hair, interlacing it with the ribbon Darcy hands her. Diane is just glad to have the parasol to herself.

"So," Lola says, "I suppose Beau will be escorting you to the ball, then, right?"

"The ball? Oh, no, it's—we're nothing like that."

"Oh, sure," Diane chimes in, her eyes shut as she sits in the shade. "Like he'd have brought you to the Gardens if he wasn't planning on asking to escort you. In front of Rachelle, no less."

Rachelle's here? My eyes dart around, frantically searching for her. I don't want to be on the receiving end of whatever vitriol she's spewing today.

Lola must notice because she straightens my head out, tightening the braid she's working on. "Don't worry," she says. "She's off with the baron somewhere."

"Well," Darcy says. "You'd better hope Beau asks soon. He's a free man now. Every girl at the university is going to try to get him to escort her. I'd try with him if I thought Rachelle wouldn't rip my head off for it."

"She wouldn't even care," Diane says. "Not much."

"Oh, she'd care," Darcy says. "But not because she likes Beau. She *hates* Beau. She'd just be mad it was me."

Rachelle hates Beau? Beau clearly wasn't that keen on her, either. So why were they even together?

"Well, I think he'll ask to escort you," Lola tells me, finishing off the braid. She hangs the excess ribbon over my shoulder, and I feel like one of Violette's dolls. "*Paper Hearts* said the two of you went to the Salle Favart together. Said you left holding hands. I'd say that's pretty serious."

Right, holding hands. I bet Beau thought it'd be hilarious to slide that fabricated detail in his periodical.

"Well"—Darcy leans in, fanning herself—"is that true?"

I shrug. "We did go to the Salle Favart. My friend Josephine came, and Beau's cousin Mia was there with us, also."

"And the part about you holding hands?" Darcy pries.

"Come off it, Darcy," Lola says, swatting her away. "It's none of your business."

"Oh, dear," Diane says. "What is he *doing*?"

We all turn to see what she's gawking at. To my great surprise, the Baron of Brittany is wading into the water, his trousers pulled up and cuffed over his hairy knees. Rachelle isn't far behind him, her face buried in her hands.

"You're not going to find it in there!" Rachelle shouts at him. She stands at the edge of the water like she might be contemplating going in, but she doesn't make a move.

I crouch down, trying my best to hide my face behind Darcy. I'm not afraid of Rachelle, but I still don't want her to find me here with Beau. And I especially don't want her to catch me laughing at her.

CHAPTER THIRTEEN

BEAU

"Pay up," I say, gloating.

"You have an unfair advantage," Dre tells me, digging into his pants pocket for what he owes me, what they all owe me.

"Exactly," Julien agrees, "the rest of us weren't raised in London playing cricket."

"Guess you'll just have to learn if you ever want to win, then," I say as I take the money that he reluctantly gives me.

We're making our way down the hill when Julien stops. He cups his hand over his eyes, shielding the sun.

"Well, well, well," he says. "Looks like your lady got a little bit of a makeover."

I squint to try and see what he's talking about. Evie is on the lawn with the other girls. They've done her hair and tied up her skirt so it mimics their own. She probably hates it. But I don't. Because she's laughing and the day is breaking on her skin, and I'm glad she agreed to come here with me.

"You know, Beau, she's not too bad," Julien quips. "If you don't escort her to the ball, maybe I will."

I grip the cricket bat tight. I don't know why his comment gets under my skin the way it does, but I'd like to lunge at him right now, send him rolling down this hill. I don't, though, because with Julien, you can't ever let him see you sweat. "Don't get ahead of yourself," I say. "I'm going to ask to escort her. On my own time."

"You're not still thinking you could make her into the Bellegarde Bloom, are you?" Julien asks.

Julien is scared. He's seeing her here now, seeing her in a different light, and he knows what I know, that Evie Clément is a real contender for Bloom. I like it when he's scared.

"What does it matter to you?" I ask.

"Matter?" he huffs, clearly bothered but trying to mask it. "It doesn't matter to me. It's you who's trying so hard. If you weren't trying to make her into the Bellegarde Bloom, why would you even bring her here today?"

I stare at him but don't respond. It *is* why I've brought her here.

Julien laughs, clutching his stomach. "Oh, no, brother. You *do* think she's got a shot, don't you?"

There's a part of me that always internally twitches when he calls me brother. He's never acted like my family, like real family should, like Evie's family does. And we've certainly never been treated as equals.

"If I made a deal like you two did, I'd still be trying, too," Dre says.

Julien's lip curls. "He's already lost. We know Rachelle will win. He can go ahead and kiss that inheritance goodbye."

"I don't know about that," Dre says. "The more I see

the baron, the more I think maybe he could hurt Rachelle's chances."

"A guy with a title hurt her chances?" Julien brushes it off. "Never."

Dre shakes his head. "I don't know. If Rachelle is already promised to the baron, the Court of Flowers may choose someone else. The crowd loves the excitement of seeing who the Bloom pins their boutonniere on."

"Rachelle isn't promised to anyone," Julien snaps back. "Did you see the two of them by the lake earlier? She's clearly embarrassed by him."

"Not according to *Paper Hearts*," Dre says back.

"*Paper Hearts*." Julien rolls his eyes. He tosses the ball in the air and snatches it when he comes down, like he's getting angry. "That bogus paper. Nobody believes what's written in there." He turns and stares me down. "If you ask me, whoever wrote it is just desperate."

Does he know? Does he know I have a printing press in my closet? How could he know? I hold his stare, never giving.

Finally, his shoulders relax, and he clasps a hand on my shoulder. "Well, little brother, I just hope you're getting something out of the deal. You are sleeping with her, right?"

I push his hand away. "It's not like that. It's a bet. That's it."

Julien smirks. "Too bad."

.ೂ⚬ఎ.

We're the only ones under the wisteria, and it feels good not to have to listen to Julien for another second.

"Thank you for taking a walk with me," I tell Evie.

"Yes, well, it was the only way I was going to get away from the girls," she says.

"They're not all that bad, are they?"

"No, some of them—they're fine," she says, fidgeting with one of the ribbons that falls down her chest. "I still don't belong here, though."

"Well, you look nice."

She shoots me a look like she thinks I'm teasing her.

"What?" I say, throwing my hands up. "You do."

"Because I look like them?"

"No! That's not what I mean. It's not the change—not the braids or the ribbons. I just liked seeing you laughing in the sun like that. That's all."

"I actually quite liked it," she tells me, grinning. "It's kind of nice to have people doing your hair and primping you. Plus, they were so busy talking about what they were going to do to me that I barely had to talk to them."

I shake my head, laughing.

Evie reaches up and grabs a low-hanging vine, pressing her nose to the dripping wisteria, savoring its sweet scent.

"Did you know the queen has her own cottage?" she asks me. We keep walking.

I shake my head. "Can't say that I did."

"She does. A hamlet built just for her and her friends

when she wants to get away. When it was built last year, she made them cover it in this stuff. The whole thing. All the windows, the siding. All of it. I bet it looks beautiful right now, bursting and blooming the whole way up."

I remember the journal I found, the one where I talked about her dress. "You like flowers, don't you?"

She shrugs. "As much as the next person, I suppose. How could anyone not like flowers?"

"I can't argue with that."

"Wisteria has always been mother's favorite. If Father ever sees it, he stops and chops her down a handful. He tried growing it over the bakery facade once, but something went wrong and we ended up with dead brown vines everywhere."

I gulp, remembering what happened all those years ago, the day I, too, picked her a handful of flowers. But I push it deep down, hoping she isn't thinking the same thing. "*You* used to come to the Gardens?" I ask.

"I did."

"I thought you hated it here."

"I do, now that the likes of you and your friends have taken it over. But before then, my parents took me here all the time. It was mainly before Violette was born. We'd always go sit under the orange trees, the ones on the far side of the lake. We'd eat oranges until we had a bellyache. I can't eat them to this day."

My mother used to take me to a strawberry field near our house. It belonged to a friend of hers. He gave her work during the summers. We'd spend all day out there picking the fresh strawberries, eating them as we went. She always said it was hard work but she liked it because it meant she got to spend the day with me. I look over at Evie, and I wonder what my mother would've thought of her. I think she'd have liked her. "They seem like good people," I say, "your parents."

"They're great," she says. "I'm lucky to have them."

"They're pretty lucky to have you, too. It seems like you're always doing something for them—working in the bakery, watching Violette."

Evie shrugs. "I do what I can. They've always done everything for me, so it's the least I can do."

"And what about the bakery? Is that your dream? To take it over one day?"

"Oh, no, certainly not," she says immediately.

"Okay, then what is it you want to do?"

She keeps walking, but her eyes shift to the grass. "I don't know."

"You don't know what you want to do?"

"No, I do, I guess. But it's—it's foolish. I'm not going to leave the bakery. I wouldn't. I wouldn't put my mother and father out like that. And I wouldn't leave Violette to do it; that's for sure."

"But what do you want? Whatever it is, I'm sure it isn't foolish. I don't think there's anything foolish about you."

"It is," she tells me. "It's silly to even think about, to talk about. It's never going to happen."

"Well, if you can't tell your hopes and dreams to a guy who you hate in a place where no one else can hear you, then who can you tell?"

She presses her hand to her temple, shaking her head. "It's nothing, really."

"It isn't," I emphasize, slowing my pace so that I can savor more of our time together, so that I can watch her think about her dreams. "Do you want to sew? I know you're good at that."

"How do you know I sew?"

"Your dress at the theater. Josephine's, too. You made those," I say. "Also, Mia may have told me about it."

"Well, yes," she confides, "if we lived in a world where I didn't have to worry about the bakery, then yes, I'd like to be a designer."

I bite my cheek to keep from smiling. It feels like I've won a prize, getting her to open up to me. "You want to make dresses for the queen? Make the king's cape? Things like that?"

"Sure, those things would be incredible. Anyone wearing my garments would be incredible, really. I've always thought it would be nice to make clothes for people like—like me also. Like Jo. Like Violette."

"What do you mean?" I ask her.

"You won't understand," she says, looking over to me.

"Try me."

"Okay," she says. "Well, walking into school every day, knowing that everyone can tell your status based on the fabric or the outdated cut of your dress—it's dehumanizing. I've gotten used to it now, but when I was younger, I wanted to crawl out of my skin. I wanted to disappear. I started sewing when Violette was born. Madame Landry at the store next door had an old sewing kit. Her hands got the shakes, so she gave it to me. I'd go to her shop every day after school and learn from her. I make almost everything that Violette wears to school now. I never wanted her to have to feel the way I did. So, if I ever could, I'd like to make garments for people like me. So that they don't feel invisible."

I watch her for a moment. She has the same twinkle in her eyes that she had the night we ran to the Seine. She looks different, like the veil she wears every day—the one that makes her appear unaffected and stubborn—is lifted for just a minute. I can see her, see who she really is. "There's nothing foolish or unrealistic about that," I say.

"Yes, well, it's just a dream," she says.

"Not if you don't want it to be just a dream," I tell her. "Evie, you don't have to spend your life at the bakery, you know."

"Easy for you to say. I'm sure you've already got a job lined up. Probably a pretty penny from inheritance, too. I don't have any of that. I've got my parents, Violette, and the bakery. That's it."

She doesn't know about the inheritance—that I have practically none, that we're only here *because* I have none—but still, she's right. Why is she always right? I should be grateful that my father wants me to work with him. It's a secure job and probably more pay in a day than Evie's family makes in weeks. But if I could win Julien's inheritance, maybe I could help them. Maybe I could help her do what she wants to do. Maybe if I did that, I'd stop feeling so guilty about betting on her.

When we finally loop back around to the lawn, the others are finishing gathering their things.

"We were wondering if we were going to see you two again," Lola says.

"Let me guess," Julien chimes in. "He took you under the wisteria?"

Evie looks up at me, like it's a joke she isn't in on, but the truth is that Julien is just an oaf.

"Yes, Julien," I say, "we did in fact go for a walk in the wisteria tunnel."

"He didn't try his little trick on you, did he?" Julien says to Evie.

"Trick?" Evie questions.

I step forward. "Julien, come off it."

But Julien doesn't back down. "Beau likes to take girls under there; he gets them talking—asks them something deep, real sentimental. And then, when they least expect it, he kisses them. That's how he got Rachelle."

"Oh, get out of here, Julien," I say. "That is *not* how I got Rachelle. A deep conversation? With Rachelle? Now we know you're lying."

"No," Evie says, and it shuts up whatever retort Julien was about to give. "He didn't. Since you're so curious, he didn't try to kiss me."

She glances over at me, and she's unreadable. What's she thinking? Did she want me to?

"Well then." Dre breaks the awkward tension. "I guess that settles it. But you two are coming to the château tonight, right?"

"Party there tonight?" I ask.

"Certainly is," Dre says. "A bit last minute, but everyone's coming."

I look at Evie. "You want to go?"

"To the château?" Evie says, her brows raised. "Oh, no."

"Why not?" Julien asks her. "You ever been?"

"No, but I've—" Evie starts. "I've got a lot to do back at the bakery."

"Your loss, then," Dre jokes.

The group disperses, going our separate ways to the carriages, Evie and I walking together.

"Can you really not go tonight, to the château?" I ask her as Francis opens the carriage door for us. "Or do you simply not want to?"

"I really can't." Probably a lie, but I let her tell it anyway. "Violette had some of her friends around, so there's mess that needs cleaning. And anyway, I have to be up early. I've got to go to the food stalls and buy the ingredients we need for the rest of the week."

"Hmm," I say, thinking. "But if you didn't have to do those things, you could go, right?"

"Sure, Beau," she says sarcastically. "If all of those things magically got done—if fairies swept the floors and brought bins of flour and sugar—then yes, I could go to your little château party."

There may be a lot I don't know how to do, like figure out if a girl wanted to be kissed underneath the wisteria or not. But one thing I do know is that money can make magic happen.

CHAPTER FOURTEEN

EVIE

I'm back at the bakery, helping my mother dust the shelves, and I'm considering lying to her when she asks me how my day at the Gardens was. I know how much she wants me to find someone the way she and Father found each other, and I know I've never given her much hope in that department.

I don't completely lie and tell her I had the greatest day of my life, but I compromise. "It was fine," I say.

And it's more truth than it is lie, because while spending time with Beau's friends is the last thing I'd ever want to do, the day wasn't awful. Beau was surprisingly tolerable, Lola made my time with her and the twins bearable, and I managed to avoid Rachelle. All in all, a success.

"I think he likes you," Violette chimes in. She has her dolls lined up on the windowsill and is brushing out their hair and putting them in their finest outfits—dresses made from napkins and washcloths—in anticipation of the day Beau comes back to play with her. I don't know how to break it to her that it's not going to happen.

"He doesn't like me, silly," I say. "We're just—classmates." I can't even bring myself to say friends.

"Well, I don't think so," Violette reiterates. "I think he likes you."

Mother keeps working, but I see the grin she's trying to hide.

"Yes, and why do you think that?" I ask Violette, teasing her.

"Because he keeps coming to see you," she says.

"He's only been here twice, V," I say.

"Nah-uh," she says, standing on her tiptoes, looking through the bedroom window. She presses her finger to the glass. "He's here again. See?"

"He's what?" I drop the dust rag and rush to the window. Violette's right. Beau is here, standing just outside the bakery, but he's not alone.

"Who is that with him?" my mother asks, peering down at the group of people now gathered in front of the bakery, none of whom I recognize except for Beau.

"No idea," I say. "I'll go talk to him."

I'm barely halfway down the stairs when I hear my father's voice.

"You brought what for the bakery?" he asks.

What could Beau have brought? I make it the last few steps, and my father is standing at the door, holding it open for the others to come in.

"Evie, have a look at this," he says, beaming. "Look at everything they've brought us. Can you believe it?"

The first few people walk in carrying open crates filled to the brim with flour, fresh eggs, sacks of sugar, and herbs that look freshly picked. Father follows them into the kitchen, giddily asking them question after question.

The next few are holding brooms and polishing supplies. They walk past me on Beau's orders. "Straight up those steps," he tells them.

Up the steps? To our home? What is happening? Who are these people?

Beau comes in after them, and the rest follow behind, a pair that come in rolling trunks. They stop and stand behind him like they're at attention, waiting for him to give them direction.

"What's going on?" I ask him. "What is all this?"

"Well," he says, clasping his hands together, "you said that if all of your work was done—if fairies came with ingredients for the bakery and did the cleaning—that you could come to the château with me tonight, right?"

"Right?"

"So, I brought you the fairies," he says, lifting his hands up like he's showing off. He points to the bakery kitchen. "Our chef has brought ingredients from our stores—I wasn't sure what you needed, so I just had them bring a little of everything."

A *little* of everything? What they've brought will keep the shop running for weeks; it will mean we can buy Violette new school shoes, and—

"Beau, this is—I can't accept this. I can't possibly—"

"Upstairs is Pietra and her team," he interrupts. "They're

here to clean the place from top to bottom. The house, the bakery. All of it."

"No, this is too much," I tell him. "I can't let you do this."

"You can repay me by going to the château with me tonight," he says before grinning.

"Beau, I don't know—"

"Please?"

It's a manipulative gesture, sure, but I glance back to the kitchen and the look on my father's face is ecstatic. His bellowing laugh is echoing throughout the room—he's so happy to have the chance to talk to a real chef for a family like the Bellegardes. I already know he's going to tell stories about this for years. My mother is secretly dabbing quiet tears on her apron, knowing how much of a help these supplies are for us.

I look back to Beau and sigh, resigned. "Sure," I tell him. "I'll go."

"Sure," he repeats with a smile that pushes his dimples in. "Just what I love to hear."

"Wait." I stop and point to the two women behind him. "If they're bringing the ingredients and the people upstairs are here to clean, then who's this?"

"Fleur," the first woman says, stepping forward to shake my hand. She has a white-blond pouf hairdo that stands about a foot tall and is woven with sparkling tulle. The girl next to her looks younger, barely older than me, with painted-on eyebrows and a star-shaped beauty patch at the corner of her lip. "I'll be doing your hair. And this is Gigi. She'll be taking care of your makeup."

"And Jacques should be around here somewhere," the woman named Fleur says, craning her neck to search.

I turn to Beau shaking my head frantically. "No, no, no. I don't need any of this."

"I know you don't need it," he says, "but I thought about what you said at the Gardens today, about how you thought it was actually kind of nice to have people primping you, so I thought I'd bring the whole team."

"I didn't mean it like that. I just meant—"

"Oh!" Gigi squeaks. "There he is now."

Someone else? Beau opens the door, and instead of a person, a clothing rack rolls through, filled from end to end with some of the most beautiful frocks I've ever seen.

The man pushing the cart finally enters. He steps to the side and bows slightly. "Jacques," he introduces himself. "Wardrobe." His outfit is simple enough—black trousers and a black blouse buttoned all the way up to his neck—but his eyes have been smoked out with a kohl and there's a hint of dust on his cheeks that sparkles champagne when the light catches it.

"Evie," I say. "Nice to meet all of you, but I don't think I can accept—"

"Nonsense," Jacques says with a clap. "Show us to your room."

I don't see that I have much of a choice in the matter, so Beau and Jacques lug the wardrobe rack up the steps where

Violette is waiting, peeking around the corner.

She's rendered almost speechless when she sees all of the gowns. Almost.

"Are these all for you?" she says in wonderment. She reaches out to touch them, but I wave her little hand away, afraid she may smear remnants of the raspberry tart, which she swiped while Father was preoccupied, on them.

"Oh, she is all right!" Jacques assures me before looking to Violette. "You see this one?" He takes the hem of a sugar-pink dress and puts it in her hand. "This one is made from a fabric the queen chose herself."

"Really? She chose it? The queen?"

"She did." Jacques smiles at her. "She's given a book with different fabrics every Saturday, and she puts pins in all of the fabrics she wants her new gowns made from. *This* is one of her favorites. Rose always finds new and interesting ways to use it."

"Rose," I blurt out. "You mean, Rose Bertin?"

Jacques's lips part into a smirk. "I do."

I'm too stunned to speak simply at the mention of her name. Rose Bertin, the minister of fashion and without a doubt the most successful dressmaker I've ever heard of, was a commoner like me before she became part of the queen's inner circle. My first year at the university, I told Madame Bissett I could never be more than a baker's daughter, and she kept me after class, made me learn everything about Rose, made me believe there was hope for me after all.

"Violette, no!" I shout, pulled from my thoughts. I'm mortified as she buries her head in the skirt, rubbing the fabric on her cheek, but thankfully, everyone just laughs. They can't get enough of her.

"Maybe one day we can come back and dress you," Jacques says to her. "But in the meantime, how about you help me pick out what your sister is going to wear."

"Oh, wait one minute," Beau interjects. "I don't think she can help you. You see, Violette and I have a date. A date with some dolls, isn't that right? Or are you going to stand me up?" He winks at Violette, who immediately races over to him.

I've never seen her give up the chance to play with pretty dresses so quickly, but she's already off, taking Beau by the hand and dragging him to her room. Before I walk into mine, I glance back at them, watching for a second as he takes a doll off of the windowsill and begins talking in an absurd high-pitched voice. Violette falls into a fit of giggles. And I'm bewildered, because—because he actually kept his promise to her.

"What are these?" Jacques asks. He's standing in front of my own rack of clothes, the ones I've made.

"Oh, no, those are just—" I begin.

He grabs a skirt from the rack and inspects it. "These are . . . *magnificent*." He turns sharply to me. "Did you make these?"

"Uh—yes. Yes. I did."

"And this." He plucks a corset from its hanger and holds

it up to the sunlight. "No boning and yet the structure is impeccable. And it's so short, so delicate. This wouldn't even come to the hips. I've never seen one quite like it. You did all of this yourself?"

I nod my head. "It's not much," I say, not wanting to gloat.

"Not much?" He scoffs. "You think this is not much? My apprentices can barely achieve this level of detail, and they are some of the best in the city." He takes his eyes off the corset and trains them on me before placing his fingers under my chin, lifting it up. "You hold your head high when you talk about your work. You should be proud."

It's exactly the thing I need to hear. And he's right, so I decide to show Jacques the drawings I keep in my bedside drawer, the ones I don't show anyone. He flips through the stack—years of ideas for garments.

"And this." He marvels at one of the pages. "The bustle. You've kept it short, no?"

"Yes," I tell him, "I know it isn't normal practice, but—"

"No, no, it's incredible. *Innovative*," he calls it. He flips a bit more before asking, "May I borrow some of these? I know someone who may be interested in them."

"Oh, of course," I say, surprised. "Of course!" Even if it never amounts to anything, it feels good to be seen.

"Wonderful," he says, sitting the drawings down and gliding over to the wardrobe rack. Gigi and Fleur have just finished setting up, and it looks like my bedroom is a boutique—rows of wigs cover my desk, and on top of the bed is an open trunk full of powders and rouge and paints of all colors. "I believe I know exactly what we're going to dress you in this evening."

He has me step into the gown he showed Violette earlier, the one that looks like my favorite strawberry frosting, made from fabric that is a favorite of the queen's. The sleeves stand puffed and full, contrary to the straight, tight style that is common. Once he zips it in the back, I'm afraid to move, afraid to dirty the bottom or loosen a seam. The shoes he slips on my feet are simple, pale and scalloped at the edges, adorned with a small bow on the front.

"One last thing," Jacques says. He takes the ivory-and-blue toile stays I've made from the rack and pulls my arms through.

"Stays on top of the dress?" I say to Jacques, confused, accustomed to stays being placed under a garment.

"You like it?" he says cheekily, tugging at the laces.

"It's brilliant," I answer, amazed at the innovative silhouette.

As he begins to lace it, Gigi stands in front of me flushing my cheeks with blush and applying a small black heart patch under my eye. Fleur holds wigs up to the dress to see which will be best, something only the French elite can afford. Her head cocks to the side a little, studying my features, before she turns to Gigi.

"I think we're going to do something a little different," she says. "Could you hand me those pearls?"

Fleur sets the wigs and hairpieces aside and begins combing through my own hair. She weaves a few thin braids, fastening them where she likes and stepping back every few seconds to examine her work. The rest of my hair is left soft and full, gathered into gentle curls. I think of Beau and Violette in the room next door playing dolls, how this isn't much different, except I'm the doll being poked and prodded and plucked. Finally, Fleur begins placing the pearls one by one in my hair the same way I place sugar pearls on a cake. Each one is tied delicately in by hand until she's satisfied.

Fleur slips out of the room as Gigi brushes a shimmering dust over my arms and chest.

"All done," she says with one last sweep over my collarbone.

Jacques stands back and stares, rubbing his chin. "Beautiful," he says. He turns and grabs a small mirror, twisting it so that I can see their work.

"Oh, wow," I breathe. I hold my fingers up to my cheeks, lightly touching my skin. Gigi has somehow managed to make it glisten, but it's still mine. I think I was expecting to not recognize myself, for them to have painted over all of the parts that made me, me. My freckles haven't been covered, and the small imperfection at my brow is still there—the time Violette accidentally scratched me when I woke her up for school one morning. The pearls in my hair sit like fallen snow or morning dew, and the stays . . . *My* stays. I move from side to side, trying to hide my amazement with how it gathers the dress in all of the right places. I usually don't enjoy wearing things I've made, worrying that they'll only be judged harshly, but it pairs so beautifully with this dress that I can't imagine anything in its place. I brush the side of it, feeling the toile embroidery.

"Say it," Jacques urges me. "Say how fine your work is."

I laugh. "Only because you've styled it the right way."

He rolls his eyes dramatically. "I tell you what—you need to come work with me. After a few days, I'll have you talking like you're the most important designer in Paris! Besides myself, of course." He winks.

The door opens, and Fleur pops her head in. "The carriage has arrived," she says.

Jacques leads me out of the room with Gigi holding the back of my dress. She doesn't have to, though, because I've never seen our house so clean. The floors are practically sparkling and the air smells like lavender.

Violette's room is empty. She and Beau must be back down in the bakery. Violette's probably showing him how her dolls love to eat the strawberry macarons, which of course means that she sweet-talked Father into giving her a few.

Fleur does touch-ups to my hair all the way down the steps. My parents and Violette are waiting for me at the bottom.

"Oh, darling, you're radiant," my mother says, kissing my cheek. Father and Violette hug me at the same time, her little arms squeezing around my thigh.

"Okay, okay, can't breathe," I say. My father lets go, but Violette has to give one last squeeze.

"Where's Beau?" I ask her. "You don't have him back there washing strawberry macaron out of Penelope's hair, do you?"

"No, he's there." She points.

I turn to see him standing outside, waiting in front of the carriage door. He's staring at the ground and wringing his hands.

Father leans in and whispers in my ear, "Think he might be a bit nervous."

"Oh, Pierre," my mother says. "Of course he's nervous. Look at her!"

"Oh my gosh, Mother! Father!" I say, throwing my hands up, needing to get out of here. "Bye. I'll see you tonight!"

The bell rings as I walk out of the shop. Beau lifts his face, and his eyes grow wide.

"What?" I say to him as he stares. "You ready?"

"Yeah, I—I, um—" He trips over his words.

"The door?" I say, pointing to the carriage.

"Oh, yes, yes," he fumbles, jiggling the handle. "The door. Sorry."

Once we're inside and the bakery is fading from view, I look at him.

"Thanks for that," I say, relaxing my shoulders as much as I can beneath the tight stays. "It was very nice of you. I haven't seen my father so excited in ages."

Beau gives me a half smile, like his mind is elsewhere.

"Do you think the queen feels like this every day?" I ask him.

He goes quiet, fidgeting for a moment and staring out of the window into the night before he looks back to me. "No," he says, straight-faced. "I don't. I think that queens and princesses and duchesses and the like all wish they could look the way you do."

I'm watching the way he's gazing at me—the same way he looked at me that night on Dom's boat—and I'm wondering why he didn't kiss me underneath the wisteria today. If he had, what would I have done? Would I have pushed him away? Or would I have let him?

More important, would I have kissed him back?

CHAPTER FIFTEEN

BEAU

Walking into a room with Evie is different than walking in with Rachelle.

Rachelle would hold her shoulders back and smirk like she was unaffected, but I knew what she was expecting. She expected every eye to be on her, and if they weren't, she'd let go of my hand and storm off to the drink table. I wouldn't see her for the rest of the night, and if I did catch sight of her, I'd sneak off into a spot where the candlelight didn't reach.

But Evie doesn't even notice that every tongue in the château has her name on it, that the whispers are about her.

I join them in watching her as she enters, taking it all in for the first time. She's like a fairy-tale princess, untouchable and enchanting, and everything about her—from the way she walks, to the way she blinks, to the way her hair slips over her collarbones—is shamelessly romantic.

I hold my arm out for her, and this time, she actually takes it. Although, to be fair, I believe she only does so she doesn't have to speak to someone she doesn't like.

"I didn't think anyone lived here," she says, eyeing the ratty furniture placed sporadically throughout the château.

"They don't," I tell her. "People have just furnished this place over the years. Everyone got tired of standing around, I suppose."

Her chest glitters as it rises and falls with her deep breaths.

"Relax," I say. "I'm going to make sure you have fun."

Mia runs up to greet us. "Oh, Jacques has outdone himself," she says. She grabs Evie's hand. "I *knew* he'd pick that one. Give me a twirl."

Evie does so reluctantly, a sort of half spin where she tries to draw as little attention to herself as possible. It doesn't work, though, because everyone is already glancing at her from the corners of their eyes and over the tops of their champagne glasses.

"I thought you weren't coming," I say to Mia. She normally hates going the château. She always says it's just a place where posh people can comfortably give in to debauchery outside of the prying eyes of polite society. She isn't wrong.

"I didn't think I was, either," Mia tells me. "But things changed!"

I study her for a moment, trying to figure out what could've changed to get her here.

"Oh, Evie, will you join me outside for a moment" Mia says, taking a hold of one of Evie's hands. "I want to talk to you about something."

"Oh, of course," Evie answers. Her eyes light up, and if I had to guess why, I'd say it's because she gets to get out of the main hall for a minute.

"I'll be back," Evie tells me.

"Yeah, yeah," I sigh. "Just leave me here alone."

"Will do!" Mia laughs as the two of them flutter away.

I walk the room searching for Dre, taking in the decaying surroundings I've spent so much of my adolescence in.

The château once belonged to the Joubert family, but there's barely a trace of them left now. Driven out in a hurry when they couldn't pay their debts, most of their things were swiped by the townspeople like vultures to a carcass. But the chandeliers still hang, and every now and again when someone is off in a dark room, they'll find an artifact buried in a closet or stashed away in a cupboard. Rachelle claimed to have found one of the eldest son's hankies once. It had his initials sewn into the corner. But if you ask me, the stitching looked brand-new.

"Beau!" someone shouts. I turn to see Darcy Chastain headed my way. She's out of sorts, already—her lipstick smeared and her walk more of a general stumble. I hurry my feet, ducking through the crowd, weaving until I spot a promising-looking hideout. Quickly, I slide behind what's left of a marble statue, holding my breath and not letting it out until Darcy has passed by.

She doesn't find me, but Julien does, and now I'm wishing I'd stopped to talk to Darcy instead. He's headed my way, his chest puffed up, and a glass of champagne in each hand. "My, my, my, little brother," he says, handing me one of the glasses. "You sure have outdone yourself."

I know he's talking about Evie, but I want him to say it. I want him to admit that he could lose this bet. "How so?"

"Your girl," he says. "The peasant one. Looks better than when she was covered in flour, at least."

The peasant one. He wants a rise out of me, but he isn't going to get it. Not here, not now. Not before the Court Ball. Not before I take everything from him, and he learns what the word *peasant* means. "You sound worried," I say calmly.

"Worried?" He scoffs before taking a sip of his champagne. "I'm only worried for you, brother."

"For me? And why would you be worried for me, Julien?"

"Well, it seems to me like you've actually gone and fallen in love with the baker's daughter."

"Fallen in love? With Evie?"

"Am I wrong?" he questions, a singular brow raised.

I toss back the entire glass of champagne in one go. "Of course you're wrong. I told you. It's a bet. Nothing more."

"Well, whatever it is, if she doesn't sleep with you after tonight, after you put her in that dress and dolled her up like that, then I'm going to start seriously questioning if you've lost the Bellegarde charm."

"Is that what everything is about to you, Julien? A guy can't do something nice for a girl just because he wants to? It always has to be a tactic to sleep with her?"

"Oh, don't get so offended, Beau," he tells me. "Don't act so high and mighty, like you're some gentleman, the epitome of Parisian refinement. Might I remind you that you're the one who's falling for a girl you've currently got a bet on. I'm guessing she isn't aware of that, though, is she?"

I stare him down. He wouldn't dare tell her. Would he?

"Thought so," he says triumphantly. He places his glass down and wipes his mouth. "I'm going to go find Diane. Or Darcy. Doesn't matter."

He begins to walk off and I just can't help but to want the last word, so I say, "Good luck with that."

He stops, turning on his heel. "I'm sure I'll find them with Rachelle," he adds. "Have you seen her yet tonight? She's with that oaf of a baron, but she looks prettier than ever. Real Bellegarde Bloom material, you know?"

I haven't seen Rachelle, but I don't care what she looks like. Evie will be the Bloom. "Can't say I have."

"Well, maybe you will," Julien says. "Maybe you can sweet-talk her into taking you back—your one last chance to go to the ball with the girl who's sure to win. Because of course, brother, you and I both know that isn't going to be the baker's daughter. Or, on second thought, keep the ruse with Evie going. I have so many plans for what I'll do with your mother's cottage once it belongs to me. I'll have to tear the drab structure down, of course, but once that's flattened, I'd wager the land could fetch me some nice coin." He pats me on the chest and deliberately bumps into my shoulder as he walks past.

I close my eyes and grip my glass until I'm afraid it may shatter. As much as I'd like to have my go at Julien now, I'm going to let him think he's won, and then I'm going to hit him where it hurts.

.ᴏᴈᴇᴏ.

I find Dre in the same place most of the party has congregated to—the library.

A fire blazes in the hearth, but no one's paying attention to it because they're all too busy watching the bumbling buffoon in the middle of the room. Nicolas, the Baron of Brittany, is standing on top of a dusty velvet sofa, shouting loudly and sloshing his drink so wildly that everyone is keeping their distance.

"She wanted me," he says with a slur. "She did. Told me I reminded her of one of her cats!"

I lean over and whisper to the girl next to me, "Who's he talking about?"

"The queen," she snickers. "Apparently they had a torrid affair." She rolls her eyes. "If I were Rachelle, I think I'd have thrown him in a carriage by now."

I stretch my neck, trying to see over to the far side of the room, to see if I can get to where Dre is. I've got to hear his commentary on this. Instead, I see Rachelle pushing her way through the crowd, parting them like a raging bull, and I'm in her path.

"Out of my way, out of my way," she hisses. Dirty looks and incoherent taunts are hurled at her as she passes.

She shoves aside the couple in front of me and stops dead in her tracks.

"Beau?" She looks surprised and annoyed all at the same time. "Why are you here?"

"Um, hello, Rachelle," I say. Her eyes are caked with turquoise shimmer, and she's wearing her mother's diamond earrings, the ones she always used to put on when she was trying particularly hard to impress someone. "Why wouldn't I be here?"

Her face sours, as though the answer is an obvious one. "Because the château is *my* place."

"Your place?" I nod, frowning. "Interesting. I thought it technically belongs to the city. Or maybe it's still in the Jouberts' name. Who knows, but I definitely don't think the name Rachelle LeBlanc is on the deed, unless of course you've made a pretty hefty property purchase I don't know about. Or perhaps the baron bought it for you."

"Ugh." She sticks her tongue out, unamused. "Blah, blah, blah. So funny, Beau."

"You think so?" I mock her. "I don't think I'm that funny, but your boyfriend on the other hand . . . he's a riot. Did you hear him tell the part about how he's the one who inspired the queen's signature hairdo? Just hysterical."

Rachelle rolls her eyes. "Oh, Beau, it's pathetic that you're so jealous. But if you'd like the baron to, you know, look over your writing or whatever little scribbles it is you make, I'm sure he knows people."

My stomach drops to hear her mention my writing in a crowd of this size, tossing it out so casually. "Oh, I'm sorry, how rude of me. Did I call him your boyfriend? I meant to say your betrothed."

Rachelle's nose scrunches up with disgust. "A baseless rumor. One I'm sure the duke hasn't heard. I'll be sure to not bring it up when I see him in a week."

I almost spit out my drink. "Are you sure that the baron's delusions haven't worn off on you?"

"What is it, Beau? Shocked I have an audience with the duke?"

Yes, actually. There must be a lie in there somewhere. Rachelle may be university royalty, but surely a duke is out of her league. "Just wondering if Nicolas over there knows what you're playing at, is all," I tell her.

"I'm sure I don't know what it is you're implying, Beau," she says, cocking an eyebrow, "but there's nothing saying that I can't keep my options open."

I gaze out into the crowd where the Baron of Brittany has finally jumped down off the sofa. Now he's shoved into a corner, and by the looks of it, his tongue is about to go straight down Grace Collier's throat. "Well, what a coincidence," I say. "It looks like Nicolas is keeping his options open as well."

She jerks her head around to see what I'm seeing, and as soon as she does, she throws her glass furiously to the floor. "Nicolas!" she shouts before taking off in a fury and finally disappearing into the crowd.

It doesn't matter how many girls' mouths the baron's tongue has been in, Rachelle will stick with him long enough to climb over him and on to someone else, someone with a better title. I'd like to think she can't do it, but I've witnessed firsthand how people fall at Rachelle's feet. Most of them know how awful she is, but they see what she has, and they want to bask in that light.

I don't want to think about Rachelle anymore—I've set the plan in motion to make Evie a real contender for the Bloom. But a duke—compared to an idiot of a baron, a duke is an opponent I don't think I can win against. If word gets around that Rachelle is favored by the duke, it's over. If the Court of Flowers thinks Rachelle is on course to become a duchess, they won't even look at anyone else. Especially not the baker's daughter.

I don't know how, but one thing is for certain: I'm going to have to get creative.

Chapter Sixteen

EVIE

The château is nothing like I imagined.

Hearing about the abandoned mansion always conjured images of a crumbling facade, empty hallways with no echo, and creepy staircases that lead to forgotten rooms. This is nothing like that.

The chandeliers are draped with cobwebs, but they still twinkle in the glow of the candlelight. The velvet curtains are coated with dust, but they're still pulled taut, as if they've just been opened for the morning sun. The lion's head statues on either side of the front entrance are creeping with ivy, but they aren't cracked or chipped, every tooth still in its place.

"She should be here any minute," Mia says to me. She's invited Josephine. I can't believe that Jo said yes to coming here—but then again, I can't believe I said yes, either. "I should've gotten her a dress like Beau did for you. Do you think she'll be mad?"

"Jo?" I laugh. "She wouldn't have accepted it even if you had. She barely lets me dress her up. The theater night was a rare occurrence. Trust me, she won't be mad."

Mia smiles. She's peering off into the thick night looking

for the carriage she sent for Josephine. It's the same way Jo looked when we were waiting for them to pick us up for the Salle Favart.

"So, you and Jo," I begin, unsure where I'm going even as the words come out. "You two are becoming good friends?"

"Oh, yes, we are," Mia tells me before she laughs. She takes a seat on the edge of the fountain, but I don't dare. The only sitting I'll be doing in this dress is in a carriage, and even then, I can't be too careful. "Don't worry, I'm not trying to take your place. I just— She's really nice. And interesting. She reminds me of some friends back in the countryside."

"That's right. I keep forgetting you didn't grow up in the city. Your father is Beau's uncle?"

"One of them, yes," Mia answers. She pulls her satin gloves tight, stretching them almost to her elbows. "The only one on his father's side. The rest are Isabelle's siblings."

"And Isabelle is Julien's mother?" I ask.

"Yes," Mia says, rolling her eyes. "You've probably heard about her, huh?"

"Um." I try to think of a nice way to put it. "A little." I've only seen Isabelle a few times, but I've heard about her enough to last a lifetime. She's a sort of legend on Rue du Faubourg Saint-Honoré, and not in a good way. The Bellegardes have hordes of private chefs and bakers, so her wide-brimmed hats and pointed fingernails have never stepped foot into our bakery, but it seems she's been in just about every other establishment on the street. Madame Landry once told me that she knocked over a priceless vase in her shop and had the nerve to blame it on the cat, Timmons. Monsieur Williamson practically gets hives simply at the mention of her name. We don't know what she did to him, but whatever it was, he locks up his shop early if he finds out she's in the area.

Mia chuckles. "You're too polite to tell the truth, but I've heard the stories. If you can believe it, she's even worse at home. Thankfully the house is so massive that Beau and I are usually able to avoid her altogether. There's a little cottage out back; we go there a lot to get away when she is in one of her fits. You know, about important things like how the boutique didn't carry her size in a specific shoe or the jeweler wasn't willing to give her a pair of earrings for free for 'publicity.'"

I crack a smile. Mia's all right by me.

"I know Beau plays the city boy," she says, "but between you and me, he belongs in the country, not here. I think fresh air does him well."

"Beau Bellegarde in the country?" I can't help but laugh. "I don't believe it."

"It's true." Mia grins. "His father would bring him to visit us for weeks at a time. He brought him for the entire summer when Adeline passed."

"Adeline," I say. "Is that Beau's mother?"

Mia nods. "It is."

"What—" I begin, wanting to ask about her, but I think better of it. Best not to pry.

"What happened there? With Beau's father?" she finishes for me. "It's all right to ask. It's always been so hush-hush around here."

I nod softly in agreement. Paris is always full of whispers.

"Well," she proceeds, "my uncle, Beau's father, met Adeline on a business jaunt to London. She owned a small apothecary there. He was married—a society match marriage to Isabelle that neither of them were particularly happy about. He went through with it because it was his parents' wishes, but when he met Adeline, he was immediately taken with her."

"But Julien was already on the way, right? I know he and Beau are only a few months apart." It feels like I've said too much, but Mia doesn't seem offended.

"That's correct," she answers. "Isabelle was pregnant with Julien at the time. Adeline didn't know. So, when Monsieur Bellegarde started flirting with her, she didn't know that he shouldn't have been. I'm sure he exhibited that famous Bellegarde charm."

I resist the urge to roll my eyes.

Mia sighs. "Either way, I'm kind of glad Adeline didn't know, because if she had, Beau probably wouldn't be here today. And without Beau, well, I don't know where I'd be."

"Do you think Beau's father loved his mother?" I ask, but I immediately backtrack. "Sorry, I shouldn't have asked; that's far too intrusive."

"No, no." Mia shakes her head. "Truthfully, it feels quite

nice to find you and Josephine, to have a real conversation with someone in this city, to talk about anything other than how many jewels you own, what the latest trends are, or who's sleeping with who. Feels like breathing fresh air for the first time." She laughs. Every few seconds, she looks back up into the distance, still searching.

"But yes," she continues, "I know Monsieur Bellegarde loved Adeline. However, he was already married to Isabelle, and his own parents would have stripped him of the family name if he'd tried to leave Isabelle for Adeline. Every bit of his inheritance would've disappeared. So, one could argue that Beau has the life he has today because Monsieur Bellegarde didn't leave Isabelle. Isabelle didn't know about Beau until Adeline died, actually. She'd never found out about Adeline. But when Adeline got sick, she faded quickly. And by that time, Monsieur Bellegarde's parents were both gone, and I don't think he cared what Isabelle thought anymore. So, he moved Beau from London to here in Paris, and Isabelle has resented him ever since. To be fair, though, I don't know if there's anyone that Isabelle likes besides Julien. And herself, of course."

I knew almost none of that. I've heard little bits and pieces, the things people whisper about—the secrets they tell others so that, for a moment, they don't have to think about their own. I knew that Beau's mother was never married to his father, and I'd heard she was a mistress, but she doesn't sound like how people make mistresses out to sound. She sounds nice.

I also knew that Isabelle was a wicked woman, but I didn't know she treated Beau poorly. I suppose I never imagined anyone being wicked to Beau. Living in a house with a woman who doesn't want him there . . . I suppose he's more of a misfit than I realized.

"Earlier," I say, turning to Mia, "you said that without Beau, you don't know where you'd be."

"Mm-hmm," she agrees.

"What do you mean by that?"

Mia shrugs. "I never had any brothers or sisters. My parents work quite a bit—our small town really depends on them. I had friends back in the country, some really great ones, but I was yearning for more. I was going mad in that place, and Beau could tell; he saw the excitement in my eyes when he told stories of the city. So, he came to visit and said something to my mother and father. The next day, my parents decided I'd finish out my schooling here in Paris."

I brush my fingers over the stagnant fountain and watch the ripples that chase after them. I don't know if a person can be all bad, but I'm starting to think maybe not. I thought Lola St. Martin was just like Rachelle, but she told me my dress was beautiful, said she wanted me to make her one. She braided my hair, and I don't think she did it because she felt bad for me, either. I think she did it because she didn't want me to feel out of place. And Beau. I can't figure him out. I can't understand why, after all of these years, he's finally paying attention to me. I'd have given anything for that attention when I was younger, back when I was Violette's age, back before everything changed and he ruined the way I saw him.

"Beau isn't so bad, you know?" Mia tells me. "I know he's arrogant and pompous and selfish at times . . . but he's not like some of the others."

I huff. "He hangs out with them, and that's bad enough."

"Yes, I know," she sighs. "Please don't tell him I said this, but I think he does it because he's afraid of what will happen if he doesn't. He came to a city he'd never been to, he didn't know anyone, his father was always working late, and he was stuck in a house with a woman who despised him. I think he's always wanted to be accepted, so he latched on to Julien and to Julien's friends. They were his path to acceptance. And if he doesn't stick to that—the persona of Beau Bellegarde that he's so carefully built—that acceptance could be ripped out from underneath him. He'd go back to being that six-year-old boy, traveling to Paris with barely a bag, alone and unwanted. What would you have done, you know?"

Thankfully, I don't have to answer her. Just as she asks, Josephine's carriage rolls into view. Mia jumps up, wiping the dirt from her backside. I've never thought about Beau that way, about what he has endured. And I don't know what I would have done if I'd have been him.

The carriage doors pop open, and my eyes bulge. Josephine has styled her hair into thick coils. My usually tomboyish best friend is wearing a skirt I made her, the one with the bow in the back, and her lips are tinted like golden honeycomb. Now I know she's smitten.

"Evie?" She gawks. "What are you doing here?"

I put my hand on my hip, messing with her. "I could ask the same of you."

"Um, well, Mia—" Jo says, stepping down. Her shoe gets caught, though, and she loses her footing, stumbling out of the carriage. I jump for her, but Mia's already there, steadying her. "Oh no, sorry, I'm so clumsy." I don't know which is stranger, seeing Josephine all dolled up or seeing her embarrassed about something so small as a stumble. If that had been her that day in the fashion show that fell flat on her face in front of the student body, she would've laughed it off and probably never thought about it again. But in front of Mia, she wants to do everything right. It's sweet.

The two of them smile at each other before Jo finally turns to me, taking in my whole ensemble. "Are those pearls in your hair?"

I can only laugh at the expression on her face. "I had to be fit for the occasion," I say, sweeping my arm over to the château.

Josephine's eyes lift upward as we step into the light and she sees the house for the first time. "Whoa" is all she manages to get out.

I hook my arm in hers, and Mia walks alongside us. "Wait till you see the champagne fountain."

We go together to see the library and then up to the master bedroom balcony, where, for no reason we can discern, a statue of Achilles sits in the center of the room. Bright purple goop is stuck to the statue's mouth in stringy webs. I recognize it instantly as the violet candies Monsieur Paulsen sells at his sweetshop, melted in the day's sun.

"Where to next?" Mia asks me as we walk back to the stairs. "Oh, I know—let's go to the observatory!"

A few others run past us, stumbling and screaming obscenities at each other, playing a drunken game of tag. One of the boys running is the boy from the fashion show, Cliff, the one who told me I'd never be anything more than the flour girl. His hat bounces off as he goes, flittering to the ground. And it gives me an idea.

"You two go ahead," I say to Josephine and Mia, ushering them on. "I'll be right back."

Once they've turned away, I snatch the hat and run inside to the master bedroom, to the statue. I don't have anything with me, so I have to use my nails and it's pretty gross, the sticky purple goo piling up underneath them as I scrape. But I keep seeing Cliff's face in my head, replaying his taunting words, and keep going.

"My hat!" I hear Cliff's voice echo down the hall. Frantically, I smear the melted violet candies all over the inside. By the time he rounds the corner, I'm standing in the doorway.

"This yours?" I ask.

He studies me, his eyes pinched like he's trying to place me, but he doesn't seem to recognize me. I must not look like the flour girl anymore. "Thanks," he slurs. He runs back to catch up with the others, and the last glimpse I catch is him shoving the hat onto his head.

I stand at the top of the stairs laughing to myself. I can't wait to tell Beau. He isn't Cliff's biggest fan, either. I start down the stairs, catching sight of him bobbing through the crowd.

When I get to the bottom, I call out his name, but she hears me before he does.

Rachelle knocks over a ninth-year boy to get to me. "Evie Clément," she sneers. "Playing dress-up, are we?"

"Excuse me?"

"You heard me." She moves closer, trying to intimidate me. "I know that you came here with Beau. Know you went to the Gardens and the theater with him, too. And now look at you, all primped, thinking you look like a princess when you're just a baker's daughter. It's cute, really, how much you want to be me. But you can't, because a weed can never be a rose and weeds have no place in a garden."

Everyone is paying attention to us now. She's done it on purpose, wanting to humiliate me with a crowd. She's almost a whole foot taller than me, too, and I don't know if it's the champagne or the adrenaline from stuffing melted candies into Cliff's hat, but for some reason, I hold my ground, moving so close to her that our noses are almost touching. "Rachelle," I say, glaring at her. "You're the last person on Earth that I'd ever want to be."

Her nose flares, snarling. "Face it, Evie," she hisses, "you're going to lose the Bloom. And when you do, no one will ever remember the name of the little baker's girl."

I sigh, my body giving way. "I never wanted to be Bloom," I tell her. "If I lose, maybe no one will remember my name. But if *you* lose, you'll never forget it."

Before she can spout whatever vitriolic response her monstrous mind comes up with, I turn to go back up the stairs, to get away from her and to go find Jo. I've had enough of the château, enough of these people. But as my foot hits the first step, I feel a tug and hear a rip. My heart drops into my stomach. I don't want to look; I already know what I'm going to see, but I have to.

The back of my dress, Jacques's dress, is ruined. The fabric, the queen's favorite, has been split in two, the frayed edges giving way to my petticoat underneath. I follow the tear all the way to the source—one of Rachelle's pointed heels, which she has speared through the train.

"Oh no, did I do that?" she says, one side of her mouth lifted into a smug smirk.

Tears well in my eyes, but I don't let them through.

"Don't worry," she continues, "it's not like you can't pay to have it repaired. Oh, wait."

Pay for it? No. No, no, no. There's no way. We could lose the bakery. This one dress is probably worth the whole building. My chest tightens. I want to say something back to her, want to find the place that hurts her the most and squeeze it until it bursts. But I can't, because people like Rachelle and Julien, and even Beau—they always win. So I tell her that instead.

I press my lips together and inhale. "You win."

She scoffs, looking back to the crowd that's gathered. "I what?"

"You. Win," I say again, enunciating. "Isn't that what you want? To show everyone here that you're the greatest. That you're the prettiest, the most popular, the richest. We all know that, Rachelle! It's been shoved down every single one of our throats for a decade. So, yes, you win. Isn't that enough? Haven't you had enough?"

Her mouth is open, but she's got nothing to say. The gears in her brain are trying their best to formulate a comeback, but I don't care. I move past her, headed for the door. Even if she hasn't had enough, I have.

CHAPTER SEVENTEEN

BEAU

"Evie!" I call out, elbowing my way through the crowd, trying to get to her as she runs to the exit.

I didn't see what happened, but Dre filled me in well enough. And if it involves Rachelle, it's never anything good.

When I finally make it outside, she's disappeared into the night. I look around, panicked, but the only people I see are a group of boys gathered around the fountain, laughing at Cliff, who is dunking his hair in and picking at a sticky purple substance clinging to the ends. Likely serves him right.

"The girl!" I shout to them. "Did a girl just come out this way? Pink dress, pearls in her hair, about this tall." I hold my hand up to my chest.

"Went that way!" one of them yells back, pointing to the road.

We're too far from her home. She wouldn't dare think she could walk there, would she? But then I remember it's Evie and I remember how stubborn she is, and of course she would.

I run to our carriage, where Francis is sitting with his feet kicked up, smoking a pipe.

"Francis," I call to him.

"Ah, Monsieur Bellegarde," he says, startled. "Are you ready to leave?"

"Evie. Did you see her?"

"I can't say that I did," he tells me. "Did she come this way?"

"Yes! Let's go," I say, climbing up to join him. "To the left, hurry!"

"Oh—okay, on it," Francis says, frantic.

The horses stir, and soon enough, we are on the road. Francis controls the reins while I steady myself enough to stand and hold out a lantern.

"She's there," I tell him. "Just up ahead."

We're so noisy coming down the road that there isn't any possible way she doesn't hear us, but she pretends not to notice, keeping her eyes ahead.

Francis slows the horses to a leisurely pace, and I lean over the side of the carriage.

"Heard you might need a ride," I say to Evie.

She takes a deep breath, still not looking at me. "Well, you heard wrong."

Her heels are in her hands as she walks, barefoot. The light from my lantern catches the back of her dress, and now I can see the damage Rachelle's done, although, judging by the tear streaks on Evie's cheeks, it isn't the only damage that's been done.

"Let me take you home," I tell her.

"I'm not getting in," she says, finally looking at me, "but

if you want to ride next to me going no faster than a snail all the way home, then by all means, do so."

"Sure," I tell her. "Sounds like a plan. We may even make it there by Wednesday morning."

She holds her shoulders back and continues walking, determined. She knows I'm right, but it's Evie, which means that she will walk well into the night before she admits it. So, much to Francis's shock and dismay, I jump from the carriage and begin to walk with her.

"What are you doing?" she snips at me.

"If you're walking, then I'm walking."

"Oh, what, this is supposed to get me in the carriage or something? Trying to make me feel bad that you're having to walk with me? Well, I don't."

I shove my hands into my pockets. "No. Just walking. Nice night for a walk, don't you think?"

She only turns her head to me and glares.

For a while, we walk in silence save for the clopping of the horses' hooves and rattling of the carriage. After a bit, I muster the courage to ask her, "Want to talk about what happened back there?"

She hesitates. "You saw?"

"No, I didn't. Dre told me. And I can see the dress, so."

"Well then, there's nothing to talk about."

"I'm sorry I wasn't there," I tell her. And I *am* sorry. I don't know what I would've done, how I'd have made it any different, but I'd like to think I would've tried.

"I didn't need you to be there," she says. "Just like I don't need you to be here right now. I don't need you to save me, Beau."

I hang my head. "I know you don't. But I'm still sorry I wasn't there."

The first splatter of cool rain falls on the back of my neck. I hold my palms to the sky to catch it.

"Is that rain?" Evie asks before a drop falls right onto the tip of her nose.

A few seconds later, the bottom of the cloud drops out. Francis offers us an umbrella.

"Still want to walk?" I ask her.

"No, it's the dress," she breathes, frantic. "It's already ruined, but—"

"Don't worry about the dress, Evie. The dress was yours to keep anyway," I assure her. "What did you think, that I was going to get you a dress and have you turn it in at the end of the night?"

"Well—well, I still don't want to ruin the fabric!" She hikes the dress up and makes a run for the carriage. Francis slows down so that we can make it in.

The rain falls in sheets around us, washing the windows, and battering the carriage ceiling. It closes in around us, enveloping us in our own small sliver of the world. I remember my journal. *She likes the rain.*

"You got out of there so fast tonight," I say, laughing. "I thought the carriage would be too slow, thought I was going to have to unhitch a horse to find you."

She tucks her stray, wet hairs behind her ears. "Yeah, well, once I started moving, everyone just sort of parted for me, let me leave. It may be one of the only kindnesses those people have ever afforded me."

After a bit, I look up at her and tell her what I want her to know, even if she doesn't care to hear it. "Rachelle has always been wicked," I say.

"Why ever would you date her, then?"

"Good question," I sigh, rubbing my sweating palms on my trousers. "Honestly, the truth is that I've never fit in with that crowd."

"But you're a Bellegarde."

"Sure," I say, "my last name's Bellegarde, and I guess that means something in Paris, but my mother wasn't a part of this world, so I've never really felt like I was, either. Rachelle and her family—they're the epitome of French high society. And I thought—well, I thought that if I was with her, I'd fit in. When I was with her, no one looked at me differently. God, it's horrible to say out loud, but that's why. That's the truth."

"It would sound horrible if it were anyone but her," Evie says, and she smiles for the first time since she left the château. "You don't need her for that stuff anyways. You've probably got a fortune with your name on it and a job to match. No one will care about where you were brought up in a few years' time, and you'll get the life you want with the people you want."

"The thing is," I tell her, "I'm not so sure it is the life I want." I sigh. "For starters, the job with my father, I'm not sure it's how I want to spend my days, you know?"

I think I know what she's going to say next—she's going to tell me that it must be nice to think I can reject a well-paying job—but she doesn't.

She looks me in the eye. "So, you should do what you want to do, then. Which is what, exactly?"

I shrug. "I've always wanted to write. Go into journalism, somehow. My mother, she lived in this cottage on the outskirts of London—I always thought maybe I'd go back there, create a new life for myself."

Evie watches me intently.

"Anyway," I continue, "that's all nothing but dreams. It's not practical. I can't leave what my father has given me. And I don't know anyone in the newspaper business, wouldn't even know where to start."

"It'd be a shame to waste those dreams, though," she tells me. "You started *Paper Hearts*. Everybody at school is talking about it. You've actually made people believe I have a shot at being the Bloom. Now *that* is a talent." She laughs, but I don't, because if the past week with Evie Clément has taught me anything, it's that she deserves to be the Bloom more than anyone I've ever met. "So why don't you just create your own?"

"Create my own newspaper?"

"Yeah, why not? You've got the money. You probably know people who could help, too."

I don't have the money, not yet, but if I could win this bet with Julien, I could get it.

"I don't know," I say. "It's—it's risky. This job with my father is a sure thing. And if I don't take it, I think he'd be really disappointed." I don't tell her what I really mean. That, if I don't take it, or if I lose this bet, the cottage is gone, and he'll probably kick me out into the streets of Paris.

"Well, my best friend once told me that you have to try at things. Even if you think there's a big chance that it might not work out, the least you could do is try."

For a while, she watches the rain and I watch her, watch how the pearls in her hair glisten, wet with rain, and how she still finds a way to shine even in the night's graying light. She's right. About all of it.

Soon, we arrive at the bakery, at her home, and Francis calls the carriage to a halt. He opens the door for her.

"Mademoiselle Evie," says Francis.

"Hey," I call out to her as she steps out. She glances back at me. "See you on Monday?"

"Sure" is all she says before closing the door.

She takes off running for the door, the rain pelting her as she goes, but right before she steps inside, she inhales and lifts her face to the sky, letting it wash over her.

She likes the rain.

CHAPTER EIGHTEEN

BEAU

On Monday, the incident between Evie and Rachelle is all anyone can talk about. I've made sure of it.

"A mean girl?" Rachelle snaps, peering down at the latest issue of *Paper Hearts*, my most recent handiwork. "As if I was mean to her. I simply told her the truth! Who is writing this anyways?"

That's right. A half page detailing Rachelle's abhorrent behavior toward Evie, and perhaps worse, about how Evie bested her with grace. I spoke with Dre later and got the full story of how it all happened. I took a few liberties, but their argument gave me a lot to work with.

"I heard it might be Florent," Darcy chimes in. "You know he's always been jealous of us."

"Florent's not smart enough for this," Rachelle says. "It has to be someone who doesn't want me to win Bloom."

I can feel Julien staring at me, wanting to know if I'm the one behind *Paper Hearts*, but I don't look at him. I only sit back and try to appear inconspicuous.

"I bet it's her," Rachelle says before turning to me. "I bet it's Beau's little girlfriend."

I roll my eyes dramatically. "Come off it, Rachelle."

"Evie's not his girlfriend," Julien chimes in. "He's made that quite clear. Isn't that right, Beau?"

I nod, trying to find what he's playing at. He's always playing at something. "That's correct," I say nonchalantly. "We're just friends."

Rachelle cuts her eyes at me. "You sure about that?"

"I'm sure about that," I mock her.

"Right," Julien interjects. "If Dre or I wanted to have her, that would be just fine."

Here we go again. His feeble attempts to get under my skin are starting to not to be so feeble anymore—they're starting to work their way in.

"Uh, speak for yourself," Lola says, glaring at Dre.

Julien throws his hands up. "Okay, okay. Me, then. You've got to admit, she's looking pretty good these days. And that dress she wore to the château . . ." He blows a kiss.

"It wasn't *that* great," Rachelle says.

"All right, that's enough," I tell him, ignoring Rachelle.

Julien opens his mouth to talk, but Monsieur Travers shuts him down.

"Gentlemen!" he shouts. "Ladies. Please quiet down."

As soon as Monsieur Travers announces the class change, everyone springs from their seats. We're all going to the same place, all headed for the courtyard to see who's made the list, to see who the five girls will be in contention for the winner of Bellegarde Bloom at the Court Ball. The list I made up in *Paper Hearts*, that was my best ploy to get Evie on *this* list— the official list of nominees as decided by the Court, the only one that really counts. It could all be over for me with this one simple list. If Evie's name isn't up there, I might as well pack it up, because Julien's won.

Mia is already there, waiting, when we arrive. "It isn't posted yet," she says, pointing to the empty wall where the parchment is hung each year.

"You nervous?" I ask her, but it's only a deflection for how nervous I am. I look around trying to find Evie, but she hasn't gotten out here yet.

"Me?" Mia says. "Of course not. I don't need to be the Bloom. I don't want to be some prized bachelorette."

I huff, teasing her. "You don't even have an escort to the ball yet, so I'd be a little more concerned if I were you."

"Who says I don't have an escort yet?" She smirks, her brows raised.

"You what?" I exclaim. "You actually accepted someone's proposal?"

"Maybe."

"Who, then?"

She clutches her books to her chest. "Josephine is escorting me. She asked at the château."

My mouth drops open. "Josephine asked?"

"She did! I was just as surprised as you."

"Actually," I say, "if I'm being honest, I'm not all that surprised."

"You knew? And you didn't tell me?"

"Evie swore me to secrecy!"

Mia playfully shoves me. "I can't believe you didn't tell me."

"Aren't you a little glad I didn't? I can only imagine how nervous you'd have been if I had. You'd have been frantic! You'd have been waiting for it to happen, and you'd have driven yourself, and me, completely mad."

Mia sighs. "I suppose you're right."

"So, do you have to match her, or is she going to match you?"

"She's asked me, which means she's going to have to match me! Plus, I already have my gown picked out, so she doesn't have much of a choice in the matter." Her gaze carries past me. "Oh, there she is now. I haven't seen her all day; I'm going to say hello."

When I turn, Evie's standing with Josephine, but she isn't the only one.

"What's Julien doing over there?" Mia asks me. "Josephine hates him."

He isn't talking to Josephine, though. He's talking with Evie, and judging by his charming smile, whatever it is, he's up to no good. "Let's go see," I say.

When we make it over to them, I realize that Julien is just finishing up his story about the time he saved a little boy who fell into the Seine. It's his party trick, the story he tells that he calls a "guarantee" to get any girl to fawn over him. Except, I'm the only one who knows his story is a lie. I'm the only one who was there. The real story from that day is that Julien pretended to throw the young boy's satchel of coins into the river. I didn't stop him because he was a lot bigger than I was back then and I half expected him to throw me in, too.

The boy jumped in after it, and Julien held the satchel behind his back while the boy flailed in the wind-churned waters. It wasn't until the boy's father came, saw what was happening, and dove in that Julien even jumped into the water. He pretended to find the satchel that he'd been holding the entire time, and he has since lauded himself as a hero.

I wait until the end—the part where he heroically swims the boy to safety, which never happened—to comment. "That's not exactly how I remember it, Julien."

"Well, brother." He cocks his head to the side, his mouth pulled tight. "We both know you don't have the best memory. For example, Evie here tells me that the two of you went on a date to the theater. You took her to Salle Favart; I remember the periodical talking about it as well. But if I'm not mistaken, just a short while ago you were telling all of us that you and Evie are nothing more than friends, right? That is what you told Rachelle this morning, isn't it?"

Evie looks at me, and I can't read the expression on her face. I don't think it would upset her that I've said we aren't together. It might upset her that I've even called her a friend given her disdain for me, but I don't think she'd argue that we were ever a pair.

"Does it really matter, Julien?" I ask.

"Well, not to me, of course," he says, his brows pinched. "But if I were Evie, I think I'd be a little offended that you didn't want to claim me." He turns to Evie. "What do you think?"

She doesn't look at him, though. She keeps her focus on

me. "You told Rachelle that?"

Oh. *That's* what she would be upset about. "No," I say. "Well, not really. It was Julien who asked. I wasn't even talking to Rachelle."

Evie just nods, but I can tell from her eyes, she's hurt. I know it isn't that she's jealous of Rachelle. I realize that, after what Rachelle did at the ball, Evie's upset that I'd even choose to be in her company. I'd be hurt, too. I'm a buffoon.

"To use your own words, Beau," says Julien, "that's not exactly how I remember it."

I move closer to him. I've had enough. "What are you doing, Julien?"

"I'm sure I don't know what you mean, brother."

"Don't call me that," I sneer.

"Oh, look at the tough guy," Julien says. "I think you should back up."

"I think you should make me."

"No problem," Julien says before shoving me in the chest.

I'm ready for it, though, my feet planted. I take a step before lunging at him, spearing him at the ribs and sending us both to the ground. We tousle, kicking up clouds of dust, and he makes it over me. Julien pins me, pressing my face into the wet grass. He was bigger than me for most of my childhood, before I hit a growth spurt, and I had to learn all of his weak spots. He's shit with his left arm, so I go for his right, making it unusable. He comes down with his left, but he misses, and I see my opportunity. I wrap my legs around him and roll, flinging him to the ground. I land a couple of solid punches before I'm ripped off him. It takes three guys to do it, but we end up a few yards from each other, both restrained.

"Beau!" Dre shouts at me. "What's wrong with you?"

"What's wrong with me, Dre? What's wrong with him?"

"It was Julien," Mia tells him. "He's the one who started it. That's who you should be talking to."

"Looked like it was both of them to me," says Dre.

"Get him over here," Evie says, pushing me toward a shaded area. "Monsieur Travers is outside. We can't let him see."

She's right. I could be kicked out. Doubtful, with all the money my father gives to this school, but they could always try to stop me from going to the ball. I follow, and when she tells me to sit down on the bench, I do it. I press my head in my hands to stop the throbbing.

"They're here," Mia says.

I've barely sat down, my knuckles swollen, and clothes covered in dirt, when the Court of Flowers representatives arrive. Seven of them are here—all now the elite of society, married to either nobility or the über-rich. Thankfully, none of them seem to have caught my tussle with Julien just now.

I recognize Cassandra, the winner from last year. She isn't the one carrying the scroll, though. That honor has gone to Vivienne de Verley. Everyone knows she's like the Court of Flowers queen if they had one. Win over Vivienne and you've won yourself the Bellegarde Bloom.

Vivienne approaches the wall and pulls her gloves off

before pinning the parchment at eye level.

The text is still too small to read from here. The Court turns to the crowd of us who've gathered, and Vivienne is the only one to speak. "Congratulations to the five women selected," she says, her body rigid with years training her posture. Not even a hair budges as she speaks. "May each of you take your nomination seriously and may the best win. We look forward to seeing all of you at the ball." Her lips twitch as though they're going to part into a smile, but they never quite make it there.

Once they've left, there's a stampede to the parchment.

Rachelle's name is first. Then Lola's, then Camille's—neither of the twins have made it—Mia's, and then . . .

"Evie!" I shout. I don't think, I just turn and pick her up, twirling her in the air.

She's slapping at my back. "Beau! Put me down! Put me down!"

I lower her to the ground. "Sorry," I breathe. "Got carried away. You're one of the five, Evie!"

She's shaking her head, but she isn't saying anything.

When I look up, I can tell that Julien has seen it, too. He wipes the blood blossoming from his split lip and stares me down. It's a look he's given me before—a look that says he's coming for me.

Chapter Nineteen

EVIE

Word travels so fast in Paris that I didn't even get to break the news to my parents, because Madame Landry has already told them. She heard from Monsieur Paulsen, who heard from the clockmaker, who heard from the paperboy.

"I want to help!" Violette squeals.

"You can come with me and Evie to Madame Landry's, then," mother says to her. "She said she has heaps of costume jewelry Evie can borrow for the ball."

"We could do some extra jobs and buy her something nice from the boutique," father suggests. "All of the girls will have dresses from there, don't you think?"

"No way," I interrupt. A hundred extra jobs aren't going to pay for any single dress from the boutique. "I'm not letting you spend your savings on this." I want to tell them that it's just Beau's silly periodical, the one it seems like he only started to get back at Rachelle, that got my name on the list in the first place. It isn't real—no one actually thinks I have a shot at winning. But they all look so happy, so hopeful, that I can't bring myself to tell them.

"You don't worry about that," my mother says to me. And

her face doesn't say it because she'd never let it, but I'm sure she actually is worried about it.

"Well, it's just that I don't *want* to buy a dress," I say. "I want to make my dress." It's a big task to make a gown fit for the Court Ball, but that's no matter right now, because my parents can't possibly argue with that. They're soon distracted, anyway.

"What's Quincy doing here?" Father asks, peering out of the window. I walk over and join him, looking down. Sure enough, it's the palace carriage that Quincy always arrives in, feathered horses and all.

"You don't have anything for him?" I ask. "No order for the queen?"

He shakes his head no. "Unless she wants something right away. Oh, I hope she doesn't; there's no time!"

We all head downstairs in a stampede, steps rumbling, to see why Quincy's here.

"I wasn't expecting you today," my father says.

"And I wasn't expecting to be here today, sir," Quincy says. He opens the carriage door, and Jacques comes bounding out. He's in a tizzy, far less put together than he was when he came to dress me for the château. His shirt is wrinkled, and his eyes look like it's been a while since he's slept.

"Oh, Evie," he says, holding his hands out to me. "Please tell me you don't have plans this evening."

"I— What?" I look to my mother and father, who are just as confused as I am.

"Plans?" he says. "This evening. Do you have them?"

"No, no plans," I tell him, confused.

Jacques rejoices. "Oh, thank the heavens! I need you to come with me."

"Is this something to do with Beau?" I ask. "Has he sent you?"

"Beau?" he responds. "No, darling, this is for the queen."

"The queen?" my father interjects.

"Yes!" Jacques exclaims. "She has a soiree tonight, the Queen's Ball, and all of her usual dressers have fallen ill. Every last one of them is unable to make it. Well, all of them except for me. And I can't get the queen ready alone."

He can't be serious. He can't mean what I think he means. "I'm sorry, you want *me* to help you dress the queen of France?" I say, dumbfounded.

Violette gasps, almost dropping her doll right in a puddle, but Mother anticipates it.

"Of course," Jacques says.

"But I've never—"

"Oh, nonsense, Evie," he cuts me off. "It doesn't require years and years of training to put someone in a pair of stockings. Now, come on, we must hurry! She'll be wondering where I've gone soon enough."

"But my clothes," I say. "I'm not dressed to go to the palace!"

"Your clothes are fine!" he assures me. "She doesn't notice us anyways unless we're absent, and then she's very aware.

Which is why I need you to get in this carriage quickly."

"Okay, okay," I say, panicked, heart ready to jump out of my throat. I turn back to my parents. "I suppose I'll see you in a bit? Will you be all right without me?"

"Evie, are you joking?" my father bellows, shooing me into the carriage. "Go! Go!"

"I can't wait to hear all about it, dear!" my mother shouts, her hardworking hands clasped together, before the door closes.

They fade into the distance as Jacques tries to teach me all the ways of the queen.

"She'll be having her mask treatment now," he says, "so we should be right on time. Léonard, Fleur, and Rose are already there. Léonard and Fleur will take care of the hair, so there's nothing we need to fuss with there unless they need you to hand them pins. She likes her—"

"When you say Rose . . ." I begin, "do you mean—"

"Rose Bertin," he says, so nonchalantly, as if she isn't the most famous dressmaker in France.

"Rose Bertin!" I yelp, almost jumping from my seat. "Rose Bertin is going to be there?"

Jacques laughs. "I forget how exciting this all is to first-timers, forgive me. Yes, Rose will be there. She's a delight, really; you will love her. You and I will dress the queen while Rose prepares the outfits and makes adjustments where she sees fit. Sometimes Rose will try a few things out, but usually with a soiree like this, everything is planned in advance."

The excitement and rush has devolved into nerves, sending butterflies fluttering through my stomach. I breathe deep. "I think I might be sick," I say to Jacques.

"No! No! Not you, too!"

Luckily, Jacques has a pitcher of water he pours me a glass from, and it helps. Still, my nerves are on overdrive. Me, in the same room as Rose Bertin and Léonard Autié? Madame Bissett is going to have a fit when she hears about this.

When you're with Quincy and Jacques, getting into the palace is a breeze. The gilded gates part for our carriage with ease, and we pull right up to the front doors of the Palace of Versailles. I don't have time to take anything in before my eyes are catching sight of the next incredible thing—darting from statue to crystal chandelier to priceless portrait until I'm dizzy.

"Just follow me," Jacques says. I don't speak back, only nodding when he gives me direction. In a place this opulent, I'm afraid to even breathe.

We aren't the only ones running through rooms at top speed, though. Even beyond the four footmen following us with Jacques's trunks, the palace is covered in chaos. Maids and butlers move frantically—dusting vases, setting tables, and shouting at one another in the most oddly polite way. One particularly young footman trips on a rug and almost drops an entire tray of silver but catches it just in the nick of time, performing a balancing act that people would pay good money to see.

"She's in her chambers," Jacques says, leading the way. "Now, when we get in there, I will introduce you. You shall curtsy—you do know how to curtsy, don't you?"

"Yes, of course," I say. One of the facets of going to school with rich kids was learning all of the proper ways to greet nobility, should we ever encounter them. A notion which, until today, has been nothing but amusing to me.

"Of course, of course," he says. "You will curtsy and stay by my side. Don't speak to the queen unless she speaks to you. And you are only to refer to her as Your Majesty."

"Unless she speaks to me?" I whisper. The queen of France speaking to *me*?

"Oh, she won't; don't worry," he says. "She only speaks to Rose and Léonard."

My stomach lurches again. "I don't think I can do this, Jacques," I whisper out of the side of my mouth.

"You already are, dear Evie," he says as we approach two towering doors rimmed with gilded filigree. "Smiles on."

A footman pushes the doors open, and I follow Jacques, one foot in front of the other, doing my best not to trip. Thankfully I'm wearing my boots and not the heels from the fashion show.

Everywhere I turn, things drip in gold. Sunlight washes over the walls, which bloom with flowers. The air smells of wisteria and sugar cookies, and all at once it reminds me of home and reminds me nothing of home.

The queen is sat underneath one of the many chandeliers, laid on a silk chaise, her back to us, never noticing the doors opening. Just like in the rest of the palace, the room is rife with people moving about, either tidying up or readying something for her. Jacques guides me to a spot in front of the window where we proceed to open each trunk and begin removing everything we'll need.

Léonard and Fleur are busy working away on the queen's hair when Rose Bertin walks over to us. I recognize her immediately.

"Jacques," she says, holding her arms out to him. They share kisses on the cheek. A hat bursting with flowers sits crooked on top of her bouffant. She leans in, quiet. "I was beginning to think you might not make it."

"Just had to take a short detour." He winks at her.

"And who is this bright-eyed girl?" she asks him, turning her attention to me.

"Rose, this is Evie Clément," Jacques says. "Evie, this is—"

"Rose Bertin," I breathe, awestruck. "I—I know who you are; I know everything about you, probably."

"Now, now, Evie," Jacques says like he's trying to calm me, and I feel like a fool for turning into a puddle at her feet. Seeing her and the queen in the same room at the same time is a little much for one day.

For a second, I'm worried that Rose might be put off by my behavior, but a smile peeks across her lips. "Charming one, you are," she says. "Pretty, too. Do you design as well?"

I gulp. "I do," I say. "Not in the way that you do, of course, but Madame Bissett, my teacher, she's taught me a lot, and my neighbor Madame Landry also."

"Jacques, this wouldn't be the young lady whose designs you showed me recently?" Rose asks him. "The ones with the cropped stays and pearled necklines?"

"It certainly is," he tells her. "One and the same."

Rose Bertin? Jacques showed Rose Bertin my designs?

"Well, Evie," Rose says, studying me with a pinched brow. "I have to say that your ideas are some of the freshest I've seen in quite some time. Reminded me of someone." She pauses for a moment, smirking. "Me."

"Oh," I manage to get out. "Well, I'm—I'm nothing of your caliber."

"Jacques, you must teach her a thing or two about confidence," Rose insists.

"Believe me, I've been trying," he jokes.

"Looks like she's ready for us," Rose notes, nodding over to the queen. She gives me a wink. "Chin up, Evie. You're about to dress the queen of France."

There's no turning back now, no making a run for it and hitching a ride on the Seine, no going home where I can wallow in shame. No, I have to do this now. I have to dress the queen, and I have to not mess it up.

Jacques hands me the stockings, and he readies the stays. We approach behind Rose, who holds a slip. I try to steady my breathing. The queen is beautiful—rosy-cheeked with eyes so clear they remind me of Violette's. She's so done up, so regal, but she's also just a human. I don't know why this startles me. I'm almost taken aback to find that she's got skin and fingers and bones just like the rest of us.

Rose curtsies and is acknowledged by the queen. Jacques gives me a nod, and I follow his lead, curtsying completely in step with him. I don't raise my head until I'm sure he has. He directs me to begin putting on the queen's stockings, and I do so, lifting her ankle with a porcelain delicacy that father would kill for me to use when constructing macarons. She watches me slide them up to her knees while Rose changes her slip. She stands for Jacques to lace her stays. Rose fetches her gown—a saccharine blueberry satin with bows lining the bodice, and bell sleeves with the subtlest gilded floral embroidery.

"Will I have a choker?" the queen questions Rose.

"You will," Rose answers. "I've brought an assortment for you to choose from." One of the maids brings over Rose's trunk and opens it to reveal rows of multicolored ribbons for the queen's neck. She moves closer, inspecting them one by one. I watch her, trying to figure out the thought process behind the most fashionable woman in France.

"Let the girl choose," she says, turning to me.

I look around the room, trying to find another girl she might be referring to, but her gaze is clear. She's talking about me.

My feet seem to be stuck with shock, so Jacques ushers me forward to the trunk.

My hands tremble as I sort through them. A bergamot

orange with transparent stripes, a ruffled vanilla linen, a honeypot satin. Finally, I land on the one that I think will suit her best, and I can feel all of their eyes on me, especially hers, so I make the choice: an ivory tulle with candied pink knots so dainty you could miss them if you didn't know they were there. I lift it and turn to her, forgetting to breathe.

The queen's matching pink lips lift into a smile. "Excellent choice," she says.

I haven't the faintest idea what to do, don't know if I thank her or if I am even supposed to speak, so I just curtsy again like a buffoon.

"Is she an apprentice?" the queen asks no one in particular. Almost everyone in the room is silent, except for Rose, who seems almost friendly with the queen. Rose takes the choker from my hands and drapes it around the queen's neck.

I look wide-eyed and mortified to Jacques. She isn't speaking directly to me, so I shouldn't speak back, right?

Jacques gives me a few looks that I can't comprehend before he finally blurts out, "Evie works at a bakery on Rue du Faubourg Saint-Honoré, Your Majesty. Her family owns Chérubin."

The queen whips around to me. "Chérubin! You're the one who makes those delightful strawberry cakes and banana cream puffs?"

I gulp. "Yes, Your Majesty. Myself and my father. Mother helps some, too." I almost begin to ramble, but I catch Jacques's eyes and stop myself.

"Well, this is a delight," the queen says.

Rose leans in. "Would you like for Evie to tie your choker, Your Majesty? I'd bet Evie's years at the bakery have proven her an expert bow-tier." She gives me a quick wink that the queen doesn't catch.

"I certainly would," the queen says, and I almost faint, but Rose guides me over and replaces her hands with mine, right where she's pinched the choker into a knot.

I take a deep breath and try to imagine myself back at the bakery, back listening to Violette playing in the next room over, my father in the kitchen preparing dough, and my mother upstairs making a racket while she whistles and dances and sweeps. I begin to tie exactly the way I'd tie a box of the queen's favorite cream puffs. Rachelle isn't here. The Chastain twins aren't here. Cliff isn't here. No one is here to call me flour girl. It's just me—me tying a bow that I learned to tie at my family's bakery, tying it in the Palace of Versailles, tying it for the queen of France.

CHAPTER TWENTY

EVIE

A fact that I was unaware of until today is that one of the perks of dressing the queen on the night of a soiree is that you then get to attend that soiree. Well, *attend* may be a bit much. You get to stand in the shadows in case she's to need a touch up—fresh powder or an extra pin—in which case you'd be there at her every beck and call, and I suppose I could imagine worse things. My first real ball will be the Court Ball in two weeks' time, but perhaps I could use this night as practice so I will know what to expect.

"She won't need us," Jacques says as we make our way to the ballroom, gliding past windows where the shades of night have fallen. "In all my years of doing this, she's never needed me. Rose and Léonard will take care of everything. Our job, along with Fleur, is to blend in and make ourselves wallflowers."

That, I can do. Although, I am still cursing him under my breath for not letting me change, for letting me come to the palace, and now to the Queen's Ball, in such a simple frock. Rose tied one of the discarded sashes at my waist, but I still feel like a peasant out of place. I still *am* a peasant out of place.

Fleur leans down and whispers in my ear. "Wallflowers have some of the best views."

I follow them into the ballroom, and I'm not quite sure what I was expecting, but this is even more than that. It seems the whole of Paris high society has been invited, with couture gowns and dress coats filling the space from wall to wall. They don pastel silks, floral brocades, and ballooning skirts that occupy three times the amount of space one normally would. They walk as though they are floating through the space, everything steeped in low rose-tinged light. The tables are draped in velvet and lined with powdered pillowy loaves of bread and towers of plums, cherries, and segmented nectarines. I've often dreamed of my father's cakes being the centerpiece of one of these parties, but it would take us a month just to make all the treats in the room, every corner piled with a confectionary of decadent sweets—chiffon cakes, crystallized lilac petit fours, and blueberry jam truffles.

Jacques and Fleur lead me down a flight of curved stairs until we finally take our place, backs against the wall, watching the night unfold. Most of the room has broken out into a dance while the others mingle and dine, and every so often, I catch a pair skittering away hand in hand.

The queen dances in the middle with a woman I don't recognize. I lean over to Jacques.

"Is the king here?" I ask. "I thought we'd have seen him by now."

"His Majesty rarely attends," Jacques tells me. "Must not

like a good party, eh?"

I grin back at him. "Must not."

He begins pointing everyone out to me—viscounts and secret mistresses, but we don't even make it a quarter of the way through the list before I spot someone he doesn't have to point out to me.

"Rachelle," I say, unaware it's out loud. I cover my mouth.

"You know someone here?" Jacques asks.

I crouch down, trying to hide behind Fleur's towering frame and a marble pillar. Rachelle is with the baron; they're talking with another couple, but it's definitely her.

"Over there," I whisper to Jacques. "In the gold dress."

"Ugh." He frowns. "What a dreadful shade of goldenrod. Is that the Baron of Brittany that she's with?"

I nod before taking another quick peek from behind the column.

"She doesn't seem very interested in him," Fleur notes. "She's been trying to get away the whole conversation."

"Don't blame her," Jacques says. "The Baron of Brittany isn't much company, I must say."

"You know him?" I ask.

"Not entirely," Jacques laughs. "I've had the displeasure of dressing his mother before. Did you know that she chooses every outfit of his? Right down to the cuff links. That's why he's wearing those horrid square-toed shoes. They're her favorite."

I glance out to see them, but he and Rachelle have moved and are migrating ever closer to where we stand.

I turn back to Jacques. "Is it all right if I go out and get some fresh air?"

"Of course," he says. He places a hand on my shoulder, and I feel him relax for the first time today. "After all, you saved me today. I promise I'll find a way to repay you."

I grin at him, and I want to tell him that bringing me here is payment enough, but Rachelle is only a few yards away, so I duck down and find the nearest exit.

I sneak out into the gardens, eventually settling behind a topiary so large it could conceal an elephant. Inside the palace, it sounds like the party could be heard from miles and miles away—like my parents could be dancing in the living room to the queen's band. But out here, it's muffled, like a scream underwater. The night is cold but the stars are out and I'm at the Palace of Versailles, and it's here in this temporary quiet that I can finally appreciate it. I take the first true breath I've taken in hours, letting the chilled air fill my lungs.

Mother and Father will wait up for me, of that I'm sure. I'll be lucky to get any sleep, lucky if they wait until morning to bombard me with questions. I'll tell Josephine first thing.

And Beau. The queasy feeling from earlier tickles my throat again. I remember Julien's words outside in the courtyard today, and I don't know why it makes me feel the way it does, why it makes me sad or mad or—something. I don't care if Beau talks to Rachelle. I don't know why he'd want to, but I don't care if he does. I guess I just don't want him talking to her about me.

A full moon rises over the gardens, washing soft light

over the Venusian statues and the queen's sweet-smelling flowers, a bath of romance and indulgence. Carnations, lilies, and roses of every color open to the stars. Violette would love to see it. Should I take one for her? Just a petal, even? Would they notice?

While I'm busy contemplating the possible consequences of stealing a rose from the Palace of Versailles, the leaves behind me shake, and I'm startled out of my criminal thoughts. Please don't let it be a guard. Worse yet, please don't let it be Rachelle.

A young man steps out from behind the hedges, breathing heavily and peeking over his shoulder, looking back at the palace.

"I'm sorry, I thought I was the only one out here," I say.

He jumps backward, clutching his chest. "Goodness, you scared me," he laughs.

"Oh, I'm sorry, I didn't mean to—"

He's hunched over, hands on his knees, still laughing, when he lifts his head. "Do you always apologize this much?" he asks me.

As he looks up to me, the starlight paints his skin, his eyes brighter than the chandeliers that hang in the palace, and his hair like a black pearl, so dark that it fades into the night sky. He's tall and broad and the way he smiles, the way only one side of his mouth curves up, is mischievous but warm.

"Do you always run away from parties?" I say back to him cheekily.

He grins, standing up straight, brushing his coat. "I could ask the same of you, out here hiding behind bushes. Have enough of the party, or are you also trying to get away from someone?"

"Neither," I lie. "Just needed some air, is all."

"Well, I wouldn't blame you if you were," he says. "Lots of people in there worth hiding from."

"Oh, I don't doubt that," I blurt out, recalling all the overheard gossip swarming through the party. The palace is a beautiful place, but apparently quite a few insufferable people walk its halls.

"Either I'm losing my mind," he tells me, "or I've had a girl following me around all night long. I thought perhaps I was imagining it at first—but I was at the buffet and I went to reach for a shrimp, and someone's hand grabbed mine." He mimics the moment, reenacting it like the hand was a claw clamping down on his.

"And it was her?" I ask.

"It was her! Standing there smiling like it was an accident, as if she hadn't been following me round the room all night. I rushed out so quickly I forgot my shrimp and now I'm out here, and I'm hungry."

I try to stifle my laughter. "How do you know it really wasn't an accident?"

"Because I know," he assures me. "I know girls like her. You can see it in their eyes."

See what in their eyes? He's undeniably handsome, the

kind that knocks you over, so I guess he's used to women flocking to him. Like Beau.

"Do men like you always assume that every girl you come across must be madly in love with you?" It comes out of my mouth before I can stop it.

"Men like me?" he questions.

"Yes," I double down. "Like you."

He cocks his head to the side, curious. "What exactly are men like me like, then?"

I take a deep breath, and then I think better of it. "No, no. Forgive me, I shouldn't have—"

"No," he says, his eyebrow arched. "Go on. You've piqued my curiosity."

"All right," I sigh. "Well, I simply mean that people who look like you, men especially—"

"Look like me?"

"Yes, like you. Handsome, dashing, charming, the works. People like that, well, they tend to think that everyone wants something from them, that we all must secretly be fawning over them." I know Beau thinks that. He must think I'm a bird in his hands. He must think that I will look past all his failings because he's Beau Bellegarde. But I won't, because I don't care who he is.

"I don't think that," he says.

"No?"

"No." He shakes his head for confirmation. "I don't think you are secretly fawning over me at all right now. What do you say to that?"

"I say that you're correct." I rub my shoulders to stop a shiver.

"Here," he says, taking off his coat. "Take this."

"No, no, I'm fine," I say.

"Nonsense." He drapes his coat around my shoulders. His hands linger for a moment, slow and warm like spring sunlight. "I insist."

I'm about to take it off and give it back when the heat of the jacket first washes over me. "Thank you," I tell him.

"What's your name?" he asks.

"Evie. And yours?"

"Oh." He hesitates, like he's never been asked his name before. "Uh, it's Heath. Heath."

I extend my hand to him. "Nice to meet you, Heath Heath."

He grins, taking my hand in his. And there it is again, that spring sunlight. "Nice to meet you, Evie." He watches me a moment before turning back and looking once more through a split in the hedges.

"She hasn't come to find you, has she?" I kid him. "The woman with the shrimp."

"She hasn't," he assures me. "Probably thanks in part to your exquisite hiding place."

"Yes, well, I suppose it's our fortune that the gardens are just big enough for both of us to hide out in," I joke with a shiver.

"Wait. I thought you said you weren't hiding out," he says with a smirk.

"Oh, yes, I did say that, didn't I? Well, I guess the secret's out, then, huh?"

"It sure is."

"It's nothing, really. It's just this girl from my school. I didn't realize she'd be here. Didn't want her to see me."

"Why's that? You'd only make her jealous?"

"No," I breathe. The thought of Rachelle being jealous of me is so inconceivable that it almost makes me erupt into laughter. "We—aren't friends is all."

He rubs his hands together, nodding. "Wouldn't want to have a spat at the palace and never be invited back, yeah?"

I laugh. "I wasn't invited in the first place."

"No? I didn't take you for a party crasher."

"No, I was sort of whisked here by someone, asked to dress the queen. I thought it would be obvious by my attire or lack thereof. Must be too dark to see."

"I can see you quite clearly," he says quietly. "And I think you look lovely."

My eyes meet his, and I can't find a moment of deceit in them. It stirs something in me out here in the darkness of the gardens, something that makes me wonder if his touch is like spring sunlight, would his kiss taste like fresh rain showers? "I, um—I should be getting back inside," I say. "I'm supposed to be on call if the queen were to need anything—supposed to be blending in, being a wallflower."

"Oh, I don't think that's possible," he says before taking a breath. "But I should be in as well. I'm sure my sister is looking for me."

We walk together back to the palace doors.

"I'll let you go in first," I tell him. "I don't want to get in trouble for talking to guests."

"Yes, well, if you see a girl with a fistful of shrimp, do me a favor, and stall her?"

I grin. "Will do."

The smile drops from his face. "It was very nice to meet you, Evie. It's rare I enjoy meeting someone."

I guess I've never given it much thought, but it's rare I enjoy meeting someone also. "Likewise," I tell him.

He nods and turns back to the soiree, disappearing through the doors.

"Oh, wait," I call out to him, rushing through. "Your jacket!" But he's already gone, lost in the crowd.

By the time I get back to Jacques and Fleur, they've both made their way upstairs and are people watching, deep in gossip. I check around to make sure Rachelle is nowhere near, but I'm just shrouded enough by the crowd that I don't worry.

"I heard she's leaving him," Fleur says in between sips of champagne.

"Never," Jacques says. "Marguerite wouldn't."

"Wouldn't she?" Fleur counters. "If there were better options."

"Like who?" Jacques says.

"Like the Viscount Phillipe," Fleur suggests.

Jacques scoffs. "Too old."

"What about Richard Renauld, then?" Fleur says.

"Too married," Jacques says, jokingly appalled.

"Or the duke," Fleur says, but Jacques just rolls his eyes at the notion.

"Like Marguerite could win the favor of a duke," he says.

"Oh, the duke," I interrupt, thinking about Rachelle. If I can spot him, I can likely spot her. If I had to guess, he's the real reason she's here tonight, not the baron. Wherever the duke is, I'm sure Rachelle is not too far behind. "Which one is he?"

"That's him there," Jacques says, pointing to the center of the dance floor.

I stand on my tiptoes, my eyes sifting through the sky-high hair and feathered plumes until I find him, the one Jacques has identified as the duke.

As it turns out, I'm wearing his coat.

CHAPTER TWENTY-ONE

BEAU

"Where've you been?" Mia demands when I walk in the house.

"Out," I tell her.

"Out? You've been out for days! Haven't been home, haven't been to school. You know I've had to lie to your father?"

I laugh. "What'd you tell him?"

Mia crosses her arms. "What did I tell him? Is this a joke to you? I've been worried sick, Beau. You almost beat Julien to a pulp right there in the courtyard, and then Evie is named one of the five and you go missing."

"I'm sorry, Mia. I just had to get away." I don't want to tell her where I've been, that I crashed the past two nights on Dom's houseboat, that I spent both evenings with him and Bash and Celeste down at one of the taverns where no one knows my name, before falling asleep just as the sun rose over the Seine.

"What's come over you? What happened with Julien? What made you so angry?"

I don't want to tell her about the bet. She'd be so disappointed in me. She likes Evie. And so do I, but I'm in too deep now. So, I tell her half-truths. "Did you know that Julien gets everything? The inheritance. Everything except my mother's home. That's the only thing that goes to me. Did you know he gets it all?"

Mia is shaking her head. "No, that—that doesn't sound right. Your father wouldn't do that."

I sit down in one of the study chairs, ignoring the dirt on my boots. "Well, he has."

"How can you be sure?"

"Because I'm reminded of it every year. Have to go down to the law offices and sign papers that detail all of it, to say that I understand."

"He's giving Julien everything?" Mia shouts.

"Shh," I quiet her. "Yes. He is. I've tried not to think about it for a long time, but now that we're graduating, I can't seem to get it out of my mind." The truth, of course, is that now I've made this bet, I keep picturing him winning. I keep picturing him taking my mother's cottage, the only thing I've got to my name, and throwing out the furniture in the bedroom or spilling coffee on my mother's favorite chair, or worse—selling the place and making it so that I never get a proper goodbye.

"Oh, Beau—" Mia begins.

"He knows it, too, Mia. You know how he is. When he finds that he has the upper hand, he clenches it tight. The other day at school, he made a comment to Evie. He's said horrible things to me about her, trying to get a rise out of me, and I've let them pass. But then he said something to her. Not me. And I could tell that it hurt her. I'd had enough, you understand?"

She nods, thinking. "I'm sorry he did that. Your father, I mean. Julien is predictable, but it's your father I'm disappointed in."

"Thanks, Mia," I say. "It's fine."

"It's not," she assures me, "but maybe time will make it so."

We sit for a moment in silence, both of us listening to the crackle of the fireplace, before she speaks again.

"You know what you said about Julien," she starts, "about having the upper hand?"

"Yes?"

"I think you're right," she says, "but I think he clenches it too tight, until it turns to ashes and falls from his grasp. Like I said, he's predictable. So, let him be predictable."

She's right. If you wait long enough with Julien, he always shows his hand.

"I suppose Isabelle's heard already," I ask her, "about the fight. Suppose my bags are already packed, yeah?"

She shakes her head no. "I don't think Julien has told her," Mia says. "Actually, I know Julien hasn't told her. There's no way. She'd have torn the city apart looking for you." She starts laughing. "Chances are I'd be on my way back to my parents' home in the country right now because she'd think I'd conspired with you."

Just then, Jacques trudges through the room, headed for

the door. He's carrying an armful of wrinkled dresses and mumbling furiously to himself, something about Isabelle. There's no telling what dreadful thing she's said to him now.

"No gig at the palace tonight, Jacques?" Mia calls out to him.

"Unfortunately not," he says before noticing me. "Oh, Beau! Where've you been?"

"Out," Mia and I both say in sync.

Jacques's brows raise, and he studies us both for a moment before he continues. "Well, I'm assuming you've heard everything about Evie's night at the Queen's Ball, then?"

"The Queen's Ball? At the palace?" I ask. I haven't spoken to Evie since school. I haven't known what to say to her, and I seriously doubt she wants to speak to me.

"Yes, of course," Jacques says. "I thought she'd have told you by now. The others were sick, so I took Evie with me to dress the queen."

"Evie dressed the queen?" Mia yelps, coming up out of her chair.

"She did." Jacques grins. "Did a fine job, too. She'd be a great apprentice once she's out of school. The queen appeared quite pleased with her as well. Seems like the queen wasn't the only one pleased with her, though," Jacques says, focusing on me.

"What do you mean?" I ask him.

Jacques clears his throat. "Well, if the rumblings in my circle are correct, I believe she met the duke. And from what

I hear, he's a bit taken with her."

"The duke?" I scoff. "Taken with Evie? How did they even meet? When? You left her alone with him?"

Jacques's hands fly up in the air in innocence. "I knew nothing of it. It wasn't until Fleur informed me this morning. I noticed Evie was wearing someone's coat when I took her home last night, but I didn't know that—"

"She was wearing his coat?" I snap.

"Well, I assumed it was his once I learned of their meeting," Jacques begins.

"Were you not with her the whole time?" I ask him sternly. How could he let her run around the palace by herself?

He searches for a response, and I realize I'm interrogating him.

"Never mind," I tell Jacques. "It doesn't matter."

After he grabs what he needs and hurries back upstairs, Mia turns to me.

"Way to take it out on Jacques," she says.

"Take out what? I was only asking him what happened."

She isn't buying it. "So, it doesn't bother you at all that Evie was with the duke, then? That someone might actually be interested in her?"

"Evie can do what she likes."

"If you say so, cousin," she says, patting my chest as she walks away. "I'm headed to bed."

I should be, too. Two long nights at the tavern followed

by barely any sleep on a rocky houseboat hasn't been good for my brain, but I decide instead to get a moment of fresh air to clear my head.

I make my way out to the front steps and take in the quiet of the streets. As has been happening lately, my mind drifts to Evie. If she hates someone like me, then she must hate someone like the duke even more, right? I can't imagine she'd be interested in someone so high born. Maybe Jacques is just playing it up—maybe their meeting was nothing more than accidentally bumping into each other in a corridor. But why would she have his jacket?

Just then, the front gate swings open. I don't have to look to find out who it is—there's only one person who would let themselves in so nonchalantly to another person's yard at this time of night.

"What a surprise," Rachelle says, sauntering down the cobblestones. "Didn't think I'd find you so quickly. Julien said you haven't been home."

"What are you doing here, Rachelle?"

"What? Can't come visit a friend?"

"We aren't friends," I tell her.

She sits down on the step next to me, and I'm too exhausted to move away.

"Oh, don't be like that, Beau," she says, looking at me from under her eyelashes. "I came over here because I wanted to see you. Is that so hard to believe?"

Yes. It is, actually. "And where's the baron, then? Does he know you're here?"

"Ugh," she scoffs. "Nicolas doesn't care where I am. He's too busy having dinner with his mother."

"Hmm. And you aren't invited to those dinners?"

"Of course not. The woman acts like I'm poisonous or something. She actually had the nerve to call me a gold digger. As if they even have enough gold to dig." She laughs at her own joke, but I don't crack a smile.

"Well, your aunt seemed to think they did," I say. "She was always looking for a way to run me off."

"Yes, well, Aunt Geneviève was mistaken. Nicolas's mother may have an in with a viscount and a few others at the palace, but the land they own is dwindling in price—mostly flood territory that they soon won't be able to sell."

"Ah, so your aunt did set you up with him, then?" I smile at her inability to keep her lies straight. "From what I remember, you told me that you ran into the baron serendipitously while you were visiting your aunt."

"Oh, um—" I can see her searching her mind for a good excuse, another lie to add to the pile.

"Don't bother," I tell her. "I knew from the start."

We sit there in silence. I'm half hoping she'll go away and half glad to have a distraction.

"I thought you'd be with Evie tonight," Rachelle says. "Seems like you've been spending a lot of time with her."

"Yeah, well, I think she's found someone else," I blurt out.

"You were too good for her anyway," Rachelle says, sidling closer to me. "She should have realized what she had. I should've, too." I look over to her and she touches my cheek, and it's comfortable, easy to fall back in with someone you hate just because it's familiar. I regret it the moment my lips touch hers.

It doesn't last long, only until I'm able to knock myself out of it. I pull away.

"Rachelle, I shouldn't have— We shouldn't have. I don't—"

"Shh." She presses her finger to my lips, going in for another kiss, but I stand to get away from her.

"No, Rachelle. I can't."

"Oh, what, because of Evie? Don't give me that, Beau. She's the daughter of a baker for goodness' sake. Do you really think you're going to marry a girl like that?"

"Wait," I stop her, beginning to put the pieces together. "Didn't you tell me that you had an audience with the duke two nights ago?"

She flips her hair out like she's unaffected. "Yes, why?"

"And how did that go?"

"Why are you interested?"

"How did it go, Rachelle?" I demand.

"Fine," she sneers.

"Yeah? What did the two of you talk about, then?"

"Talk about? Well, we . . . you see, we . . ." She fumbles over her words. "As it turns out, we didn't get the chance to talk. I was being bombarded all night, you know. The Queen's Ball, it's quite hard to find a moment to talk to everyone, of course."

And I finally put the pieces together. The duke wasn't interested in Rachelle that night because he was interested in Evie. And Rachelle has just found out that the baron is close to penniless. I'm her last resort. "So, that's why you're here. You've got no other options."

"What? No, no, of course not," she says. "I only wanted to see you, wanted to tell you how much I've missed you." She stands and tries to wrap her arms around my waist, but I don't let her.

I should've known better. "You know, Rachelle," I say, "Nicolas's mother is right. You are poisonous."

CHAPTER TWENTY-TWO

EVIE

I'm almost asleep when the first pebble hits my bedroom window.

I jolt upright, startled, heart pounding. Did I imagine it? The only light in my room comes from a dwindling streetlamp. I wrap my cotton slip tight and head to the window, my feet cold on the floor. I'm not even halfway across the room when the second pebble hits. This time, it bounces off and almost shatters the lamp. Kids, probably.

But when I make it to the window, I realize it isn't kids. Instead, he's there, standing in the warmth of the hazy light, waving up to me.

"Beau?" I mutter to myself, rubbing my tired eyes. I stand quietly for a second, listening to hear if the sound has woken anyone else, but nothing stirs, so I fidget with the window latch until it opens.

I lean out and try to whisper as loudly as I can. "Beau! What are you doing?"

"Come down," he says. Even from up here, he doesn't look well. Looks like he's been awake for days.

"Do you have any idea what time it is?" I say, but then I

hear a creak from the other room. Either someone's shifted in their bed or someone's awake. I hold my hand out to silence Beau, who thankfully gets the message. I hold still, ears perked, but hear nothing else. I pop my head out of the window and motion down to Beau. "Stay there."

From all of my excursions with Jo, and our late nights at Dom's houseboat, I've perfected the art of sneaking out. I know exactly which floorboards to step on and how far I can turn the knobs before they squeak.

Once I make it outside, I realize I should've taken a moment to grab a jacket.

"Have you lost your mind?" I ask Beau. "My father would be furious if he knew you were here this late."

"Where?" Beau jokes. "I just happen to be on your street."

I look at him, unimpressed. "Have you been drinking? You smell sour."

"I haven't been drinking," he says. "I had been, but not today." He laughs so loud I think the whole block might have heard him.

"Be quiet!" I hiss, but he only muffles his laughter.

I shake my head. He thinks it's funny. What's gotten into him? "So why are you here, then? Something I can help you with at midnight?"

"Is it a crime that I wanted to see you?" he asks, his voice somehow louder than before.

"My parents' room is right there," I say, pointing upward before I have an idea. I grab him by the arm. "Come with me." I lead him down the alley and to the back of our building. "Up here," I tell him.

He follows me up the fire escape to the roof. "Whoa" is all he manages to say when we reach the top. I can't blame him. If the top of Dom's houseboat is my second-favorite view of Paris, this is my first. There isn't a thing you can't see from up here. "This is—incredible."

"Yeah," I say, peering up at the stars. "It's not so bad. Being the baker's daughter has its perks after all." He joins me as I sit on the ledge, and I ask him again, "Why are you here, Beau?"

"It's like I said. Just wanted to see you."

I glare at him. "I don't believe you."

"I did, really," he says, but after a moment, he follows it up with the truth. "And I may have seen Jacques earlier."

My eyes narrow. "Okay? And?"

"We talked about your big night at Versailles, of course. You weren't going to tell me?"

"I haven't seen you in a couple of days," I say. "Am I supposed to run to your house every time something happens?"

"Yes!" he insists. "You are!"

"Well, if you must know, it wasn't awful. It was nice, actually. I'd like to hurt Jacques for letting me go to the palace in such plain clothes, but still, it was pretty grand."

"He said you'd make a good apprentice one day."

My lip twitches as I try not to grin. "He did?"

"Don't act so surprised." Beau nudges me. "You should go for it."

"Go for it? Yeah," I say sarcastically.

"What? You'd be great at it."

I look at him to see if he's joking, but it's clear he isn't. "I can't, Beau. You know that."

"Right, the bakery, the bakery. It's always the bakery."

"It *is* always the bakery," I say. "I can't just abandon my family to go and—do what? To follow Jacques into the palace every weekend?"

"To live out your dreams," Beau interjects.

I sigh. "You'll never get it, Beau Bellegarde."

"What is it, then?" He stares at me, awaiting my answer. "What is it that I don't get? Tell me."

"You have options; you have opportunities. You want to go work with your father, you can do it, but if you don't want to, then there are so many other things you can do. You don't have to worry that you might not be able to afford food or the rent payment. That's not how it is for people like me. People like me don't get to dream. If I dream, that means that Violette has to take over the bakery, and I'll never let that happen. She, at least, should get to have a dream."

Beau leans back, eyes to the sky. I think he's going to argue with me about it, but he doesn't. "I shouldn't have pushed," he says. "I apologize."

I fold my arms over my stomach as the breeze from the Seine comes around, a cold chill that prickles goose bumps on my skin.

"I'd give you my coat if I had one," Beau says.

"I'm fine."

"Jacques may have told me that you already have one, though."

"One of what?"

"A coat," he says. "From the duke."

My eyes widen. "Jacques knows about the duke's coat? How does he know about it?"

"Ah, so it's true, then," Beau says with a sly grin, but it's not his usual. For once, he doesn't look happy about being right.

I look back out over the city. "It's nothing. We met in the queen's gardens, is all. I didn't even know who he was."

"Well, he must have thought it was more than nothing. From what Jacques tells me, the duke is quite taken with you."

"Taken with me?" I laugh. "Yeah, sure."

"Just telling you what I heard," Beau says, but I'm convinced he's heard wrong. "Could be a good thing, you know? A duke could give you those options and opportunities you were talking about."

I stop and look at him, waiting for him to crack, but he doesn't. He's serious.

"A man isn't an opportunity," I tell him.

"Sure, but still doesn't change what the duke could do—"

"What's it to you, Beau?" I cut him off. "The duke. Me. Any of it? I can promise you that there isn't a nobleman out there who's interested in me, no matter what Jacques may have said. But even if he was, what's it to you? Why would you care?"

"You're right," he says, wringing his hands. "It's none of my business."

"That isn't what I said. I asked why you would care."

"I wouldn't, I guess," is all he says. And I don't know why exactly, but I hate that that's his answer. I don't know why I want more from him. Why, over the past few weeks, I've come to expect more of him. He's still Beau Bellegarde.

We're dangerously close to having to confront whatever it is we've been doing for the last couple of weeks, so I say the only thing I can think of to change the subject. "Rachelle was there. She was at the palace with the baron."

"I heard," he says.

"You heard? Jacques told you?"

"Oh, uh—no. She did. Told me at school."

"Ah," I say, nodding until silence falls around us.

"About Rachelle," Beau says finally. "I've been meaning to apologize."

"Apologize for what?"

"What Julien said," he says. "About me telling her that you and I were just friends. I shouldn't have done that."

I shrug. "It's not a big deal."

"Maybe not, but I still shouldn't have been speaking to her after what she did to you."

"Yeah," I say. "I guess I just—after that night at the château, after I saw what she really thinks about people like me—I don't know why you want to be around someone like that. . . . It made me wonder if you think about me like that, too."

After I've said it, after it's out in the open, hanging in the air between us, I wish for nothing more than that I could reach out and grab it, and stuff it all back inside.

Beau moves toward me like he's going to take my hand but thinks better of it, dropping his own in his lap. "Evie, I'd—I'd never think any of those things about you. And Rachelle. She's—" His head drops for a moment, watching the empty streets below, before he looks back up at me. "I won't be seeing her anymore. That's all."

I only nod. I could tell him that I don't care if he does, but that would be a lie.

"You going to put that in *Paper Hearts*?" I joke.

He smiles. "I'd rather not swat at that hornet's nest."

"Yeah, well, thanks to you, everyone now thinks I have a chance at winning Bloom," I tell him. "I hope you won't be too upset when I don't win."

He doesn't look at me, doesn't laugh, just keeps his eyes on the stars. "If people knew about you and the duke, you could win."

I wrinkle my face. "There's nothing to know about me and the duke," I say, but he still doesn't look at me. He only sighs. "But you don't actually think I have a chance at winning, do you? Beau, the whole thing is a joke. Something you did to make Rachelle jealous. Isn't it?"

He shifts uncomfortably before getting to his feet. "You know," he says, running a hand through his hair, "you were right before. It's—it's late. I should get going."

"Well, okay," I say, half laughing, confused at his abrupt-
ness. He's already starting down the ladder before I even
make it to my feet.

His head peeks over the roof one last time. "See you at
school?"

"Sure," I say with a shrug of my shoulders. "See you."

Chapter Twenty-Three

BEAU

Julien's home. His boots are strewn outside the front door. I stand alone under the night sky and exhale, readying myself for whatever might be waiting for me. Surely, he's told Isabelle by now. She's probably already planning my departure from Paris.

Much to my surprise, though, on the other side of the door, no candles flicker and no torches burn. The rooms are dark and still, Mia and the others long asleep, which means I've managed to avoid Julien for one more day.

I begin unfastening the buttons on my shirt as I walk up the stairs. He'll have a lot to say at school. He'll most likely try and turn everyone against me somehow. Probably will want a rematch, too, as if that's even what this is about. I don't know, though. He hasn't told his mother yet. I know that to be true because my bags aren't packed, waiting at the door for me. And why hasn't he? She's always been the first person he runs to.

When I open my bedroom door, though, it's clear he isn't going to wait until school tomorrow. He's there, standing by my window with a scowl on his face, staring daggers into me.

"Can I help you?" I say flippantly.

Julien begins to pace back and forth behind my bed, rubbing his chin. "Yes, I think you *can* help me, as a matter of fact."

"What do you want, Julien?"

"Let me ask you a question, little brother," he begins, still pacing. I don't say anything. Instead, I watch him, ready for the moment he might try to rush me. "You know the new periodical at the university? The one that seemed to have popped up overnight?"

My heart quickens a little. Still, there's no way he could know it's me. I shrug, trying to seem aloof. "Sure. What about it?"

Julien scratches his head and turns to me. "Don't you find it curious that the author could have so much information about the people in our inner circle? The author knows things about Rachelle, about me, about the twins. Hell, they barely ever talk about anyone else."

"Never really thought about it," I tell him. "Now, if you'll excuse me, I'd like to go to sleep." I start toward my bed.

Julien holds his finger up as if to stop me. "Well, you may have never thought about it, but I did think about it. And I realized that there was one person who was consistently in *Paper Hearts* who wasn't a part of our group." He turns toward me. "Evie Clément."

"Okay?"

"So," Julien continues, ignoring me, "I realized that

whoever the author was had to be close to us, but they had to be close to Evie Clément also. Every time they mentioned her, it was always positive, always made her look shinier than she really is. Dusted the flour off her, if you will. I couldn't figure it out."

I glare at him. He knows. He may have suspected before, but now, somehow, he knows for sure. I can see it in his eyes. Still, I hold out. "What's your point, Julien?"

"I couldn't figure it out until," he says, bending down, picking something up, "I found this." My stomach lurches as it comes into the light, as he tosses my mangled printing press onto the bed. "Everything was still arranged from the latest periodical. Isn't that something?"

My knuckles go white from how tightly my fists are clenched. The whole machine is ruined, a wrecked heap of gears and ribbons.

"Sorry about the state it's in," he says with a smirk. "Accidentally tripped over it."

"Tripped over it?" I scoff. "Tripped over something in my closet and smashed my printing press to smithereens? And you just happened to have a hammer in your hand?"

The same devious grin slips across his lips. "What can I say, Beau? Accidents happen."

"What's it to you, Julien?" I press him. "What's this about? Is it about Rachelle? Huh? Even after all these years, you can't handle that she chose me over you? Or is it that she still doesn't want you? Is that it? Because she came by the house tonight and it wasn't you she was looking for. Wasn't you she kissed, was it?"

I know I've said too much, but I don't care. I keep looking at my printing press, or what's left of it, and all I want to do is say something that hurts him.

"You shut your mouth about Rachelle," he snarls.

"You know what I think it is, Julien? I think it's that you can't stand to see me get something that you want."

I've always thought it, but I haven't said it out loud until now. There's a feeling that comes with being the second son, especially with being the other woman's son. It feels like you're an afterthought, forgotten—a book fallen behind the shelf, collecting dust. If I had to guess, Julien's life has come with certain expectations, too—like an expectation of entitlement. I suppose he thinks he was entitled to Rachelle—entitled to the prettiest, wealthiest, most popular girl in school—or at the very least, entitled to anything over me.

"You think I care about your little meaningless relationship with Rachelle?" he says, stepping closer. I stand my ground. "What did you get out of it, Beau? You got to sleep with the best-looking girl in school? Big deal. She's moved on and left you behind, and now you've got nothing. No girl. No inheritance, unless you call that shack in London an inheritance. And soon, when I tell our father everything, you won't have a job prospect, either."

"Get out, Julien."

"Oh, someone's mad. Is it because I said you didn't have a

girl? Oh, Beau. You don't count that poor little baker's daughter, do you?"

"I don't know, Julien," I say, closing the gap between us. "Do you mean the poor little baker's daughter who attended the queen's last soiree and captured the eye of a duke? Is that the one you're talking about?"

"Ha!" He bends backward with laughter, clutching his stomach. "Evie Clément catch the attention of a duke? Well, now I know you're dreaming." Julien smirks. His lip twitches before he turns from me. "Have a good night, Beau."

Just as he's reached the door, I look back at him. "Are you happy now, Julien?" I ask.

"Oh, no, brother," he says. "I'm not happy. Not just yet. But I will be."

When the door shuts, I realize, it isn't Julien I hate. It's me. Because Julien is right about what he said. I don't have an inheritance. Soon, I won't have a job. And I don't have a girl, either. I don't have Evie. I've never had Evie.

She deserves better than someone like me—better than me. She deserves to marry a duke and travel the world with him, to be renowned for her designs and for her heart that's too big for this city.

She's everything, and I'm just a guy who made a bet on her.

CHAPTER TWENTY-FOUR

EVIE

Josephine says everyone knows about high tea with the Court of Flowers. Everyone must not include me, because when I received the invitation, all gilded and scented like the one before, I could've fainted.

Well, duh, Josephine told me when I waved the invitation in her face, begging her to help me find a way out of it. *The five Bloom hopefuls always have to attend high tea.*

Yeah, *duh.*

Jo didn't help me find a way out of it, so while she's off with her father delivering letters, I'm finding out that Vivienne de Verley's house is somehow even grander than I imagined it to be. Although, I'm not sure the word *house* even covers it. It's more of a mammoth estate with sprawling manicured gardens, a guest house, a carriage house, a greenhouse, and stables. It's fairly new, but the place is entirely grown over with roses, like they wanted it to look as though it's been here for ages. When I arrive, I'm led over the marble floors, following a footman through the parlor to the gardens, where a long banquet table has been set up.

My heart races, quick as ever, my fists clenched so tight

that I'm afraid I might bust the seams of the gloves Madame Landry has lent me. The whole outfit is on loan from her, actually, and it's obvious. Out of all the garments I've made, Madame Landry declared that not one was fit for a formal tea. She's keen on keeping with tradition, and although I wanted to insist on wearing something I've sewn, I couldn't say no to her. We managed to cut the fraying from the hat's ribbon, but I can still smell the mildew. A couple of the jewels at my neck have been glued back into place and the frills blooming at my breast combined with the drab shade of rosewood ages my high-tea dress more than the fresh ivy ages Vivienne de Verley's mansion.

I'm stopped by a footman before I step out onto the pristine lawn. He blinks, giving me a confused and judgmental look when I hand him my wrinkled name card that's been crushed in my anxious fists.

The man clears his throat. "Mademoiselle Evie Clément," he introduces me, his voice deep and resounding. It's much louder than I expected, and now every eye in the gardens is on me. I dip my head, accompanying it with a curtsy, but not too low, just the way my mother taught me. Another man appears, younger than the other, and escorts me to the table. Thankfully, the seat I'm directed to is right across from Mia, who is guzzling lemonade when I arrive.

On either side of me is Cassandra Hardy and Hester O'Brien. They both greet me as I sit. Mother had me memorize all of the Bellegarde Bloom winners for the past thirty years, and then she and Violette quizzed me on them. I was dreadful at first, could barely get past Vivienne, but when I pictured sitting here with no idea who anyone was, I suddenly knew all their names backward and forward. I could probably tell you their pets' names, too, if I had to.

Rachelle is sat near the center of the table, in between her mother and Vivienne de Verley—not an accident, I presume. Lola is a few chairs down, engaged in conversation.

Mia reaches across the table and squeezes my hand. "How are you?" she asks.

"Well," I choke.

"Oh, here," Mia says, handing me my glass of lemonade. "Drink."

I'm unsure if it's proper etiquette to go ahead and drink before the meal is served, but my throat is so dry that I do it anyway.

"The two of you are friends?" Hester asks me. It startles me so that lemonade dribbles down my chin, and I have to catch it with a gloved hand.

"We are." Mia redirects Hester's attention, and I'm thankful because it gives me a split second to dab my chin and shove my damp glove underneath the napkin in my lap. "Evie's friend Josephine and I have class together, and Evie and my cousin Beau have been friends for a while." Mia is so kind and so optimistic that I don't correct her. "We met through them."

"Ah." Cassandra enters the conversation, readjusting the

coveted rose pin at her breast. "Beau Bellegarde. Fine family of yours, Mia. Are you two a match, Evie?"

I'm glad I'm not still drinking the lemonade because I think I'd have spit it out.

"A match?" I say with a small laugh. "Oh, I'm not so sure of that."

"Hmm," Cassandra muses. "That's too bad. He seems a catch, that one."

I resist the urge to roll my eyes. If she only knew.

"Well, I think they'd make a fine pair myself." Mia winks at me just before the last few girls arrive and are announced.

My stomach churns as they're seated. Both Cassandra and Hester have already turned their attention to the late arrivals, seeming to have grown bored with me. Something tells me I've messed up by saying that Beau and I are not an item, but it's the truth. We aren't. But it makes me realize why I'm here, and I'm not sure why I didn't get it before. These women, they're evaluating us, studying us, and measuring us so that they can determine our worth. Being attached to Mia gave me points but being attached to Beau would've been a golden star, a value only determined by one's proximity to powerful men.

Vivienne clinks a spoon on her glass and stands. Her dishwater-brown hair has been pulled so taut that it arches her graying eyebrows. When the chatter dies down, she begins to speak.

"Ladies," she says, her thin lips pursing into something

resembling a grin. "I want to thank you all for coming here today. Today is a special day because today our table is not only filled with women of the Court, but it is also filled with five Bloom hopefuls. These are the five young women that have risen above the rest, the five we've deemed the most eligible for the Court of Flowers. However, as is customary, only one of them can be chosen at the Court Ball. I've called this high tea so that we can get to know our hopefuls a little better—find out what makes them Bellegarde Bloom material. In just a moment, I'm going to have each of the girls stand one by one and tell us a little about themselves. Please, help me welcome them."

My breath catches as all the others raise their gloved hands and delicately clap them together. No. No, no, no, no. Stand up and tell them about myself? What, that I'm a baker's daughter with no real prospects and have only ended up here because Beau Bellegarde thought it would be funny and would possibly make Rachelle jealous if he put me in a gossip periodical?

"Wonderful," Vivienne says before turning and motioning to the servers who are lined up and ready to go, each one holding a silver tray. They disperse at her cue, one server for every one of us. The same boy who escorted me in now approaches and, in unison with the others, places the tray in front of me and removes the silver dome to reveal a bowl of shocking orange soup. I go to reach for a spoon but realize I have two. Actually, I have eight utensils in all, each shaped only a bit differently than the others.

I look to Mia for direction, still sick to my stomach that in mere moments I will have to formally introduce myself to the most influential women in all of Paris. Mia gives me a slight nod and picks up the largest spoon in the assortment. I follow her lead and do the same. I force myself to take small bites like the others, relishing the notes of carrot and tangerine and pistachio, but all I really want to do is inhale it as fast as I can. I try to think of how much it might cost just to make one bowl of this stuff, but it's no use—some of the ingredients aren't even things we could find at the market.

"You know," Cassandra says to us, "I hear the queen grows these apricots in her gardens."

"These same ones?" Hester asks, jabbing at the dried fruit floating to the top of her soup.

"Oh, no, I don't think Vivienne would have access to the queen's personal stores," Cassandra answers before leaning in and lowering her voice to a whisper. Her pink lipstick has smeared onto her front two teeth, and I'm not sure if I'm supposed to tell her, so I keep it to myself. "Although I'm sure she'd like for us all to think that she does."

I fake a small, awkward laugh because it seems like that's what Cassandra wants, but if I'm being honest, the thought of being Bloom is becoming less appealing by the second. None of these women even seem to like each other.

"Evie's been in the queen's garden," Mia blurts out. "She could probably tell you about the apricots."

I shoot Mia a look, but Hester is already questioning me. "You what?" She gasps. "Is it true that her peonies are the largest in the city? I've heard they're bigger than the head of a toddler."

"I—I didn't see any peonies," I say. "It was dark out."

Cassandra opens her mouth to speak, but Vivienne is calling for our attention again.

It's time. My hands start to sweat as Lola stands—the first to tell the Court about herself, or as I see it, to plead her case.

Lola does just as well as I think she'll do. She's charming and graceful and effortless. She tells about her family, about the St. Martin ink fortune. She mentions her relationship with Dre and his family's import business. The ladies of the Court look intrigued.

Camille goes next and she's nice enough, but she rambles on and on about her family's history as royal cabinetmakers. It's once she begins detailing the techniques that go into crafting a carriage that I realize half the Court has taken to staring off into the sky while the other half look like they are seconds from falling asleep.

Camille has been going on for so long that Mia finally coughs, trying to help her out. If the faces of the Court are anything to go by, Camille's as good as out of the running.

"And that's about everything, I guess," Camille says with a confident smile that makes me wish for a fraction of her blissful ignorance.

Mia's next, and she wows the women with tales of the French countryside. She's so likable and so easily cool that her every word, even if simple, commands attention. She could win Bloom if she wanted to. She could beat Rachelle and stun everyone. But I know Mia, and I know she doesn't want to. She makes it clear, too, because right at the end, she adds, "Oh, and I'll be escorted to the Court Ball by Mademoiselle Josephine Fabre." Besides a fork clattering onto a plate, the table is deadly silent.

When Mia sits back down, she kicks me under the table. She's glaring at me, motioning for me to go next.

But Rachelle and I make eye contact, and she hurries to jump to her feet. Great. I'll be going last.

Rachelle has brought out some of her finest jewelry, or if I had to guess, her aunt's finest, for the tea. Her dress, a deep fuchsia, perfectly complements her soft champagne-blond hair. She hasn't even won yet, but she looks like a part of this group already.

"As you all know, I'm Rachelle LeBlanc," she begins. She pauses, almost as though she's waiting for their applause at her name. When it doesn't come, she moves on. "I'm a fourth-generation Bloom hopeful. My great-grandmother Edna Archambault was one of the first members of the Court."

Almost every lady at the table, save for the other hopefuls, has a pleased grin on their face.

"My mother here as well as my aunt Geneviève, also a

member, have been particularly helpful in raising me like a lady of the Court already. I've grown up so familiar with your traditions and practices that being here feels just like home."

Rachelle giggles, and if I thought no one would see me, I'd roll my eyes as dramatically far back in my head that they could go.

"Mother and Aunt Geneviève have also been instrumental in teaching me the ways of a lady in dealing with courtship. As is no secret, I'm currently being courted by Nicolas Farrow, the Baron of Brittany. The two of us were most recently invited to the Queen's Ball at the palace."

The women all perk up and lean forward with interest, each one of them eating up Rachelle's every word.

"It was lovely," Rachelle continues. "Nicolas and I danced the night away."

I don't remember Rachelle doing much dancing, but I do distinctly remember her desperately trying to catch the attention of the Duke of Berry.

"The baron fell a bit ill, so we regretfully had to leave before the party concluded," Rachelle says. "Likely a tainted bit of cake. Actually"—she gestures to me—"Evie's father supplied the confections that night. Oh, but Evie, I'm sure everything else at your family's quaint bakery is lovely."

The ladies of the Court have turned their attention to me, but my sights are still set on Rachelle and the smug look of satisfaction smeared on her face. *Tainted cake. Quaint bakery.* She knows exactly what she's doing.

"Were I to be chosen as Bloom," Rachelle says, calling the focus back to herself, "I assure you that I would take my position very seriously and would be a worthy representative of the Court no matter if I were shopping on Rue Saint-Honoré or at the Palace of Versailles having an audience with the queen."

She finishes with a smile and takes her seat, and now it's my turn and I can't cool my blood. I can't quiet the hatred I feel for the girl who seems to have made it her life's mission to ruin mine.

Hesitantly, I stand. I look around at their faces all trained on me. Mia gives me the slightest of nods as if to tell me that I've got this—but I don't have this. All I have is the truth, and I know that these women won't be impressed by it, but I'll be damned if I have to lie about who I am to get anything in this world. I don't want to end up like them—making snide remarks, judging women's worth by the men who claim them, and gossiping about each other when they're only a few chairs away—so, I tell them the truth.

"Hello, everyone," I manage to choke out before clearing my throat. "Um, my name is Evie Clément. I am the daughter of Pierre and Matilda Clément. As Rachelle mentioned, my family owns the bakery Chérubin on Rue Saint-Honoré. We've been there for decades. My father has taught me everything about the business and I help him with the daily duties as well as helping with my younger sister, Violette, who is about as useful as a jackrabbit in the kitchen."

I see smiles appearing on most of their faces, and I don't even care that they're never going to consider me. There's something liberating about telling the truth.

"When I can find the time, I enjoy sewing, creating garments from scratch pieces of fabric that my teacher Madame Bissett is gracious enough to let me have."

I catch Rachelle lowering her head, laughing into a handkerchief. She thinks it funny that I have to use scraps, but that's okay because sometimes scraps can be pieced together in just the right way, sewn in just the right pattern, to create something beautiful.

"Yes, well," I say, "I suppose my life is pretty uneventful, but it's honest work and I'm glad to spend the time with my family."

I curl my dress in behind me, preparing to sit, knowing I've just blown it, but also knowing they were never going to choose me anyway. An older woman with graying hair speaks up. "Could you tell us more about your sewing, dear?" she asks. She isn't looking at me, though. She's glaring with contempt at Rachelle, who is still obviously caught in a laughing fit. The woman turns to me and continues. "Oh, how I've always wanted to learn. Whenever I would try, mother always said, 'Angélique, you're going to end up a pincushion if you're not careful.' She was right. One prick too many and I stopped trying altogether." The woman laughs along with a few others. "Oh, and are you courting anyone, Evie? We'd love to hear."

I straighten the bend in my knees, standing back up.

"Ah—y-yes," I stutter. "Our shop neighbor Madame Landry taught me how to sew when I was younger, and I fell in love with it. Anyone can learn how to sew, really. Well, except for my best friend, Jo, she's pretty dreadful at it." This garners more laughter from them, especially Mia, and I remember a detail they might be happy to know something about. "Just last week I helped dress the queen for her soiree. I even had the pleasure of meeting Rose Bertin and Léonard Autié." I forget to watch their faces for a reaction because I get lost in the story. Even remembering that night still feels like a dream.

Once I'm done telling it, I fall silent, but the same woman again asks, "And courting, dear? Anyone you have your eye on?"

"Oh, well—" I pause because I'm inclined to say no, that there isn't anyone, but that isn't the truth. The truth is that the invitation to the Court of Flowers high tea wasn't the only invite I received yesterday morning. I wasn't sure if I'd accept this new invitation, but I look at Rachelle and the snarl her lip is curled into, and now I know that I'll accept. "I do have a date tomorrow night." Rachelle's lip falls, and the others lean in, waiting. I take a deep breath. "With the duke."

CHAPTER TWENTY-FIVE

BEAU

I'll never be able to put the printing press back together.

Julien's smashed it into such shattered pieces that even Monsieur Williams at the shop near Evie's couldn't fix it.

A knock comes at my door, and I ready myself for more of Julien's wrath, too exhausted to show him some of my own.

It isn't Julien, though. It's my father standing in the doorway. His jacket is tossed over his shoulder and his eyes are tired, his glasses resting over the bruised-looking circles under his eyes.

"Father," I breathe, clutching a handful of gears and no time to shove the broken pieces under my bed.

He squints down at the wreckage. "What's all of this?"

My heart picks up speed, but I think it's telling me that it's time. Julien will tell him anyway, so it's best he hears it from me.

"It's a printing press," I say quietly. "*My* printing press."

"A printing press?" he says, confused. "I didn't know you had one of those."

I nod.

"Well," he says, moving closer, "whatever has happened to it?"

I don't want to tell him about Julien because it doesn't matter. I don't want to be involved in Julien's choices anymore. I used the printing press to make Evie look better, to make her a favorite for the Bloom, all to beat Julien in a pathetic bet for an inheritance that my father never intended for me in the first place. I want out of it. All of it.

"I was careless," I lie. "Had it perched on the windowsill arranging the letters in the last light of day, and I bumped into it and sent it crashing to the ground."

My father crouches down, joining me on the floor. He takes one of the letters, one of the only ones that isn't cracked, and holds it up, studying it.

"What were you doing with it in the first place?" he asks.

This time, I don't lie.

"I made a periodical for the university," I say. I pause but he's only looking at me, curious. I gulp. "I've actually been making them for a few weeks now."

I'm almost afraid to look at him, afraid to see the disappointment in his eyes, but I lift my head anyway.

He doesn't look disappointed, though. He looks interested, and I'm nothing short of shocked. "You?" He grins. "The boy who used to beg the maids to write his essays for him? Now you've got your own periodical?"

I laugh. "Those essays were horrible. Monsieur Travers loves a meaningless, soul-stealing assignment."

Father laughs, too. "Well, did anyone like it? The periodical? Or did it get binned?"

I smile. "It's become quite popular, actually, the talk of

school. Made a lot of people mad. Made some people happy, too, though."

A wide grin spreads across his face, and I realize how long it's been since I've seen him smile. "Sounds like you've a natural talent," he says.

My hands fidget. "So—" I try, choking on the words. "So, you're not mad, then?"

"What ever would I be mad about?"

"About the printing press—or just about me," I say.

"What are you really trying to say, son?"

I lift my eyes to him and decide it's time to start being honest. "Father, what would you do if I told you that I don't know if my future is in finance?"

My father's eyes widen, but he rubs his chin, thinking. "Is that how you feel?"

I look down to the floor. "I don't know. Kind of. Yes." I meet his gaze again. "Yes, that's how I feel."

"And is this what you'd like to do instead? Writing?"

"Yes." I gulp. "It is." I brace myself for the judgement, for the speech about low-class professions and how a Bellegarde can't possibly disrupt the family name with such fantasies.

"Well then, it's settled," he tells me. "I have a friend in London we can speak to. He runs an impressive periodical there and will know just where you should start."

"Really?" I can't believe I've been so afraid to have this conversation with him before now. "You're not mad? Not mad that I don't want to work for the family business?"

He frowns. "I could never be mad about something like

that. I'm sad, sure, but only because I imagined you having an office next to mine, a place I could see you every day. I missed so very much of your youth. I thought it would be a way to get those years back. But I can't think of anything else I'd rather you do than whatever makes you happy. It's the least I owe you."

My father has never been one for affection, so I resist the urge to fling my arms out and wrap them around him in a much-overdue hug. Instead, I hold my hand out to his, clasping it in a tight embrace. "Thank you, Father."

He locks his other hand over mine, and we stay like that for a moment until I summon the courage for the other question I've been too afraid to ask before now.

"May I ask you something?" I say, dropping my grasp from his.

"Of course," he answers.

Everything goes quiet again, and I hope I don't overstep, hope I don't ruin the ground we've gained. "Why are you giving him everything?" I ask. "Julien. I don't—it's not the money I care about. It's just, I don't understand why it all goes to him if I'm your son, too."

My father shakes his head. "I'm not sure I know what you're talking about."

"At Olivier's," I say. "At the law office. When we sign our papers each year, it says the same thing every time. That Julien gets everything and that I get my mother's cottage. And it's fine, really, it is, but I just can't stop wondering . . . is it because of Isabelle? Is it because—"

"Wait a minute," my father cuts me off. "The papers say what? They say that you get your mother's cottage in London and that Julien gets everything else?"

"Well, yes. That's what they've always said. I thought you wrote them."

"I wrote no such thing!" He raises his voice, his cheeks flushing red as he stands. "Julien, get everything? Not ever. I'd never hear of such blasphemy. You're telling me Olivier has been facilitating this? That snake. I always had a feeling something wasn't right about him, and now I know for sure. I'm going to see him." He turns to leave but stops before he gets all the way out. "Beau," he says, glancing back at me.

"Yes?"

"You've thought all these years that I was giving everything to Julien?"

I don't answer him at first, because I'm not sure how to. "I thought it was Isabelle, mainly. Thought she didn't want me to have anything because—because of my mother."

He hangs his head, and it's the first time I've seen him like this. It's the first time I've seen him ashamed.

"I'm sorry, son," he says finally. "I'm sorry you've had to think that."

I nod in understanding, because I can see that he means it.

"You're a lot like her, you know?" he says. "Your mother. She was resilient, too."

It's the nicest thing he's ever said to me. And after a

moment, he leaves, fire under his feet as he storms off to Olivier's office.

I slump down, sitting on my bed. He never knew about the inheritance. He doesn't hate me, doesn't think I'm a burden. He knows now that I don't want to work in finance and he's—he's fine with it! Suddenly, it dawns on me. The bet. It's rendered meaningless now. The inheritance isn't Julien's to give or take. He has nothing to hang over my head anymore.

I lay back into the pillows and take the first real breath I've taken in eleven years.

CHAPTER TWENTY-SIX

EVIE

Of course we're meeting at Notre-Dame. I should've known a date with a duke was never going to be a simple affair.

I chose the blue dress I made for Madame Bissett's show last year, and it's fine—simple and romantic with puffed sleeves and a thin line of beads at the hem. It's nothing compared to the things my mother, Jo, and Madame Landry picked out for me from Madame Landry's trunk. After feeling so out of place in my high-tea outfit, I was not going to let that happen again.

As the carriage putters to a stop, I can't help but wonder why I'm here, why the duke would ever want to ask me on a date. I told him that night in the Gardens that I was only there to dress the queen. Did he think I was joking? When he finds out I'm a baker's daughter, what will he say? Will he run? Do I care if he does, or am I only here because I needed something to say at the tea that would get under Rachelle's skin? Are my actions no better than Beau starting *Paper Hearts* to get back at her?

Once I'm out of the carriage, I'm greeted by a short, older man.

"Mademoiselle Clément," he says, bowing slightly, "right

this way." I follow him inside the cathedral, past the rows of pews and back to a concealed set of stairs. Once at the top, I'm led out onto a balcony overlooking the whole of Paris. The sun has only begun to fall, casting everything in a dusty lavender haze—dyeing the soft waters of the Seine, which flows underneath bobbing boats and the feet of the people gathered on the bridge. Waiting for me on the balcony is a table and chairs lit only by a single gilded candelabra. And there, standing with his back to me, eyes across the city, is the duke.

When the doors shut, he turns to me.

"Evie," he breathes, walking over, keeping my gaze.

"I brought your coat," I tell him, holding it up.

He laughs, greeting me with a kiss on my cheek. His skin smells of wild ivy and torched wood. "Keep it," he says. "It's yours."

"No." I shake my head as he guides me to my seat. "Doesn't fit. And if I'm being honest, I would only cut it up to make a gown anyway."

"Okay."

"Okay?"

"Yes. Okay. So, do it, then," he says, laughing. "Cut it up and make a gown. But the next time we meet, you must wear that gown. Deal?"

He already wants there to be a next time. Either that, or he's just being polite.

"Deal," I say.

As we get to the table, he pulls my chair out. Soon after he sits down across from me, the same man from before arrives and pours us each a glass of water.

"I hope this is okay," the duke says.

I grin. "What, you're worried that dinner on top of a Notre-Dame balcony at sunset might not be enough?"

A smile spreads across his face. He's even more handsome here in Paris's last light than he was under the stars at the palace. He has the kind of demeanor that draws you in—a warmth that radiates from every fiber of him, and I like that he doesn't even seem to know it.

As we make conversation, he sometimes stutters instead of speaks—I think he might be nervous. It's sort of sweet, because he's a duke and I'm just . . . me.

As the night wears on and the sun drops deeper into the skyline, he starts to relax. I want to do the same, but I know I still have to tell him who I am. I don't want to. I think I'd rather just have a nice night and leave and maybe when I'm old and gray I'll tell people that I once went on a date with a duke. But I know that's not the right thing to do. The right thing to do is to tell him about me—to tell him everything.

After we've eaten, he nods over to the balcony railing. "Come with me," he says. "I want you to see something."

He offers me his hand, and together we walk to a spot overlooking the dusky city.

"You see that building that over there?" he says, pointing outward over the Seine. "The one with the iron door?"

"I do." I see it, but I'm also squinting, searching over the rows to try and see if I can find our street from here. I'm also looking for Beau's street, and I don't know why.

"There used to be a bookshop there," he says. "Decades back."

"Dukes do their own reading?" I tease him. "Or does someone sit fireside with you and read you whatever you wish?"

He returns my smile and playfully brushes his shoulder against mine. "Always teasing," he says. "Although, I do have to admit, I've heard a few tales of the king having bedtime stories read to him."

"I'll never tell," I kid him before looking back up to the building he's fixated on. "Was it a bookshop you went to often? I thought you said that you didn't spend most of your childhood in Paris."

"Oh, no, I didn't. I never got to visit the bookshop unfortunately. My grandmother talked about it quite a lot, though. She was rather enamored with the place. It's my favorite thing about this view."

"What was it about the bookshop that she loved so much?"

"Well," he begins, "she was a duchess, of course, and that meant that she couldn't travel anywhere without making a fuss. She always said the bookshop was the one place she could feel normal. They never made a big deal of her title."

His eyes are set on the skyline, but I don't think he's looking at anything, not really. I think he's dreaming about a place of his own. So, I ask. "Do you have a place like that? Somewhere you can be yourself?"

His smile is the sun. "I don't," he confides. "I often dream of it, though. Her stories, they were—well, they were certainly something to aspire to."

We linger in the silence for a bit, both of us with our elbows resting on the railing, the wind on our necks.

"You should buy it," I tell him.

"Buy the bookshop?"

"Yes. Or the whole building, even. I don't mean to intrude on your finances, but I'm sure you could afford to."

"Why would I buy it?" he asks.

"Because it means something to you. And even if it's a run-down building, that still makes it precious."

"You're special," he says, gazing over at me as if I was a creature he'd never seen and was attempting to identify.

"Special?" I eye him.

"Yes, very."

"I hope you aren't going to tell me that I'm not like other girls. You know, women are quite spectacular individuals, and I'm no different."

He laughs, covering his mouth in his hands. I wish he wouldn't because his smile is one of the nicest I've seen. "I don't mean that you're different from other women. I mean that you're different from everyone."

"Everyone, yeah?"

He nods. "Everyone."

"Hmm," I mumble. "Different how?"

He looks off to the city for a moment, but I don't. I watch him, watch the wheels turning in his mind, and I'm realizing I enjoy watching him. He looks back to me. "Because of how you treated me the other night in the gardens. You didn't know who I was, and you were still kind to me."

"Well, I don't know that I was *that* kind."

"You were," he says with a grin. "But more than that, you were a person. A real person. You've no idea how many people I meet who don't even meet that basic criteria. They're all looking to see what they can get from me, what I can do for them. You didn't do that."

"Well, perhaps I'd have looked at you like that, too, if I'd known who you were," I joke with him.

"No," he says with certainty. "You wouldn't have. And that's what sets you apart, Evie."

He's easy to be with, and I'm not sure why. How someone raised in such wealth and high status could turn out like him is beyond me. But the reality is that I have to tell him sooner or later that I've nothing to offer him, that I'm a baker's daughter, that I'm what those in his circle would call a peasant.

I've put it off long enough, not wanting to spoil the night, but it's time. He shared with me about his grandmother, so it's the least I could do to tell him the truth. "Heath, I think I should tell you something."

He looks to me, surprised. "All right? I'm listening."

I take a deep breath and look back out over Paris, not wanting to look at him when I say it. "I'm not sure who it is you think that I am," I say, watching his eyes narrow in confusion, "but when I told you that night at the palace that I was there to dress the queen, I wasn't just being funny. I meant it."

He nods. "Yes, of course, I know."

"And so," I continue, unsure of how to say it, "that means that I wasn't there as an official guest of the queen. I've never been to the palace before. I'd never receive an invitation like that. I was actually only there helping with the dressing because a whole host of people got sick, and I had to fill in for them."

"I'm not quite sure I'm following—"

I'm stalling and I know it. "Well," I breathe, "I—I say all of that to tell you that I'm not . . . of high status."

Much to my surprise, the duke smiles. "Your father is Pierre Clément, and your mother is Matilda. Together they own the bakery on Rue Saint-Honoré, a shop which has been in your family for over fifty years now. You have one sister, Violette, and your best friend since grade school is Josephine Fabre."

My eyes must be wider than the moon because he smirks at me.

"How did I do?" he asks.

"You—you knew all of that already?"

"Of course I did," he laughs. "I may do my own reading, but there are certain constraints that come with the title. Do you think I'm even allowed out unless my uncle knows exactly who I'll be with?"

"You knew everything, and you still came?" I ask. "You still wanted to be here? With me."

"You find that hard to believe?"

"A little," I say.

He slips his hand over mine, his skin warm to the touch.

"I'm here with you because I want to be here with you. Because, to tell you the truth, Evie, I can't think of anyone else I'd rather be with. I don't remember the last time I've been able to be myself around someone that wasn't family, someone I didn't grow up with. But with you, it's—it's—"

"Different," I finish his sentence.

"Yes," he says. "Different."

I'm not sure what to say to him. Because I'm looking at him, and he's beautiful, and he knows all of the right things to say, and I suppose if he tried to kiss me right now, I'd be glad to kiss him back. But there's something I can't shake from my brain. No matter how present I'm trying to be, my mind keeps straying to Beau. I wonder if he'd like it here, or if he'd make a joke about the cheesiness of choosing Notre-Dame. I wonder if he walked through the door right now, if I'd pull my hand away from the duke's. I wonder, if they both reached out to me, whose hand I'd take.

Silvered moonbeams drip over his skin as he leans in close and I'm ready for it, but he pulls away before our lips touch, and I think it's because he wants to be a gentleman. He squeezes my hand and asks if we should get going.

"Yes," I say. "My parents will be waiting up."

"As they should," he teases. "Perhaps one day I'll be lucky enough to meet them."

"Perhaps," I answer. "They would like that very much, I'm sure."

I try one more time to hand his coat back over to him, but he refuses.

Just as we make it outside to the carriage that's waiting for me, he takes it and drapes it over my shoulders. "You have to make it into a gown for the next time we see each other," he says. "We have a deal. Remember?"

The wind has turned chilly, so I hold on to the lapels and pull the fabric closer. "Sure." I grin. "Gives me an option for a gown to wear to the Court Ball."

"I have heard about this ball," he says. "It's being held this weekend, yes?"

"It is."

"I also may have heard that you are up for the big prize," he says. "The Bellegarde Bloom."

I shake my head. "Not really," I say. "There's another girl who's going to win. My name was more a joke gone bad."

"I doubt that's true. They'd be out of their minds not to choose you."

"Yes, I'm sure the eligible men in Paris would be thrilled to know that the newest Bloom was a baker's daughter."

"I would," he says.

"Well, we don't have to worry about that," I tell him as the carriage driver opens the door for me. "Be glad you don't have to be there to endure it."

"I don't know," the duke says. "I think a ball can be fun, with the right partner."

Chapter Twenty-Seven

EVIE

Afternoon unfolds like a daylily, bright-petaled and sun-swelled. Rue Saint-Honoré spills over with life: music and blue skies and intimate, meaningless chatter. It's days like these, the ones where the shutters are all flung open and the shops aren't hurt for customers and the air is perfumed with a pervasive tenderness, that make Paris feel infinite.

Josephine stretches, lying back across the fountain's stone ledge, sucking on a sweet peach. "He sounds quite romantic, the duke," she muses.

We've gathered together a misfit picnic—fruits from Josephine's neighbor, Celeste's rose lemonade, and my contribution, the last slices of an almond sponge cake filled with plush layers of raspberry jam and vanilla custard.

"Yes," I say, "but it's fleeting, don't you think? Someone of his status showing someone like me attention. It can't last forever." I dip my fingertips into the sunlight-dappled fountain and pretend nonchalance, pretend I haven't been flipping this over in my mind through the night.

"You don't know that," Josephine disagrees. "Not everyone of high status is controlled by their families."

I roll my eyes in her direction.

"Okay, okay, perhaps they are," she laughs, "but he could be different."

The pigeons have started to gather on the cobblestones nearby. Dom tosses them a few crumbs before rolling his pants into cuffs at his knees. "What about our friend Beau Bellegarde?" he asks. A welcome spray of cooling water mists mine and Josephine's skin as he jumps in the fountain. "I thought the two of you were getting along, Evie?"

"Oh, not you, too, Dom," I say. "Has Josephine been filling your head with nonsense about me and Beau?"

"I haven't! I swear!" Josephine denies, throwing her hands up.

"Nah," Dom laughs, "just thought he was an all right guy, is all. You think the duke would scuff up his trousers and crawl under a theater stage the way ole Bellegarde did?"

"He might," I answer. Although, truthfully, I'm not sure. I think everything in Heath's world is likely very polished and controlled—an empty Notre-Dame, and royal guard always somewhere nearby.

I take a sip of rose lemonade, savoring the tangy relief from the heat of the day. A group of ladies glares at us as they pass, paying particular attention to Dom, who has taken to cupping the spilling fountain water in his palms before splashing it on his face, streaked with dust from one of his odd jobs.

"Speaking of, there's a Bellegarde carriage now," Dom

points out, drying his cheeks on his shirt.

He's right. Bellegarde carriages are distinct. They have their own fleet. Most of them are coal black with gilded trimmings and spokes, and a sharp letter *B* adorning the doors. They frequent Rue Saint-Honoré, traveling between the family's many properties.

I shield my eyes from the sun to watch it pass by, wondering who or what the carriage holds, my mind drifting to Beau. But I don't have to wonder for long, because the spotted horses come to a halt outside of a familiar storefront—the blue-and-white-striped awning of our bakery.

Josephine is propped up on her elbows, and she's noticed the same thing I have. "Are they stopping at your place, Evie?"

"Looks like it," I answer. "Can't imagine why, though."

Soon after, a short, plump man appears from the carriage door holding a vase of flowers almost the full length of him. He has to crouch down just to get in the bakery door.

"Is that—" Josephine starts. "Did Beau send you flowers?"

"Not a chance," I tell her, pulling the crinkled linen sleeves of my dress back over my sunburnt shoulders. It couldn't be. They've got the wrong address, is all. Josephine and I both stand to get a better look.

"I told you he was an all right guy," Dom teases me. But it can't be. Beau doesn't think of me that way. He wouldn't—

My father's large frame appears in the window, and he looks just as confused as I am.

"I should go check what's going on," I tell them.

"Yeah, yeah, right, we should go along, too, you know just in case," Dom says, and I catch him winking over at Josephine.

When we arrive, my mother is directing the man with the flowers to a sunny spot up front.

"You can place them there," my mother tells him.

"What's all this?" I ask her.

My father emerges from the kitchen in the back, wringing a dishrag, seeming less than enthused. "It appears someone has sent you flowers, Evie."

"Oh, come now, Pierre," my mother says. "She's perfectly old enough to receive a gift from a suitor."

Father doesn't answer and instead knits his thick black eyebrows into a displeased grimace.

My mother can't help but laugh at him. "Here you are, dear," she says, turning to me, holding out a rolled-up piece of parchment secured with thin ivory ribbon.

I unfurl the parchment, scanning the thin, flourished cursive script. My heart picks up speed.

"Well, what's he said?" Josephine pries. "What's Beau said?"

Everyone, except perhaps my father, is waiting silently in anticipation.

My eyes flicker up to her. "They're not from Beau," I tell her. "They're from the duke."

"What!" Josephine screeches, snatching the parchment from my hand.

Dom peers over her shoulder. "'Dear Evie,'" he reads, "'A flower for each time I've thought of you.'"

"'Yours,'" Josephine continues, "'HL.'"

"Heath de Lyons," I explain.

"I told you he was romantic," Josephine says, sinking her nose into the towering bouquet. "The roses smell like they've come straight from the ground. Oh, do you think? Perhaps he's sent you an arrangement from the royal gardens."

"I don't think so," my father steps in. "This came with it also." From his apron, he reveals a small, speckled card emblazoned with the Bellegarde Blooms wax seal. That's why it was delivered in a Bellegarde carriage. It didn't come from the royal gardens as Josephine hoped, but was sent through the luxury florist owned and managed by the Bellegarde family.

"Well, I shall thank him next time I see him," I say before turning to my parents. "Would you prefer I take them to my room so they don't crowd the window?"

"No need, darling," my mother assures me. "It's only one arrangement, and I think it looks quite nice where it is. I wish we had a matching one on the other side."

My father's red face has dulled to a slight blush. He gives a sort of caveman grumble in agreement.

"Well, Madame Clément," Dom says, craning his neck out of the open shop door, "it looks like you may get your wish." He turns back to us, his mouth twisted into a crooked, unsure grin.

We make a dash to the door and peer out. My stomach

drops. Lining the street, as far as the eye can see, is a convoy of black Bellegarde carriages, all of them bursting with flowers. Footmen, each of them wearing the same pale coats as the first man, carry arrangements our way, enough to cover the bakery wall to wall. It's the duke's gift, a grand gesture like one I've never seen. And yet, it has Beau's name all over it.

His carriages on our street, his family's legacy on the Court Ball title—the ball held just tomorrow night, his name brought up in every conversation—and now his flowers given as a gift from another suitor. No matter how hard I try, I can't seem to escape Beau Bellegarde.

CHAPTER TWENTY-EIGHT

BEAU

The next day at school, I'm ready to formally ask Evie for the honor of escorting her to the Ball—a real offer, not one tied to a bet.

After class, I find her exactly where I expect to. It's customary for the five Bloom hopefuls to pitch themselves to their peers one last time before votes are cast at tonight's Ball—though the Court of Flowers has the ultimate say, the vote is a suggestion to help them with their choice. The five girls have all gathered in the cafeteria, but Evie is sitting at a small table with Josephine. They've positioned themselves in the corner—probably Evie's doing if I had to guess. If her plan was to go unnoticed, it's failed, because the line to get to her is longer than any of the others. It seems Rachelle has noticed this fact also. I chuckle watching her smug expression fade as she very clearly counts Evie's ever-growing line.

"We have cupcakes over here!" Rachelle shouts, agitated.

I don't have to push past the others. They let me through Evie's line with ease, all the way to the front. Josephine grins when I arrive, but Evie hasn't noticed me yet—her head is down, and she's signing a card that reeks of lavender.

Mechanically, she extends the card to me, saying, "Vote for Evie . . . if you want." She blinks, taking the card back. "Oh, Beau, it's just you."

I lean down on the table. "Well, that's not exactly the best way to get my vote, now is it?" I pluck the card from her hand. "What do we have here?"

She swipes, reaching for it. "Beau, give it back."

Evie Clément for Bloom has been written on the front, decorated with clumps of purple glitter and hand-drawn stars.

"Violette helped me make them," she explains, embarrassed.

"They're great," I tell her, placing the card in my jacket pocket. "You've got my vote."

She rolls her eyes, but she's smiling when she does it.

"Hey," I say. My heart quickens, and my palms start to sweat. I didn't expect to be this nervous about asking her. "Do you think I could talk to you for a sec—"

I don't get to finish my question because I'm interrupted by the last voice in the world I want to hear right now. "Casting your vote for Evie?" Julien asks, sidling up to the table. His lip twitches as I turn to him, but he manages to keep his brilliant white smile intact.

"Might be," I tell him. "Keeping it a secret, you know?"

I turn back to Evie, hoping he'll get bored and walk away, but he doesn't.

"I can't imagine you'd vote for anyone else," Julien says.

"Given the circumstances, she could use all the help she can get. So could you."

Evie looks at me, confused.

Julien is fragile, like a grenade. He could explode at any moment, so I play the fool. "Doesn't look like she needs much help to me," I say, motioning to the line at Evie's table.

"Excuse me," Evie interjects, her attention turned to Julien. "Given the circumstances? Given what circumstances, exactly?"

"It's nothing," I hurry to tell her, but Julien speaks over me.

"Oh, well, the bet, of course," he laughs. "Beau *has* told you about the bet, right?"

His eyes flash to me—dark and cunning—and my stomach drops to my feet.

Evie looks to me. "What bet?"

My mouth opens, but I can't manage any words.

Julien grins. "We had this bet, you see. After Rachelle dumped him, he said he could turn any girl in the university into the Bellegarde Bloom, so I bet him for it."

"You what?" she breathes.

"More specifically," Julien continues, "I bet him my inheritance for it. We chose you. And I guess he took it quite seriously, because here we are." Julien puts a hand over his heart, faking sincerity. "I never thought he'd actually try to do it."

"Is that true, Beau?" Evie asks me. "Did you make a bet on me?"

I move toward her, but she draws back. "Evie, it's not—"

"It's a yes-or-no question," she says, her tone cold. "Did you or did you not make a bet on me?"

Julien has drawn a crowd. Even Rachelle, like a vulture, has swooped in to see what remains of me.

I take a deep breath, feeling the air sucked into my lungs, and finally exhale the truth. "Yes."

Evie's shoulders fall. Josephine grabs her arm and stares at me, her eyes boring into mine.

Rachelle lets out a squealing laugh. "You didn't actually think Beau Bellegarde was interested in you, did you?" She looks at me, cocking her head to one side. "Did you tell her about our kiss the other night?"

"Rachelle," I say through gritted teeth, "stop."

Evie stands from the table and looks at me, her eyes growing watery.

Rachelle leans her head on my shoulder, eyeing Evie. I don't stop her because I'm shocked stiff. "Aw, look at her," Rachelle says. "She really did think you liked her, Beau."

I meet Evie's eyes for a split second before Josephine guides her away. I snap out of my trance just as they reach the cafeteria door. I shake Rachelle off and make my way through the crowd. This time, no one lets me pass. They stand like statues, staring at me, daring me to move them.

I run out into the courtyard and catch sight of the back of her as she passes the fountain. Finally, I catch up. "Evie," I shout to her, but she keeps walking. "It isn't what you think."

But after a few more steps, she stops. Will she let me explain? Will she believe me?

"Let's just go, Evie," Josephine says. "He's not worth it."

Her words sting, and I deserve every one of them.

"It isn't what I think?" Evie says, turning.

"Well, it's—" I mumble.

"No, Beau." She stops me before I get a chance to plead my case. "That's where you're wrong. Because it's exactly what I think. You are exactly what I thought you were. And I'm the fool for ever believing that you could be different."

"I *was* different, though," I tell her. "With you. You made me different. And Rachelle, she—"

"I don't care about Rachelle! You placed a bet on me!"

"I didn't know things would happen like this. I didn't know it would go this far."

"You didn't know it would go this far?" she asks. "Just like you didn't know about the flowers that day at school, right?"

Oh no. The flowers. I want to look away from her, look at the ground or the sky or anything other than her eyes, because they're full of hurt, and I'm the reason why.

"Maybe you've forgotten about that day," she continues, "but I haven't."

I haven't forgotten, either. I remember it almost every time I see her. It's why I hadn't spoken more than a few words to her until the past few weeks, until the bet.

"There was a moment," she says. "A moment out on Dom's boat, after the theater, when I thought you really had changed. I thought maybe I could let you in—and I guess I kind of did. But I was wrong. You're still the same Beau Bellegarde from that day. But I refuse to be the same stupid little heart-broken girl. You know, I had the biggest crush on you back then. But people like me, we're invisible to people like you. We make your food and deliver your papers and shine your mirrors, but you don't see us. Not really. So, when you came to me that day at school on my birthday with a bundle of daises, an armful of my favorite flowers just for me, I thought it was all starting to happen for me. I thought, *Finally. Finally, he sees me.* And then it started to rain. I remember watching the rain from the school doorway, and then you came up and offered me a spot under your umbrella. Beau Bellegarde said he wanted to walk me home, and I felt like the luckiest girl in Paris."

She drops her head, taking a deep breath, and all I want to do is reach out to her, but I know what happens next.

"That's when Julien thought it would be funny to push you down, to make you fall face-first into the mud. But he missed, and it wasn't you who fell. It was me. And when the rest of our classmates burst into laughter, making me the punch line of their joke, I thought you would help me. What a fool I was. I can still see your face now, the look of shock that froze it before, like a coward, you began laughing with them. Laughing at *me.* You left me sitting alone in the mud on my birthday in the only dress I owned. You, Beau Bellegarde, will never know what that feels like. I watched my mother scrub a washboard until her hands were sore that night trying to get the stains out. As I was watching her, I told myself I'd never forget it, and now I remember why."

"Evie, I'm so sorry," I breathe. I want to tell her the truth, that she's right. I was a coward. I wanted so desperately to fit in, to impress everyone, to be more than my father's child out of wedlock. But the words get trapped in my chest, and all I can do is repeat myself. "I'm so sorry."

"All I wanted back then was for you to see me," she says, shaking her head. "But you know what I realized, Beau? I don't want to be seen by you."

Her lip quivers, and Josephine takes her by the arm. I stand still, watching the two of them walk away.

They've barely made it off school grounds, when Julien sidles up next to me, flashing me a wink. "You really blew it, huh?" he sneers.

I don't try to fight back as he walks away, smiling to himself. I don't try fight back because he's already won, and there's nothing I can do, and he knows it.

CHAPTER TWENTY-NINE

EVIE

I never imagined that on the night of the Court Ball I'd be facedown in my pillows, wishing that sleep would come fast so that I could forget this day, forget Beau Bellegarde, and forget his bet.

A knock comes at my door, and I roll over, pressing the pillow to my ear.

"Not right now, Violette!" I call out, my words muffled in the sheets.

"Evie," says a calm voice on the other side. It's not Violette, it's my mother. "May I come in?"

I sigh, loosening my grip on the pillow and sitting upright. I quickly fuss with my hair and dry my eyes. "Sure," I tell her.

When she opens the door, I already know she knows. My mother has never been able to hide things well—her face will always give away a surprise, but when she's sad, her eyes gloss over and her lips purse like she's trying to keep them from dipping into a frown.

"Hey, sweetie," she says, but her voice is heavy.

"So, you heard, I suppose." I go ahead and say it, breaking

the wall of ice between us because I can't stand feeling pitied
for a second longer.

"I did," she says, sitting down on the edge of the bed,
hands clasped. It's the only place to sit in my room full of
flowers from the duke.

"Who told you?"

"Josephine came by on her way to the ball," my mother
says. Her mouth turns up into a smile. "She looked beautiful."

"Did she wear the purple dress?"

Mother nods. "She did. She even wore the gloves you
made her."

I sniffle. "No way!"

"Mm-hmm. She wanted to stay with you, but Mia was
on her way to pick her up and I wouldn't dare let her miss the
ball."

I tear up again because I love Jo, because she was ready to
give up her big night with Mia for me, because she's my best
friend in the world. "Thanks for that," I say. "Wish I'd have
gotten to see her in her dress."

Silence lingers between us until her eyes flicker up to
mine. "You still could, you know," she says.

I shake my head no. "I can't, Mother."

"Why not? Because some foolish boy did something
cruel to you? Are you really going to let Beau Bellegarde ruin
your chance to go to a real ball?"

"I'm not letting Beau ruin it," I say, twisting my hair
over my shoulder. "I don't belong there. My nomination was
because of him, because of the bet he made, not because of

who I am. Not because people like me or think I'm worthy."

"Beau Bellegarde didn't get you a job dressing the queen of France, did he?" she asks. "Beau Bellegarde didn't bribe the duke to ask you on a date, did he? He didn't force Josephine to come here tonight, to be ready to throw away the Court Ball all for you. No. Those things happened because of who you are, Evie Clément, because of how you treat people, because of your goodness, because of your heart. No one, no boy, not even the Court of Flowers, gets to determine your worth except you."

I nod, and the tears finally break through. Sometimes when you're hurting, the people you love know exactly what to say.

My mother strokes my hair and wipes my eyes with a handkerchief. "There's something I want you to see," she says. "I'll be right back."

While she's gone, I muster the strength to get out of bed and go to the window. Outside, every streetlamp is lit, illuminating the procession of carriages moving down the street. A few are stopped outside the shops, picking up someone inside. Either they're being escorted to the ball by someone of high status or their families have scrounged up enough coins to hire a carriage for the night.

The door creaks open, and it's my mother again. She's holding a small shoebox at her waist.

"What's that?" I ask.

"Come," she says, patting the edge of the bed. "Sit."

The box is from a shop I don't recognize, and it's too old

and worn to be a new pair of shoes, so I stare at her, confused.

"I should've told you about this sooner," she says, tugging at the box, "but I wasn't sure how to."

When the lid is lifted, it reveals an array of disorganized memorabilia. Dried, crackling flowers the color of rust lay on top of stacks of parchment and fabric scraps. I recognize the scent coming from the parchment—the same perfume the Court of Flowers douses their invitations in. I reach in and pull out the first piece of parchment. It has the same gold lettering, the same smell, although a bit stale.

"This is the invitation from your Court Ball?" I ask her, studying it.

"It is," she says.

"You've never talked about it," I say. "I wasn't even sure you went."

"Well, of course I went. I'm not that much of a dud."

I shoot her a look that makes her laugh before carefully sliding the flowers over and digging farther into the box.

I take out the wrinkled fabric scrap. It's a deep olive velvet with traces of golden thread. "What's this?"

"That's from the gown I wore. The gown your grand-mére sewed for me."

"I didn't know she made your gown for the Court Ball." I knew my grand-mére was a seamstress. I watched Violette grow up in the hand-me-downs grand-mére made for me, but I was too young to know her, too young to learn from her.

I rub the velvet between my fingers. "I bet you looked

beautiful in this color," I say. When I place it back in the box, a glint of metal catches my eye. I fish down in the corner until I touch it. When I bring it up, rattling off everything on top, my breath catches.

I trace the metal pin that's been punched through a roll of parchment, feeling the ridges and the curves of the rose. I've seen these before. I saw them pinned to the breast of almost every woman at the Court of Flowers high tea. I unfurl the parchment to find five names.

Adrienne Chabert
Vanessa Archambault
Anne-Marie Masson
Scarlett Fraise
Matilda de Hollande

Matilda de Hollande. My mother.

"You were—" The words fall from my mouth as I try to arrange them. "You were in the running?"

She nods. "I was."

"To be the Bellegarde Bloom?"

"Well, don't act so surprised," she jokes.

"Why have you never told me?" I gasp. "This is—this is magnificent! And you've kept it from us all these years. Why?"

"Because I didn't want either of you girls to think it was important," she says. "I didn't want you to think that becoming Bloom was all you had to strive for."

"But you were so happy when I was nominated. I thought it was what you'd always secretly hoped for."

"That you'd be nominated to be put on a pedestal for every Parisian man to gawk at and fight over?" She laughs. "No, never a dream of mine for you. But it has always been a dream of mine that you'd be given an opportunity to change your fate, to take your talents and bring your dreams to life like you've always wanted. When I found out you'd been chosen, I thought maybe this was it—this was how you got the opportunities we have never been able to give you."

A single tear rolls down her cheek, and I catch it before it falls to her lap.

"Oh, Mother," I say, "you and Father have given me everything."

She places her warm hand over mine. "I just wanted more for you. The world deserves to know Evie Clément the way that we know her. And you deserve to be known, to have your designs worn not just by the queen of France, but by everyone."

I smile for the first time since I found out about the bet. "Thanks, Mother."

I've had it wrong all this time, wrong about my mother and her intentions and wishes for me, and it pains me to realize that I've thought all this time that she only wanted me to get married. It's a good kind of pain, though, because it's the kind that pushes through and opens new possibilities. I think of all the conversations I wish I'd had with her before, and the ones I can have with her now. I see now that she's only ever wanted what's best for me.

"Wait," I say, looking down again at my mother's Bloom pin. "So, what was it like? I mean, Vanessa Archambault—that's Rachelle's mother's maiden name, and of course we know she won. Rachelle won't let anyone forget it."

"Well," my mother says, fidgeting with her skirt, "she *sort of* won."

"What do you mean, 'sort of won'? I saw Madame Le-Blanc at the Court tea."

"Oh, yes, she is the Bloom from my year. But she wasn't chosen first. She isn't aware of that, of course, but it's true."

"She wasn't chosen first? Then who was?"

Mother exhales. "I was."

"You were chosen as the Bellegarde Bloom?" I yelp, and I almost come up off the bed.

She nods, laughing. "Again with the tone of surprise."

"Well, I *am* surprised! You can't keep this from me for seventeen years and not expect me to be utterly shocked that my mother, my *own* mother, was chosen as the Bloom. So, what happened then? How did Madame LeBlanc win? Tell me!"

"Okay, okay." She grins. She takes a deep breath. "Back then, Vivienne de Verley was just another member of the Court, she wasn't the head of it. The head of the Court of Flowers was a woman named Angélique D'aureville."

Angélique. That's the name of the older woman who helped me that day at the high tea. I wonder if they're the same.

"Angélique was different than the others," my mother continues. "I think many of the younger members disliked her for her—how should I say it?—radical ways of thinking. She's the only unmarried member of the Court, you know."

"I didn't even know you could be unmarried and be on the Court."

She giggles. "No, I suppose they don't advertise that. Angélique used her position as Bloom not to get a husband, but to start her career. She owns one of the largest textile companies in France now."

Now I'm wishing I'd stopped to talk to her, to thank her for what she did for me, at least.

"I always liked Angélique," Mother says. "And I think she took a liking to me as well, because the night of the Court Ball, when everyone was absolutely sure that either Vanessa or Scarlett would be pronounced Bloom, Angélique took me aside. She wasn't supposed to, but she told me that I was going to be the winner."

"She did? Why?"

"Yes, she did. I'm not sure why she told me, but I think she wanted me to know that I had options, that I didn't have to take it if I didn't want it. She told me what I just told you, that becoming a Bloom would certainly give way to opportunities, but that it wasn't all a woman had to strive for in this life. She wanted me to know that I could make my own way, without pinning a boutonniere to some young man."

"So, what did you do? You told her you didn't want it?"

"I did."

"Why?"

"Because I'd already met your father, and I loved him. I didn't want to choose a path that was already forged for me—a path where they'd never accept the man I loved because he was considered a peasant."

"They'd have never let it happen," I breathe. "You and father. They'd have bombarded you with rich men until he ran off."

"Exactly," she says. "They like to turn women into exactly the socialites they think they should be." An ache runs through me. Beau, dressing me up, taking me to the château. The braids and the ribbons in my hair at the Gardens. He thought the only way I could win is if I became one of them.

"I didn't want to be what they wanted me to be, though," she tells me. "I wanted to spend my life with your father and I wanted to be a mother. I wanted to raise strong-willed, good-hearted children, so that maybe the world would have a bit more light in it. And then you came along, and it wasn't being nominated for Court that made my dreams come true. It was you. Because you made me a mother. And every day, even if it's a bad day, you make them come true over and over again, you and your sister both. Because I've done what I set out to do. I raised good children. That's never been more apparent to me than it is now."

I spend a long time hugging her, longer than I've spent in her arms in the past few years combined, probably, and it's really nice. It's nice to feel the people you love loving you back.

After a while, my mother pulls away, looking down at me with a grin. "So, are you going to get dressed, or what?"

"Dressed for the ball? I don't even have an escort! I can't walk in alone!"

"Who says you need an escort?" She holds up the invitation. "Nowhere on here does it say you must have an escort. They'll still announce you, escort or no, and you didn't spend days sewing that gown for nothing. So get up! And let's get you to that ball."

"But, Mother—"

"No, I won't hear another word of it." When she stands, I do, too, because she's right. I don't want to miss the only ball I'll ever be invited to just because of a stupid boy.

When she opens the door, all I hear is Violette's little feet pitter-pattering down the hallway, trying to hide the fact that she was listening at the door.

"And where do you think you're going?" Mother asks her.

Violette pokes her head out from the steps, afraid she's about to be reprimanded.

But instead, our mother's cheeks raise to reveal a sly smirk. "Evie's ball gown isn't going to fluff itself, now is it, Vi? We need your help!"

Violette squeals and comes racing down the hall to us.

Once they've zipped me up and tugged and pinched, my mother scurries out of the room muttering something under her breath. Violette grins as I look in the mirror for the first time. The gown is patchwork, made from the marshmallow-pink remnants of the gown Rachelle ripped, the lavender brocade of Josephine's disaster dress, and the soft tobacco velvet of the duke's coat, all finished off with the glittering choker that Rose Bertin gave me that night at the palace. Even I have to admit: it's so beautiful, and it's so—me.

None of us are particularly good with hair, but Mother has done her best—pulled part of it back and let two thin braids fall on either side of my face. It isn't fancy, but just like the dress, it feels like me. I swipe my mask from the table—a combination of my mother's lace and sugared pearls from the bakery—and get Violette to tie it on, making a perfect bow just like I taught her.

"I hope I look like you one day," Violette says, peering up at me, her eyes aglow.

"Even better," I say, crouching down, twisting one of her tightest curls in my fingers, "you're going to look just like you."

Her pink cheeks rise with a toothy grin until her eyes squish together.

When I stand back up, I catch myself in the mirror one more time, and it occurs to me, a thought that I can't seem to shake from my brain. I wish Beau were here. I hate that I wish he were here. Not the Beau he turned out to be, but the

Beau I thought he was. And if that wasn't Beau, who was it?
A hollow straw man I stuffed full of my own fantasies about
what love should be, what it should feel like, what the person
I fell in love with should be like. Was I so blind?

But no matter how foolish the thought, no matter how
much I don't want to be thinking it, I still wish he were here.
I wish he'd have been better—if not for me, then for himself.

The door opens back up. "One last thing," my mother
says, kneeling down near my hem. She picks up the bottom of
my skirt, stitching in the last piece of fabric—the olive-green
velvet that grand-mére used to make her gown for the Court
Ball. When she's done, she drops the skirt and ruffles it, fanning it on the floor. "There, now it's perfect."

There's a knock at the door followed by my father's bellowing voice. "Everyone dressed in there?"

"Yes, come in, darling," my mother says.

"Good, you're ready," he says, relieved.

"Good?" I say, confused. "Why?"

A smile peeks at his lips. "Because someone's waiting for
you downstairs."

"Did Josephine come back?" I ask. "Tell her to get out of
here and get to the ball!"

"Not Josephine," my father says. "You're just going to
have to go downstairs and see for yourself."

I rush to the window and sure enough, there's a carriage
parked right outside, the last remaining one on the street. Is it
the duke? It can't be. There'd be guards swarming the place,

right? But if it's not the duke . . . but no. Beau wouldn't dare show his face here after what he did.

I'm heading for the door, flipping over the words in my mind that I might string together, the perfect combination of syllables to tell him off, when my mother touches my shoulder, stopping me.

"Evie," she says just as I reach the doorway.

"Yes, Mother?"

"I only wanted to say . . ." she starts hesitantly. "Well, I wanted to say, if it is you who wins, if they call your name tonight, I hope you know that you have a choice. You get a say."

"I know, Mother," I say, and give her a kiss on the cheek. "Thanks to you." I know I won't be chosen, but it feels good to hear it. Every girl should know that they have a say in their life.

I hike my dress up and make my way down the stairs, a heat sizzling at the back of my neck, ready to tell Beau Belle-garde that I wouldn't go to the ball with him if he were the last man on Earth. But when I reach the bottom of the steps, I realize I don't have to tell him that. Because it isn't Beau who's waiting for me there.

It's Julien.

CHAPTER THIRTY

BEAU

The stars have announced themselves in the night sky, and my head swims with every shimmering wink that they give me. If I could just get away, maybe it would all stop, maybe everyone would forget, maybe she would forgive me. So, I go to the best place I know to get away.

When I arrive at the docks, Dom's hanging over the stern of the boat yelling something unintelligible at the fish that pass by. Celeste is sitting with her legs dangling off the roof, a stream of smoke hanging above her now-powder-blue hair like a halo. She sees me first.

"Beau!" she calls out. Dom twists around and lets the fish he's angry at live to see another day.

"Bellegaaaaaaaaaarde!" he shouts, his hands thrown to the heavens.

He hops over the rocking boat and onto the dock, hugging me so hard that my feet leave the ground.

"Where've you been?" Dom says. "You left without a word."

"Ah, you know," I say, "had to get back home, back to school. Thought my father might have me for it but turns out the old man's all right."

"Shouldn't you be at that fancy ball right about now?" Bash asks, jumping down from the roof with ease, like it isn't a ten-foot drop. He clasps my hand when he lands. Bash and Celeste and Dom, they're some of the good ones. Better friends in these few weeks than the ones I've had all my life.

"Yeah, if you're standing our girl up, we'll have to hurt you," Celeste teases as she comes down to join us.

"Oh, no," I say, "I'm, uhh—I'm not escorting Evie. I'm not escorting anyone at all, actually."

"You just walk around Paris looking like that, then?" Bash asks, his eyes scanning my dress outfit up and down.

"Had to pretend so that I could get out of the house without any questions," I tell him. "Didn't want anyone to come looking for me."

"Always coming round when you don't want to be found," Dom kids.

I try to laugh it off, try to smile so they don't see it in my eyes, but he's staring at me and it's like he's looking through me, like he knows.

"Why don't you come up here with me for a minute," Dom says, motioning to the roof. "Got something I want to show ya."

"Yeah, all right," I say.

As Dom and I head up, Bash and Celeste start arguing over who can tie the better knot. Celeste takes a frayed piece of rope from the docks and shoves it into Bash's chest, challenging him.

Being on the roof only makes me think of Evie. And

even though it hurts to do so, I don't want to get down. I like thinking of her.

"What did you want to show me?" I ask Dom.

He turns over a crate and fishes out a flask. "Didn't want to show you anything," he says. "Just wanted to ask you what was wrong. Why aren't you at that snooty ball with Evie?"

"You don't want to know," I say, taking a seat on the edge of the roof.

He sits down next to me and takes a drink from his flask. "Sure I do."

After some deliberation, I tell him about the bet, about Julien and Rachelle. It all comes pouring out of me, a confession of sins made to the most unorthodox of pastors.

When I've finished, Dom looks out over the Seine. It's an empty stare, like he isn't looking at anything in particular, like he's only thinking.

The old Beau would've spent this time searching for anything else to say, anything to try and convince Dom that what I did isn't who I really am. But now I know: if I did it, then it must be who I am. I made a bet on a girl—a girl who is wonderful and brilliant and enigmatic. And even if she weren't any of those things, she still should've never been a pawn in a bet. I am the person who made her into that pawn. But I don't want to be.

"I knew who you were," Dom says finally, interrupting the silence. "Before you came to the theater that night, I already knew who you were."

"You know who I was? How?"

"Evie'd told me about you. Guess she'd forgotten she did, but it was a long time ago. Something about flowers and a heap of dirt."

I bury my head in my hands.

"Yep." Dom nods, taking a swig of whatever soured liquor sloshes in his flask. He pulls it away as I grab for it. "Felt a bit like I was meeting a celebrity that night—the infamous Beau Bellegarde." He winks at me, and I nudge his shoulder, both of us laughing quietly.

My chest pangs like my heart's trying to gnaw its way out, trying to find a new host, one that treats it better. I should've apologized to Evie years ago, should've ditched Julien and Rachelle and everyone else who only befriended me because of my last name. I should've told her how sorry I was. She said that people like me don't see people like her, but the truth is, I saw Evie Clément every day. I was just too much of a coward to look at her. "Guess I messed it up big-time, huh?"

Dom pushes his hair back. "Big-time? Try colossally."

I sigh. He couldn't be more correct.

Silence hangs in the between me and Dom. He screws the top on his flask and tosses it aside. "I think you should go get her," he says.

"Go get Evie? She doesn't want anything to do with me."

"Oh, nonsense." He waves me away, standing. "How could you be so sure?"

"Well, for one, because she told me so," I say. "And did you not hear what I just said? She's got a reason to."

"She's got a lot of reasons to," he tells me, a tipsy smile

pulling at his lips. "But I don't think you're a bad guy. Not really."

"No?"

"Nah," he says, eyes set on the horizon. "I'd heard a lot about you before I met you, Beau Bellegarde, and none of it flattering. But as it turns out, the guy I've come to know is a good guy. And the guy I know, he wouldn't give up this easily."

I wring my hands in my lap, thinking. "But what would I even say to her?"

"You don't *say* anything. You show her who you really are," he says. "I think she saw it once. But you've got to show her again."

Suddenly, I remember something Evie said to me that night at the theater. We'd just evaded Monsieur Thomas to nab our front of stage seats, and I was admiring the view. *You have to see things up close*, she told me. *You stay far away from everything, and there's a lot you'll miss*. I have to tell her the truth, about all of it. I have to show her who I really am, who I want to be—not who I've been so that I could fit in. If anyone's earned the right to see me up close, it's her.

"You do need to change, though," Dom says gravely, his brow raised as he flicks at my ruffled collar.

"What do you mean?" I ask, mock incensed. "You don't like my look?" In response, he plucks the collar from my neck and tosses it overboard into the dark waters of the Seine.

"Take that wretched coat off," he says before calling out, "Celeste, I need your assistance!" He turns back to me and grabs at my blouse. "What about this?"

"Well, it's my father's but . . ."

In one fell motion, Dom rips the top couple of buttons of the blouse clean off. He leaves the cuff links, says they're cool, but it's about the only thing on me that he doesn't change in one way or another, and I'm glad for it.

"Oh, wow," Celeste says as she makes her way to the roof. "Looking better already."

"Need help with the hair," Dom says. "What do you think?"

Celeste cocks her head to the side. "You've got curls, no?"

I nod. From my mother Julien has always tamed his flat, straight hair with pomade, and I guess I thought I should do the same.

"Come with me," she beckons with a devilish grin.

One head dunk into the Seine later and my hair is dripping wet.

"Don't worry," she says, shimmying her fingers through my hair and mussing it until the curls fall wild onto my forehead. "It'll dry on the way."

Dom steps back, rubbing his chin as he studies me. Finally, he grins, pleased with his work.

"On the way?" I ask, confused. "On the way where?"

"Bash, grab the oars!" Dom shouts before throwing his fist in the air. "We're going down river. We've got a ball to get to!"

CHAPTER THIRTY-ONE

EVIE

Julien, normally so confident and arrogant, looks like a sad puppy dog standing in the middle of the bakery.

"What are you doing here?" I ask. I reach my hand around my back and shoo my family away—I don't have to look to feel them behind me, standing at the top of the stairs pretending not to eavesdrop.

Julien takes a step toward me. "I didn't want you to go to the ball alone," he says. "And it's my fault you don't have an escort, so I thought this was the least I can do."

"I don't need your charity."

"It's not charity," he says. "I *want* to go with you. What I said to you today was the truth. The bet was all Beau's idea so that he could have a chance to win the inheritance. I was only trying to help him out and it went too far, and I can't apologize enough for it. Let me try and make it up to you."

I don't know if I believe him or not, but I don't much care, because I need a ride. I suppose there are worse things than showing up to the Court Ball with Julien Bellegarde. Showing up with Beau Bellegarde, for example.

I sigh, heading for the door. "Let's go, then. You've got a lot of making up to do."

As we approach the front of the Palais-Royal opera house, Julien gives the doormen our names. He holds his arm out, and instinctively, I hook mine through it.

The doors part, and we're announced, the squatty man's voice bellowing over the orchestra. "Introducing Mademoiselle Evie Clément, escorted by Monsieur Julien Bellegarde." Every eye in the packed room flickers to us as we enter, an unexpected pair.

"Well," Julien says, glancing over to me as we make our way through the buzzing crowd. There's a crooked, cheeky smirk on his face like he's enjoying this. "Regretting your decision yet?"

"Don't push it," I say. I'm used to everyone's stares by now, but it's a relief when they look away to gossip about us.

The Palais-Royal has been transformed. Wind whispers through the open windows, rustling the gossamer drapes. Candelabra flames seem to sway along to the symphony, mimicking the spinning students on the dance floor who move like waves in step with one another, all engaged in the contredanse allemande. Bouquets of candy-colored flowers cascade down, melting from the chandeliers. The moon circles, and we're surrounded by gilded bannisters and paintings of pastel goddesses, enveloped in romance.

Julien slithers his hand down to mine and attempts to intertwine our fingers, but I pull away. He licks his lips in controlled frustration.

We're picking over sugar-frosted grapes and honey cakes

when I hear my name called out by a familiar voice.

"Jo!" I shout as she hurries over to me. Some of the tension in my chest gives way. Julien slides off to the side to talk with Dre and Lola, and I'm glad for it.

Josephine pushes through the crowd, Mia in tow, and I can see Jo fully now—her hair twisted like a dollop of cream, her cheeks glittered, and her body draped in the amethyst gown I made for her. But it isn't her gown I'm looking at, and it isn't her pearled gloves, either. It's what those gloves lead to—her hand interlocked with Mia's.

"You're here!" she squeals. "I thought I was going to have to drag you out of bed. Your mother wouldn't let me, though."

"Well," I say, my mouth crooked, "I made it."

Jo's eyes narrow. "Did you really arrive with Julien?"

"I can explain," I say, unsure. "It's simple, really. He showed up, and I needed a ride."

"Evie," Mia gawks, changing the subject, "this dress!" Much to my chagrin, just like she did at the château, she makes me give an awkward twirl so she can see it from every angle.

"Wait," Josephine says, "is that—"

"Pieces of your disaster dress from Madame Bissett's class," I finish her sentence. "It is."

"Glad you didn't let me throw it away," she says before running her palm over the velvet from the duke's coat. "And this—wow. Where's this from?"

"Ah, well—" I start, but Josephine's mouth droops into a frown.

"Ooh, speaking of Madame Bissett . . ." she says.

I turn to see our high-browed teacher making her way through the crowd, headed straight for the two of us.

Josephine nips my arm. "We're going to go to the dance floor," she says. "I'll find you in a bit." She winks mischievously at me, and I widen my eyes. *Thanks a lot, Jo.*

"Well, well, well, Evie," Madame Bissett says, her lips pursed in contemplation. "I would suspect this gown is a Clément original, no?"

"Um, yes," I say, fidgeting with the waist, unsure about what to do with my hands. There's something unnatural about seeing teachers outside of school. "Yes, it is."

She studies me for a moment longer before declaring, "Best piece of student work I've ever seen. I hesitate to even call it student work given the precision, the attention to detail, the innovation. . . . I find myself rather speechless, Mademoiselle Clément. A rarity for me, you'll know."

She's right. I *definitely* know it's a rarity for her.

"I didn't have much time," I tell her. "The zipper isn't perfect, and if you lift up the skirt, the hem gets a bit wonky."

"Nonsense," she says, clasping her hands together. "I won't even hear of it. What you've done here is remarkable. I just hope you're ready for all the designers who are going to bombard you the moment you finish school. They're all going to be putting in their bid to get you as their apprentice."

"Oh, I don't think so," I say, but the truth is that I have thought about it. I've thought about it ever since Jacques mentioned it that night, but when my thoughts stray there, I have to stop myself. It's the bakery for me. And that's okay, because if I do it, then Violette won't have to.

Madame Bissett opens her mouth to speak, but she doesn't get the first word out before a towering figure steps in.

"Pardon me," he says to Madame Bissett. A black mask shields a sliver of his face, but I can tell immediately that she doesn't recognize him. No one seems to. No one except for me. "May I have a word with Mademoiselle Clément?"

"Of course," Madame Bissett says before slipping away.

Once she's gone, I turn to the duke. "Are you lost?" I breathe. I have to bite my lip to keep from smiling.

He grins and moves closer. He smells like he did the night we met, like springtime, the same scent that lingered on his coat. "I told you I thought a ball sounded fun."

"You really came," I say. "Why?"

"I heard a rumor that the most interesting girl in Paris was going to be here tonight, and I knew I couldn't live with myself if I didn't stop by and ask her for a dance."

"Is that right?" I tease him. "I'll help you look for her."

He laughs, and I'm reminded of how much I like his laugh, but the way he throws his head back when he does it and the way his dimples press in makes me think of something else, too. It makes me think of Beau and the stupid face he makes when he thinks something is really funny, the way his breath catches and the way he grasps on his chest like he might choke on the laughter. I hate that I can't look at the duke without thinking of him.

The orchestra descends into a split second of silence before drumming back to life. "So," the duke says, eyeing me. He extends his hand to me. "What'll it be? May I steal you away from your date for a dance?"

I don't look for Julien. I don't care who he's spending his time with, and I certainly don't care how he'll feel about me spending mine with the duke. Instead, I nod and place my hand on top of Heath's. "Absolutely."

I follow his lead on the dance floor, stepping with him, moving with him, his hand on my hip and mine grasping his shoulder as we spin.

"You look radiant," he says, leaning in. "If it's not too bold to say."

"Thanks in part to your coat," I say. "I fulfilled my part of the deal."

"Your dress!" he says. "You actually made it."

I grin back at him. "I promised I would."

"Always full of surprises."

"As are you," I tell him. "Imagine my surprise when hundreds of flowers showed up at the bakery."

His soft lips slide into a warm grin. "I hope it wasn't too much."

I muffle my laughter in his chest. "It was the grandest gift I've ever received," I tell him, "although, my father might have something different to say. He's couldn't move for flowers in his way, so he's been gifting them to the neighbor shopkeepers. The whole of Rue Saint-Honoré looks and smells lovelier than ever thanks to you."

"I'm glad to hear it," he replies.

"I didn't expect you to show up here," I say after a moment. "Weren't you worried you'd be met with a stampede of young ladies?"

He sighs. "I wasn't worried about that, not when it meant I'd get to see you." His voice lowers into a whisper. "Although, I must say, I think people may be starting to catch on."

I keep in step with him but look around to find that a crowd has gathered around the dance floor. I see not only the faces of my peers ogling us but an array of members from the Court of Flowers also.

"I'm sorry," I say, shaking my head. "You don't need to risk all of this just to see me."

"If it means I get to spend time with you, it's worth it."

His fingers slip over my shoulder blades, the slightest touch causing my heart to quiver, and when it does, I catch sight of someone at the edge of the dance floor, over the duke's shoulder. *Beau*. I almost say it, but I trap the word in my throat. He's just walked in. His body sighs when we lock eyes, when he sees me here dancing with someone who isn't him. And it doesn't make me feel the way I thought it might. I thought maybe it would feel good to see him jealous, to see him sorry, but it only makes me feel sad for him. I'm angry, and that anger still burns like hot coals, but whatever part of me cares about him has yet to be ripped from me, like a plucked flower whose roots have already taken hold.

"Everything okay?" Heath asks.

I shake my thoughts away, turning my gaze to him. "Fine," I lie. "Everything's fine."

"You could be crowned Bellegarde Bloom tonight," he says as we glide across the floor. "How does that feel?"

Bloom. My mother's secret. *Bellegarde*. The surname coming off his tongue swallows me like a secret of my own. I can feel the eyes of the Court boring into the both of us, intrigued. "Can we get some air?"

The duke stops, his hand never dropping mine, not worrying what the others will think of our abrupt departure. "Of course," he says as he leads me through the crowd. Beau watches us go by, and it's clear that someone's told him who it is under the mask. He looks like he wants to say something to me, but he doesn't. His fingers brush mine as we pass.

We exit out a side door and into a row of tea olives and lavender bushes.

"Back in the gardens, I see," he says.

"How appropriate for us."

We don't walk but a few steps before he asks, "Are you sure you're all right? Or are you just being the strong-willed girl I know you to be?"

"I don't know," I say.

"You don't know, or you don't want to say?"

I turn back to him slowly. "I thought things were fine," I say. "I thought I was fine when I came here tonight. I thought I didn't care about being the Bellegarde Bloom and . . ." My voice trails off, my mind always leading me back to Beau. "Thought I didn't care about a lot of things."

"But?"

"But it turns out I might."

"Hmm," he says, rubbing the back of his neck. "Why do I feel like we're not talking about the competition anymore?"

I bite the inside of my cheek, trapping everything in. I don't want to tell him about Beau. This past week with him has been nothing short of a dream. But I can't help how I feel, and if the events of today have taught me anything, it's that good people deserve the truth, no matter how much it may hurt. "No," I say. "We're not talking about Bloom."

He takes my hand in his, his skin like bathwater. "Would I be right if I said that you don't want the same thing I want?"

"Heath, I—" His thumb rubs the top of my hand, and there's a part of me that wants to give him what he wants, a part of me that wants it, too. But at the last moment, I'm pulled away, called back by my heart, because it already lies elsewhere. "I can't."

His chin drops a little, sorrow in his eyes. "You can't or you won't?"

"Both, I suppose."

Heath nods, and his fingers interlace with mine for a moment before they fall away. "I thought you might say that."

"You did? Why?"

He leans against the Palais-Royal wall and peers up at the stars. "Remember when I told you that my uncle researched you before I was able to take you out?"

"I do."

"Well, while in his research, he may have happened upon a certain Beau Bellegarde. He said he didn't think it anything serious, and I'd all but forgotten about it until tonight. Until I saw him look at you just now, and I knew. I knew because it's the way I look at you as well. It isn't the way you look at me, though. And that's okay. But I do wish it was."

My chest feels like it could cave in. I want to reach out to him, because I know it will be the last time I can, but I don't. Because he's right. I don't look at him the way he looks at me. I tried to, and maybe I could have if things were different, but things aren't different. So I tell the duke the truest thing I can think to say. "I'm sorry," I say.

He nods. "I know. Me too."

I watch him watch the skies until the silence between us becomes too heavy a load to bear and I have to look away.

Finally, he speaks. "I did what you said."

"What I said?" I ask. "What do you mean?"

"I met with the owner of the building. The one on the Seine, the one where my grandmother's favorite bookshop was. I made him an offer."

"You're buying the bookshop?"

"The whole building, actually," he laughs.

"Oh, how wonderful, Heath."

"It is," he says, nodding. "I think she'd think so, too. But I want to thank you."

"Thank me? For what?"

"Without you, I wouldn't have done it. I don't know if I'd have ever even thought to do it. But you made me want more. You made me want to treasure the things I care about. I only regret that I could not hold on to you."

He leans down and kisses me softly on the cheek, his skin so warm that I savor it.

"Will I ever see you again?" I ask.

"I don't know," he says, taking my hand with a half-hearted smile that makes me think he does know. "But, Evie?"

"Yes?"

"If you ever change your mind, you know where to find me."

"The bookshop?"

He smiles, a real one this time. "The bookshop."

And with one last squeeze of my hand, he turns from me and disappears as mysteriously as he appeared—a handsome moonlit man lost in the shadows of a garden.

The night's almost over when they call us to the stage. *Belle-garde Bloom announced at first starlight.*

The five of us in contention for Bloom stand in a row, every face staring back at us, and I feel more like a spectacle than a person.

Vivienne de Verley stands center stage and announces that the student votes have been tallied.

"As you know," she says, doing her best to project her

smooth, stern voice in a ladylike way, "the Court of Flowers takes a great deal of consideration into the student vote, but it is we who make the final decision. This year was a tight race among five worthy young ladies, each of whom we would be delighted to have on the Court. However, we may only choose one."

Cassandra steps forward with a small silk pillow in her hands. Resting on it is the Bloom pin, the gold version of the one found in my mother's shoebox, the one that only the winner receives. After this year, Cassandra will no longer be the newest inductee. It will be Rachelle who has to clean up after the Court's parties and fetch ice cubes for their drinks.

Vivienne clears her throat, and my heart speeds up, wanting it to all be over with so that I can go back to my life as it was before. "This year, the honor of Bloom, and the newest member of the Court of Flowers is . . ."

The ballroom goes deathly silent in anticipation. I'm not looking at Vivienne, though. I'm looking over at Rachelle, watching her primp, fluffing her hair, and pushing her shoulders back. She was always meant to be a Bloom.

"Evie Clément."

A gasp pulses throughout the room before the surprised clatter of applause begins, a wild and raucous sound. It seems to hit me last.

No. No. No. Me? The Bloom? Not possible.

I don't know what else to do, so I look at Rachelle. By the

look on her face, I don't know whether she's crushed, or she wants to crush me.

I turn back to the crowd, searching for Jo, but everything's a blur. I only snap out of it when Cassandra floats over to me, her thin plum lips pulled tight, pleased. She lifts the pin from the pillow, and in her eyes, I see the next years of my life playing out in front of me. Parties and balls I don't want to attend with women who talk about me when I leave a room and men who only act like they like me because I've got a golden flower pinned to my breast.

Cassandra starts forward.

"Wait," I breathe, stopping her hands from securing the pin. "Just wait."

Her brows raise, perplexed, as I take the pin from her. I don't even know what I'm doing, but whatever it is, it feels like the right thing to do.

I make my way over to Rachelle, who looks like she could tackle me off this stage, but I don't care. "You were right," I tell her.

"I was?" she says, confused before crossing her arms and straightening her posture. "I mean, of course I was. But about what exactly?"

"When you said a weed could never be a rose," I say. "You were right. A weed cannot be a rose. But it can be a wildflower." I place the Court pin in her palm and curl her fingers around it. "It's yours. Take it."

CHAPTER THIRTY-TWO

BEAU

It happens so fast, Evie—stubborn, independent, magnificent Evie—turning down the Court of Flowers and giving her pin to Rachelle. She's off of the stage and disappeared into the crowd before I can wrap my head around it.

Gossip is swarming, her name on the tip of every tongue in the room.

I crane my neck trying to see above everyone's heads, see if I can catch sight of her, but it's no use. I push my way to the front of the stage to see if I can get a better view there.

The Court, scrambling, unaware of what to do in a situation where someone rejects them, finally announces Rachelle as the winner. Her crooked smile hides her annoyance well, but I have to laugh. Rachelle will always be a little angry that she came in second place. Especially when she lost to a girl she sees as nothing more than a peasant.

Even with this view of the crowd, Evie is still nowhere to be found.

"Where'd the duke go?" I hear Rachelle crying out behind me, waving the prized boutonniere in the air, aggressively making her way off the stage. "Does he know I won? Someone get him! Someone bring him to me!"

She shoves into my back, and I turn around to meet her glare.

"Beau?" she says, her thin brows knitting into a deep crease at the center of her forehead.

"Rachelle." I smirk. "Congratulations. I didn't know that they'd allow a runner-up on the Court."

"Oh, shut up, Beau," she sneers.

"The baron get lost on his way here?"

"Never mind him. Have you seen the duke? I suppose he won't be wanting Evie anymore after that little stunt she pulled, and I have a boutonniere with his name on it."

"That little stunt she pulled?" I say. "You wouldn't have that pin or that boutonniere without her. Oh, and good luck with the duke. Because the only reason he came here tonight was to see her. And I simply don't think a person that's interested in someone as kind and wonderful as Evie would ever be interested in someone like you."

Her mouth drops open, her breaths labored, like she's trying her hardest to find a fitting comeback to cut me as deep as she can. But I'm done acting like I care what a person like Rachelle LeBlanc has to say about the fortitude of my character, so I leave her standing there, alone in a sea of people who've just seen her lose.

Finally, I sigh, ending up over by the Royal Palais doors. Huddled together by the entrance are Josephine and Mia.

"Josephine!" I shout. "Have you seen Evie?"

"Yeah, she just left with Julien," Josephine responds.

"Julien? Why would she leave with Julien?"

"She said that he told her he'd take her home," Josephine explains. "Did he not tell you?"

"No, he didn't. He didn't say anything about—"

Just then, Lola approaches. "Beau," she says, relieved, grasping my wrist. "I've been looking for you everywhere. I should've told you sooner."

"Should've told me what?" I ask.

"He—" Lola starts, trying to find the words. "Julien. He told Dre that he was going to tell Evie he was taking her home but take her to the Gardens instead. I thought you should know."

"The Gardens?" I shout. "That rat!"

"We're coming with you," Josephine says.

"No, I—I need to do this," I tell her. I can see it on Josephine's face—Evie's strong, loyal best friend and confidant—how much I've disappointed her. If only she knew how much I'd disappointed myself as well. "Please," I beg. "Just let me do this for her."

"Hurt her again and I'll hurt you," Josephine says. And I can tell she means it.

"Deal," I say before rushing off, bursting through the opera house doors and out onto the streets. I run and run and run until I get to the Seine, and I can't help but think about how the last time I was running through the streets of Paris at night, it was with her. And it was the first time I knew I loved her.

I end up in the same place as we ended up that night, too, and thankfully, Dom's boat is still waiting.

"Dom!" I yell, sprinting down the docks, feeling them rattle beneath my feet, my lungs burning with the night air. "To the Gardens!"

CHAPTER THIRTY-THREE

BEAU

As it turns out, drunken sailors aren't that useless. Especially when they're angry.

"You sure she's there?" Dom calls out to me from the other side of the boat. My arms ache with the continuous, furious rowing, but we're so close now I can see the docks up ahead.

"Yes!" I shout back. All I have to go on is hearsay, but I know Julien. I know how he thinks. I've watched him play these same games for years—telling girls whatever they want to hear, charming them, and then taking them to the Gardens, to his notorious hookup spot, only to break up with them the next day and divulge all of the intimate details to everyone at university.

"Over there," Celeste directs us to a shorter dock I hadn't seen before. It's closer to the Gardens and closer to us.

Finally, we make it, and I have to hold the three of them off because they're all ready to pummel Julien. And as much as I'd like to see it, I've got to do this alone. Begrudgingly, they agree, but I don't think it's because they've given up. I think it's because all of that rowing has churned up the liquor in their stomachs and they're all feeling like they might need a lie-down.

Dom places his hand on my shoulder. "Go get her," he slurs before stumbling back to the bow.

If Julien's in the Gardens, I know exactly where to find him. I run through the night, passing by barely lit shops and straggling partygoers, until the sound of hooves startles me. Just a carriage, I think. But as the sound nears and the carriage dips under the streetlamps, I can make out the driver.

"Francis!" I call out to him, running over. It's our carriage.

"Monsieur Bellegarde," he says, "what on Earth are you doing here at this time of night?"

"Where is he?" I shout. "Did you take them to the Gardens?"

"I—I did, sir," Francis answers, frazzled. "Monsieur Julien instructed me to take him and Mademoiselle Evie to the Gardens, but—"

"But what?"

"Well," Francis continues, "when we got there, it seemed Mademoiselle Evie was rather upset. She got out of the carriage, and I saw her shouting at your brother, and then she left, and he ran off after her."

"Which way did they go?"

Francis points out into the distance, toward one of the Garden's many entrances, and I take off in that direction. Before I even make it far, though, I run into him. There—all alone on a bench, dripping wet from head to toe, slimy moss nesting in his golden locks—is Julien.

"Come to save your princess?" he hisses, his angry spit only adding to the puddle gathered at his feet.

"Where is she, Julien?"

"Who knows?"

"If you touched her, I swear, Julien—"

"Oh, come off it, Beau," he interjects. "The moment we got in the place, right as I was about to plant a kiss on her, she pushed me in the lake. That little brat."

Before tonight, I'd have probably slung him from the bench and tossed him out onto the street, but I won't bother tonight. Because I've realized that people like Julien and Rachelle just hurt everyone else in an attempt to dull their own hurt, and I pity them for it.

"Well"—I grin—"looks like the princess doesn't need saving after all, does she?" His lip curls and I leave him sitting alone, drenched in filthy lake water, just as he deserves. "Have a good night, Julien."

The Gardens have gone dark, and the moonlight serves as my only guide. The place goes on forever with hedges as tall as carriages and a hundred ways to get lost, but thankfully, I think I know where to find Evie.

I make my way through the tunnel of wisteria and out the other side to the lake's edge, the waters calm and silver. And suddenly, the mirrored night sky in the water is disturbed—pebbles tossed in, creating rippling halos that make the moon dance.

And there the pebble-throwing culprit is, sitting in a glittering gown underneath the orange trees, just where I thought she might be.

"Have enough of the ball?" I call out to her.

She tosses another rock, a bigger one this time, and it sinks into the water with a tall splash. "What are you doing here, Beau?"

"Oh, I don't know. Just came to pick some oranges." I motion down to the empty grass next to her. "May I?"

Evie shrugs. "Whatever."

She runs her fingers through the stones that surround the lake. She looks at them and she looks at the water, but she doesn't look at me.

I let the silence stay for a while. I think we both need it. But finally, I remember what Dom said, about showing her who I am. The only way to do that is to tell the truth, so I tell it.

"I know it doesn't mean much to you," I start, "but I want you to know how sorry I am about what I did. Julien was right about one thing. I did agree to that bet—his inheritance if I could make you the Bloom. And at first, that was all it was about for me. It's why I started *Paper Hearts*. It's why I did a lot of the things I did in the beginning. I didn't imagine that you'd change my whole life, Evie, but you did. From that first night at the theater—crawling underneath the stage to get a better view, meeting Dom and Bash and Celeste, learning about how you grew up, talking to you about my mother—I'd never felt more alive, more like myself, in my entire life. I meant what I said when I told you that you taught me to believe in myself. And if you never speak to me again, I'll understand. But I want you to know what you did for me, and that I'll spend the rest of my days being thankful for it. For you."

She's quiet for a long time. Cicadas slip into song, and tadpoles shimmy, skittering across the lake's surface. The warm wind licks the fallen leaves, carrying them to a new home. Under it all, Evie breathes, soft and quiet.

She lifts her face, blinking back at the stars, and sighs, a deep, heavy sigh. "I know Julien didn't tell the entire truth about the bet," she says. "He let it slip that you'd lose your mother's cottage if you lost the bet."

"He told you that?"

"Kind of," she says with a half-hearted laugh. "I don't think he meant to, but he's a loose-lipped drunk."

I nod, knowing that it's true.

"I don't think it's okay what you did," Evie says, "making me your bet. I don't deserve that. No one does. But I think I know now why you stuck with it for so long. If someone tried to take the bakery away from me the way Julien did with your mother's home, I'd do just about anything to keep that from happening." She picks a rock up and tosses it from palm to palm. "And I also know that you didn't really kiss Rachelle.

She kissed you. Julien didn't tell me that one, though. Turns out Rachelle confided in Lola, and well, Lola's not all bad, so she told me. Not that I ever cared about that part anyway. I've always known Rachelle's a liar."

She looks at me for the first time since I've gotten here, and I feel that same ache in my heart from before. I can't believe I've spent the last ten years without her.

"She is a liar. Turns out she's a loser, too," I say with a grin.

"Yes, well," Evie sighs, "she got the pin she's always wanted, so she hasn't lost much."

"Oh, I think she has," I disagree. "Why didn't you take it? Bloom. What made you give it up?"

"Because a very smart woman told me that I had a choice in the matter," she says. "I don't doubt that every woman on that Court has their reasons for being on it, and I don't judge them for it. But that's not my life. I don't care about having every man in Paris want me if they only want me for the rose pinned to my gown."

"Not even if they're a duke?" I ask. It comes out before I have the chance to stop it, and I hope it doesn't anger her. But seeing her with him tonight . . . it was like watching the sun fade away.

"The duke's quite nice, actually. Kind, selfless, and caring. But as it turns out"—she pauses, and looks at me for the first time since I arrived—"my heart was elsewhere."

"Well," I say, biting my lip to try and hide the giddy joy, "I'm glad to hear it. Although, I do think I may have messed

up your first real ball. You never even got to dance through
a whole song."

"That's okay," she says. "Too many people. Plus, I've got
two left feet."

I stand, brushing off my trousers and extending my hand
to her. "Let me make it up to you? I don't care if you step on
my toes the whole way through."

She looks up at me, her skin frosted with the light of the
moon, and just when I think she might leave me standing here
by myself, she takes my hand and lets me pull her up.

I weave my fingers with hers until our palms meet, but it
isn't enough, so I guide our interlocked hands over my chest.
We exchange breaths as my other hand slides across her bare
collarbones and down her waist, reaching the small of her
back. I tug, pulling her in close to me, as close as I can get.

We dance there, under the stars we've both been looking at our whole lives. The ones that look the same whether
you're at the bakery or the Palace of Versailles or under the
orange trees, the ones that she used to come to with her family when food was scarce, the ones whose scent has always
reminded me of my mother.

"How'd you get here so fast anyway?" she asks me, breaking the silence. "Took us ages just to get back to the carriage."

"Well, you see, as it turns out, I have a few new friends
who have a boat, and the Seine will take you anywhere."

"You didn't!" she gasps, intrigued. "Dom and the others
brought you here?"

"Sure did," I say, and I motion back to the river. "They're

probably still docked out there, having a right good time. Had to talk them out of coming with me. They all wanted a piece of Julien."

"Ugh, Julien," she scoffs. "If I never hear that name again, I'll be glad for it."

"I saw him on my way here," I tell her. "Looked like a wet dog. He said you pushed him in the lake. Only wish I'd have been here to see it."

"Me too," she laughs. "I realized what he was up to the moment Francis didn't take the turn for the bakery. I thought about just getting out and walking back, but I just couldn't let him go unpunished. So, I made him think his little plan was going to work out. Made him think he might have a story to tell about me tomorrow. And I guess, in a way, he does. I suppose he won't tell it, though." Her plush lips pull back into a grin.

I laugh with her. "I suppose not."

"Wait. What are you wearing?" she asks, her brows raised as she studies my outfit. "And what did you do to your hair?"

"Just a little Dom-and-Celeste makeover," I say.

"Hmm," she says. "Finally, a makeover for you and not for me. I like it."

"Good." I smile.

After a moment, she sighs. "So, what happens now with your mother's house, now that I haven't accepted Bloom?"

"Nothing happens. It's mine. Turns out Julien's threat was an empty one."

"Glad to hear it," she says.

I clear my throat, trying to find the words to ask her what I've wanted to ask ever since my father told me the house was mine. "You know, London's a pretty interesting place. Lots of high-profile designers there. People you could apprentice under."

"Is that right?"

I nod. "Mm-hmm. There's a really great newspaper I'm going to send my work to after graduation. If I make it out there, maybe someday you could come visit."

"Well, we'll just have to see about that," she says. "Maybe we'll make a bet on it." Her mouth breaks out in a sly grin.

I run my thumb along her cheekbone until the space between us feels like too far a distance. I move my hands into her hair and pull her to me. I kiss her softly at first, but when she tugs at my chest, drawing me nearer, kissing me back, I realize I don't want to drink her in little sips. Our lips part for each other, again and again, blossoming breathless. She tastes like lilac honey and clementines, like the first day of summer.

At last, we draw back, and there she is, her face dipped in starlight. The baker's daughter, and the girl who's taken possession of my heart.

"If you ever lie to me again—" Evie starts.

"Oh, you don't have to worry about that," I assure her. "I'm too scared of Josephine to do that."

She grins and I kiss her again, because I've spent too much of my life not kissing her.

CHAPTER THIRTY-FOUR

EVIE

I'm putting the last finishing touches on a skirt for one of Jacques's clients when my father pokes his head in the door.

"Working even on your birthday, huh?" he asks.

"I just wanted to finish this one last thing," I tell him, looping the stitch through and securing the last knot. "There! All done."

"Perfect timing. You've got a visitor."

I shoot him a look. The last time he told me someone was here to see me, it turned out to be that weasel Julien Bellegarde.

His dark mustache crinkles as he smiles. "I think you're going to want to see this one," he says with a wink.

I hang the skirt over the back of my chair and head downstairs.

Beau's standing by the counter, his back to me, tapping on the display case.

"Father'll get you if you smudge fingerprints on the glass," I say.

He turns around, grinning only the way he can. Close to his chest is a fistful of daisies. "Heard it was someone's birthday," he says, extending the flowers to me.

I lean down and inhale. "Can't smell anything but cupcakes," I say as he kisses me softly. I'm still not used to it, the chill on the back of my neck each time our lips touch, but part of me hopes that never goes away. I don't think it will.

"Looks like your father has been putting in some long nights here," Beau notes, looking around at the new displays.

"Sure has," I tell him. "New menu. A whole host of new ingredients he's experimenting with. Lines down the street every day now. He's even been putting Violette to work. She's not as much a fan of the secret investor as the rest of us are, but I think she'll come around."

"Secret investor, huh?" Beau teases. "Don't know anything about that."

I jokingly nudge him with my elbow, and we fold into each other's arms. We still call it the "secret investor" when we talk, but the truth is that there's nothing secret about it. Once Monsieur Bellegarde found out what his eldest son had been up to—the stories from the Gardens, the way he treated Beau, the deal he made with his uncle to forge the will, and his rampant gambling, just to name a few—he took a chunk of Julien's inheritance and doled it out to the shops on our street. Madame Landry's got enough to retire now, something she didn't think she'd ever be able to do. And with the bakery and my family taken care of for a while, I'm planning out a trip with Beau to London to go see his mother's house, to see the place where he grew up.

"Hey, come with me," he says. "I want to show you something."

"You know I hate surprises," I tell him, reluctantly taking his hand.

"I know, I know," he says. "But this one's worth it."

He leads me down the street and around a corner until the Seine comes into view.

"Is that—" I start, shielding my eyes from the sun to try and get a better look. "No way. You've got to be kidding."

Floating on the Seine, right at the end of the dock, is Dom's boat. But it isn't in its usual drab state. Now it looks like a party has exploded on it—ribbons of every color hang from the planks, and the whole lot of them are standing on the roof shouting my name.

As Beau and I get closer, they break out into song, and I'd be shocked if the whole of Paris isn't covering their ears from the noise.

Jo's the first one to greet me. She wraps her arms around my neck. "You're getting old, friend," she says.

Mia knocks into me from the side, joining the embrace, squeezing as tight as she can. Ever since the Court Ball, the two of them haven't left each other's sight. "So," Mia says, "did we surprise you or what?"

Dom hops down from the roof. "Yeah, did we, Eves?"

"You did," I admit. "It was a good surprise."

Dom throws an arm around me and rubs his knuckles against the top of my head, tangling my hair. It doesn't matter, though, because Bash and Celeste have strung together a crown of flowers, which they toss on top of the mess Dom made.

I follow them all up onto the rooftop to soak in the light of my eighteenth trip around the sun. The air up here is just right—warm, but not too warm, with a breeze that smells like juniper and blows at exactly the right times.

Beau walks up behind me as I look out over the river and wraps his hands around my waist, cradling his chin in the crook of my neck.

I push to my tiptoes and kiss him, the boy I love. Arm in arm, we both turn back to the river and to the city that beats on around us.

Some say there's nothing more beautiful than Paris, but as I look around at my friends, and at Beau Bellegarde, his blue eyes looking back at me, I have to disagree.

ACKNOWLEDGMENTS

I wrote this book in isolation. No, really. It was Christmas, and everyone except for me had COVID, so I began typing out what is now *Bellegarde* while locked away in my bedroom, searching desperately for a joyful escape.

As it turns out, though, the support you're given each day carries on even when you're alone. For the people who gave me that support, no amount of thank yous will ever suffice.

Mama, for believing in me even when I didn't believe in myself. I could thank you forever and it still wouldn't be enough.

Kyle, for never questioning the silent hours spent at the computer or library, for sitting in the sun with me and the dogs, and for always telling me that my stories would make it.

Mommee, for teaching me what it means to be good. You asked me to write you a story about a girl who could be a princess if she wanted. I think you would have liked Evie.

Grandmama Gay, for being the first writer I knew. Before you left, you gave me a pair of bookends. "To one day fill with your own books," you wrote. I finally have something to put between those bookends, Grandmama.

Victoria, for always encouraging and championing your introverted little sister.

Joshua, for being the twin I never had, and for speaking this language of stories with me.

Carter, for always keeping me on my toes.

Dad, for letting me read stories and watch movies I probably shouldn't have.

Gray and Scarlett, for making me realize how precious and fleeting time is.

Banks, Reese, and Lavender, for being the biggest distraction and the biggest joy of my life.

Erin Sims and Caitlin Wright, for being the kind of friends who made it easy to write Evie and Josephine's bond. And for all the venting you've let me do.

Leira Lewis, Kiana Krystle, Morgan Mackey, Maria McGee, Janet Ingram, Allyson Dahlin, Kristy Boyce, Robby Weber, Kaye Asher Edge, Brian D. Kennedy, Heather Candela, Kelly Ohlert. Thank you for believing in me and this book.

Kristy Hunter. You believed in Evie and Beau, in *Bellegarde*, first. But mostly, you believed in me. There is nothing I can do to repay you, but I'll spend my time trying. Thank you for being the perfect agent for me.

Elizabeth Lynch. You saw the heart of this story and made it shine. Thank you for taking a chance on me.

Clare Vaughn. Thank you for carrying this story through so effortlessly.

Erica Sussman, Danielle McClelland, Melissa Cicchitelli, Rye White, Gwen Morten, Julia Feingold, Alison Donalty, Sabrina Abballe, Audrey Diestelkamp, Katie Boni, and Taylan Salvati, and every wonderful person at HarperTeen. Thank you for being such a great team.

To everyone at The Knight Agency. I am truly the luckiest author to have the privilege of being part of your world.

To the booksellers, librarians, and book influencers. Without you, we wouldn't be able to do what we do. Your love of stories, and your voices, will never go unnoticed or unappreciated.

You, dear reader. Thank you for being here with me. I hope *Bellegarde* gives you the escape I was looking for when I wrote it. I hope it's a book you come back to when you need joy. I hope it feels like home.

And finally, to my little girl. At the time I'm writing this, I haven't met you yet. Even still, you are the driving force behind all that I do. Every line sings of you.

I love and cherish you all.